WE PLANNED A MURDER

ONE MURDER. FIVE SUSPECTS. AND ONE OF THEM IS NEXT

DEREK D WHEELESS

www.DerekDWheeless.com

Published by Invisible Think Books

ISBN -979-8-9859335-1-2

Cover design by BeauteBook

www.beautebook.com

For Franklin W. Dixon

who taught this boy the value of a hardy mystery.

"The two most important days in your life are the day you were born...
and the day you find out why."

MARK TWAIN

MONDAY

"My psychiatrist said we teach people how to treat us. A week later, he was dead. I guess he wasn't a very good teacher."

It was 1:35 and I'd been sitting at my desk in Mrs. Cervantes' fifth period Junior English class catching up on assignments I'd dodged the previous week. The girl who stood in front of me was a welcome relief to that monotony, and I tried her at a glance.

Her hair was platinum blonde, long and straight. She wore a blue skirt with pink leggings and a snug "Keep Austin Weird" baby-blue tee. She wore an Apple watch on her left wrist, an older one, I judged, by the scratches across the glass. On her right wrist, three pink rubber bands. The girl pushed a shy smile through a slight overbite and adjusted red Rodeo Drive glasses further up the bridge of her nose. I don't enjoy being interrupted. I don't like drama. And this girl had TikTok influencer wannabe written all over her. She smelled good too, like a mixture of rose petals and sweet almond milk.

"What if it wasn't the teacher?" I asked. "What if it's the student who's rotten?"

I knew I shouldn't have said it. I knew she had just moved to the town of Ten Spot and to Milo Winkler Academy. I also knew she wasn't here to talk about her therapy sessions.

She looked past me toward the lonely schoolyard outside. Rain smattered the windowpanes, the hypnotic pelting a soothing contradiction to the noisy chaos taking place in the classroom.

"What can I do for you?" I asked.

We succumbed to an uncomfortable silence, and she folded long thin arms across her chest, pinching and pulling her bottom lip with a forefinger and thumb. I watched her scan me, from my unimpressive parted hair down to my black Allbirds and back up again. She cocked her head to the left, then to the right, and a slight curve formed in her upper lip. I'd seen it before. She was testing me, measuring me, gauging if I merited her attention. I wondered about her too. In my line of work, I take nothing for granted. I let the client make all the assumptions.

She lowered her arms, took a deep breath, and straightened herself, facing me, as though she'd finally resigned herself to fate. My fate, anyway. "I understand you can help me."

I reached inside my desk and pulled out a business card. I'd made another dozen that morning over soggy Cheerios and lukewarm OJ. Had the school bus been on time I would've been fresh out. But then again, when was the bus ever on time?

"I don't know who you are or what you've heard, but if you ask me, you should be on the other side of the room with the spirit squad."

She turned to look at several girls who were making up cheers and trying to perform them for Mrs. Cervantes. Mrs. Cer wasn't watching them, nor anyone else in the class. She'd dumped her purse and was now frisking through the contents strewn across her desk. God only knew what she was looking for.

She snorted as she took in Mrs. Cer's frantic behavior, then twisted back as quickly as she'd turned away.

"I'm Zadie," she said, flashing a Colgate smile. "Zadie Abernathy."

I slipped the card across my desk, and she scooped it up before it slipped over the edge.

"Nacho Blanco." She looked up from the card. "PSI?"

"Problem Solver Investigator."

"Is that like a private eye or a detective or something?" She popped a pink band on her wrist.

"Something like that," I said. "Let's just say I make complications go away."

She got quiet again, and still. She was struggling, hesitating like the most sought-after girl on campus trying to decide if she should go to prom with the least suitable boy in school, all because he's the only one brave enough to ask. I could tell she wasn't impressed with me, my moniker, or my penchant for skepticism. I'm good at speed-reading people. It's what I do best. I was all she had. She knew that. And even better, she saw I knew it too. I was the only boy on campus who had the guts to ask her to the big dance.

"Do you enjoy the work?" she asked. "I mean, making complications go away." Her voice was soft and raspy, and I strained to listen.

"Here in Ten Spot, the armpit of the Lone Star State? First chance I get I'm on the next train out."

"Why do you do it?" she asked.

"You tell me and we'll both know," I said.

"And this town? Doesn't seem so bad to me."

"Depends on how low you set the bar." I picked up the pencil on my desk and studied the point. "Two more years at MWA and I'm out. You'd do well to consider the same."

I returned to the still unattended assignment. She bent over my desk. "You have gorgeous brown eyes, Nacho. They match your hair, and the color of your skin." She tilted her head to the left, and a faint smile slipped across pouty, blood-red lips. "Will you take the case?"

I looked up and shook my head in disbelief. Was she seriously trying to seduce me into taking on some spurious something or other? I didn't know whether she was a plant sent in by an upper classman to set me up or a vixen working alone to prove her prowess at the art of persuasion.

I let loose a sardonic laugh. "Take your case? How would I know? I just met you. Why me? Even better, why you? Tell me your story, and I'll tell you if it's worth my time."

"I can't, not now, not here. Meet me after school?"

I surveyed the room. Two guys were trying to set up a GPS tracking device for a set of keys. Three girls were sitting together, texting on their phones. Most were getting out their English journals. And Mrs. Cer was reapplying her Revlon. Everything was copacetic. There was only one thing peculiar about this setting. I was bantering with some hot mystery blonde who wanted to charm me into taking her case sight unseen. And it was working.

"Yeah…okay…bike rack…after school," I said.

She stood and smiled and padded back to her desk, leaving me with the soft scent of rose petals and sweet almond milk.

"You asked to see me?"

I'd gotten a note from Mrs. Cer at the end of class. Ms. Baxter, the school counselor, wanted to catch me before trig, and I had a feeling it wasn't to talk about polynomials.

"How are you, Nacho?" she asked.

Ms. Baxter rose behind an oversized desk littered with stacks of state testing documents. Her blue eyes more than suited the navy dress that skimmed along her trim figure. Her hair was pulled high in a no-nonsense pony, and she wore only enough makeup to highlight her natural beauty. I'd always judged her to be a conservative woman, careful with her words, guarded with her feelings. For certain, Milo Winkler Academy was not this counselor's first rodeo.

I ignored her question and proposed my own. "Don't you ever get tired of talking difficult teens off the ledge and designing next year's block schedule?"

She raised a brow and settled back into the chair behind her desk.

"You're typing me now?" she asked. "I thought that was my job."

"Call me an armchair psychologist."

"Some people have a lot more under the counter than what's on display." She leaned back in her roll-away. "How's your work? Any new mysteries or unsolved crimes at Milo Winkler?"

"Ms. Baxter, surely you didn't invite me here to discuss my upstart career in crime fighting, did you?"

"Always checking on the constituents." She paused. "The last time we visited, you were concerned you might be in the wrong program of study here. Are you still following the Innovative Technology track?"

I moved over to a shelf across the room, adjusting a tipped book, Howard Gardner's *Multiple Intelligences*. "No. Switched to Law and Public Service, but only because I had to pick something."

"We have other programs at MWA, you know." She pursed her bottom lip. "Culinary and Hospitality. Health Science. Art."

"Somehow I don't see myself going to college to cook, draw blood, or paint." I said. "In fact, I'm not sure college is in the cards for me at all."

"Are you still living with your grandmother?"

"Unfortunately, yes. We never seem to get away from each other since she's in the school cafeteria every day and at home every night." I tilted my head to the right to read the spines of some of the other books the counselor had paired with Gardner: Erikson, Jung, Wiesel. "And now it seems she has a new love interest, a woman who calls herself Rusti."

"How do you feel about Rusti?"

I sniggered. "She's got money but doesn't work, looks but

doesn't try, and friends who drive her crazy. She's a pretty dress, but I bet she's a bitch to iron." I picked up the book by Wiesel and studied the barbed wire on its cover. "I guess the main thing is she makes my grandmother happy."

"Your grandmother's a good woman. Hasn't missed a day of work in thirty years. She's a good cook," she said, her eyes widening. "And you're a good investigator. Your sleuthing abilities must make her proud."

"Proud is not the word I would use for how she feels." I plopped myself into a bulky faux leather office chair across from her desk. "Reminds me daily she doesn't want to lose me like she lost my dad."

"And your mom?"

I shrugged. I didn't really want to think about her.

"Can I ask you a question?" she asked.

"Nobody's stopping you."

She knitted blonde eyebrows together and bit her lower lip, as though pausing for her brain to parse just the right words. "Do you ever feel abandoned? I mean, you didn't even get to say goodbye to them."

"Honestly, I don't think about it."

"You must think about them sometimes." She paused again, her eyes drawing down. "What does the silver diamond logo on top mean?" she asked, dipping her head toward a black band on my right finger.

I threw up my arms, feigning surrender. "You got me."

"What do you mean?" she asked.

"You do your job well," I said, lowering my arms.

"Do I?"

"You look like the quintessential touchy-feely shrink, but you ask questions the way grandmasters play chess, always three or four moves ahead of your opponent."

"I'm not your opponent, Nacho."

"I guess." I began rotating the ring around my finger with my thumb. "It was my father's. I have no idea where he got it. I'm still surprised he wasn't wearing it the day his plane crashed."

"That's good," she said.

"Is it?" I stood and shuffled over to a jigsaw puzzle spread across a card table on the opposite wall. I studied the puzzle's box top standing to one side. On it was a picture of a bunch of dogs sitting around a table, cards in paw, smoking, drinking, playing poker; an odd choice, I thought, for a counselor's office. About a third of the puzzle had been completed, presumably by the students who trundled in and out of Ms. Baxter's office.

"It means he's still with you. You have his ring to remember him and how it felt to be in his presence. In a way, when you wear that ring you've taken his place."

I popped in seven random pieces. "Working a case is similar to working a puzzle."

She didn't say anything and waited for me to continue.

"You can sit at a puzzle for hours and might put in one or two pieces. But if you walk away from it for a day, or even an hour, when you return, it only takes a few minutes to put in half a dozen."

"Is that how you solved the mystery of the missing PTA money last spring?"

I checked my appearance in a mirror on the wall above the puzzle and gave my hair a couple of finger strokes to make sure it was staying in place.

"I'd suspected Principal Allan from the start. His inclinations didn't match his income, if you get my drift. But I didn't have proof until my grandmother forced me to visit my uncle in Alvin over spring break. Then it hit me. That first Monday back I pulled three hundred dollars in twenties out of the bank and planted an envelope with two hundred of them in the PTA mailbox. The other five bills I kept in my wallet. The next day I asked the principal if he could break a hundred and flashed him a Benjamin. He gave me five twenties, and the serial numbers on those five were in sequential order with the other five I still had in my wallet. Ten Spot PD arrested him an hour later during a faculty meeting."

"Impressive." She searched my face. "Is this the kind of work you want to pursue long-term, or is there something else you want to do with your life, Nacho?"

"I want to get out of this two-horse town. The last thing I want is to end up like my old man, stuck here until I die."

"Remember what they say," she said. "The grass is only greener when you take the time to water it."

I pulled out some Juicy Fruit, removed its foil, and folded it in my mouth. "There's not enough water in this world to make the grass in Ten Spot green enough for me."

She scooted some testing booklets over to one side, revealing a clandestine business card beneath, passing it to me. "I have somebody I want you to meet."

"Thomas Brockett. Retired." I tapped the card in my hand. "Listen, I appreciate your kindness, but I don't think…"

The radio on her desk squawked, something about a fight between two students in the girls' restroom. Ms. Baxter jumped up. "I'm sorry, Nacho, I have to run." She headed for the door but stopped short. "Call that number!"

She darted out, leaving me alone in her office.

I stuck the business card into my wallet and returned to the puzzle. I picked up another piece, popping it into place, completing the ace of clubs the bulldog had concealed beneath the table. Ms. Baxter was right. Some do have a lot more going on beneath the surface than they let on.

Then I pulled my dad's ring from my finger and slipped it into my pocket.

Ten Spot is one of those big little towns, a bastion of old-fashioned values. Only a thirty-minute drive from Austin, it's always been everything the capital of Texas is not. Predominately retired, Republican, and related, Ten Spot's a town where everybody knows everybody, and everybody knows everybody's business. It has money, but it's old money. A girl like Zadie doesn't just show up in Ten Spot or Milo Winkler Academy. The way I figured it, this girl was hiding something, or more likely, hiding from someone.

I found her after school at the bike rack, fidgeting like a pup waiting for his pal.

"Let's get one thing straight," I said, my tone harsher than I'd intended. "There are two kinds in this world: problem-solvers and drama-makers. The last thing I want to do is get mixed up in crazy."

"Maybe this will change your mind." She opened her backpack, producing a small slip of paper I recognized right away.

"It's a receipt for frozen yogurt from Mr. Dream's Ice Cream," I said.

"You're as brilliant as you are charming. Turn it over."

Someone had scrawled a message on the back, and I could barely make out the abysmal chicken scratch.

Cutters get what they deserve

"It was in my desk this morning." She brought her hand forward. "This was on top." She opened a clenched fist. In her palm lay a flat, silver, single-edge razor blade, and I took it from her.

I let out a low whistle, flipping the blade over with my fingers to get a better look. "I've hacked my face shaving with cheaper blades than this. This is a Merkur Super, made in Germany. Somebody has a cutting sense of humor and spared no expense to express it."

"Who would do this, and why?" Her eyes darted around, as though somehow, with a bit of providential luck, she might identify a suspect who lay in wait. "It's only my third day. I barely know anybody."

The air was crisper, fresher, now that the sun had driven away the rain, and it emitted an enticing, earthy aroma. I looked across the school's yard to the mass exodus of students walking home. I'd be one of them today, seeing as I'd missed my bus.

My friend, business associate, and sometimes case partner wandered over to us. With a sandy brown shaggy mop, dark brown eyes, and a toothy smile that wrapped from coast to coast, most figured him to be a future male model. I saw him as the next Warren Buffett. He had a brain for making money, and lots of it.

"Same as always, Steele?" I asked.

"For sure." He slipped me a small stack of class assignments.

I dipped into my wallet and forked over two Jacksons.

Steele pulled out a wad, adding the pair. "By the way, I got a new beauty last night. She's certified, genuine government issue. She can fly and she can spy!"

I turned to Zadie. "New drone."

"She's all guts, Nacho," he continued. "No bigger than a quarter and the HD on her is crazy." He smiled at Zadie and gave her the once-over. "What's the fly tonight, baby? Going home or going out?"

She wrenched up her face and raised a middle finger. "Go home."

He grinned good-naturedly, his eyes crinkling in the corners. "Dope." He turned to go. "Good luck, Iggy!"

I wheeled back to Zadie.

"Steele's an entrepreneur. And he knows technology. Everybody's gotta make a buck, and he's diversified. Don't judge him by his cover, or his career choices."

"It's not him I'm judging."

"Kinda ballsy to judge anyone." I grabbed her left wrist, yanking up the sleeve. She had scars on her arms from cutting. The cuts had healed, but the scars still revealed a troubled mind, and that troubled me.

She jerked the sleeve back down to hide her past. "I don't do that anymore."

Her eyes darted away from mine, and I could see she was either debating on which lie to tell or deliberating on how much truth to share. Her eyes dropped to the red Chuck Taylor high tops on her feet, and the longer we waited, the more I realized which it was. The truth is always a lot slower to come around than a lie.

"I'll take your case," I said.

"You will?" She drew in a deep breath, her eyes widening. "Thank you!" she exhaled.

"Don't thank me yet. So far, I've done nothing for you. I get twenty dollars a day plus expenses. That's fifty up front. What I don't spend I'll return to you. Don't count on any being left."

Her shoulders drooped.

"What's the matter?" I asked.

"All I have is ten. But I can get you the rest. I promise." She reached into her purse and handed me the partial payment. "I'm not getting many babysitting offers these days. It might take me a while to pay you."

"Keep it," I said.

She gave me a wary eye. "You're still taking my case?"

I don't know why, but this girl, despite the fact I was sure she wasn't telling me everything, looked like she could use a break. Maybe it was the note. Maybe it was the blade, or that she'd only been at MWA a few days. Still, my gut told me to take a chance on this one.

"Keep it for now," I said. "A girl's gotta eat, right?"

She let out a breath and placed the money back in her purse. "Why would anyone write something like that to me?"

"The answer to all your questions, the ones you have now and the ones you're gonna have in two minutes when I'm gone, is the same. I don't know." I whipped my backpack over my shoulder and slipped a pair of Maui Jim's over my eyes. "Go home. When I hear something, I'll text you.

She gave me her number then scurried off. I studied the blade still resting in my hand. There was blood on it. Zadie's, or someone else's? I pocketed the blade and headed across the street to Mr. Dream's.

CHAPTER 2

MR. DARWOOD

Mr. Dream lit up like a fifty-cent sparkler on the Fourth of July when I ambled into his place.

"Nacho! What brings you in today?"

He had on his customary white ballcap repping the Winkler Cougars. Beneath the hat, he wore a pair of black glasses with thick bifocal lenses, a generous gift, he once told me, from the government. He also had a black handlebar mustache, the kind men wore a century ago. He wasn't much to look at, but as far as I was concerned, he slung the best ice cream this side of the Mississippi. He had a great product. Unfortunately, he had a bigger problem. He couldn't get the people through the door without a promotion giving the gelato away for free. Right across the street from Milo Winkler Academy, and still I'd never seen the place slammed. Mr. Dream was a good guy, even somehow had gotten himself elected to the school board. But I was getting the impression he was about as savvy a businessman as an organ grinder's monkey. He had the chops to entertain but was too willing to work for peanuts. Still, in the five years since he'd opened, he and I had become good friends, and I always looked for an opportunity to throw some business his way.

"Just trying to turn a buck," I said.

He puffed out his chest, clapping me on the back with one

hand, gesturing toward the dining room with the other. "Look around, Nacho. I know it isn't much, still just barely out of the wrapper. Haven't even had our sixth anniversary opening yet. But it's mine. And one day you'll have your own place, too. You're building quite a reputation in Ten Spot."

I grimaced. "That's the last thing I want." I laid the receipt with the cryptic message on the stainless-steel countertop. "Recognize this?"

He squinted through the bottom portion of his glasses. "That's mine!"

"Turn it over," I said.

He read the penned scribbles, then flipped it back around. "Whoever it was bought yogurt at 12:08 yesterday afternoon. Let's check the video feed from the security cameras."

"I thought you'd never ask."

Mr. Dream veered toward the employee behind the counter. "Porter, bring my good friend an 1885."

"Only if I pay," I chimed in, digging a fiver out of my pocket.

Porter rubbed his forehead with his fingertips. "What's an 1885 again, Mr. Dream?"

"It's a combo drink, Porter. Dr. Pepper with a quadruple shot of Hershey's chocolate syrup." He turned his attention to me. "You're the only customer I got who appreciates such a tasty tipple."

I tossed the half-sawbuck on the counter and followed Mr. Dream to his office, a small windowless chamber no bigger than one of those cheap metal sheds you get at Home Depot. On the wall hung a free calendar from Farmers Insurance. On a table next to a computer monitor was a copy of *Reader's Digest*. And taped to the monitor was a photo of Scout, his trusty golden retriever who, like Dream, was also a veteran. Dream reveled in stories from his military days, particularly those that involved him and Scout on K-9 search-and-rescue missions. I'd met Scout once, and as far as I knew the retriever was the only family Mr. Dream had. He was an ice cream man, through and through.

He fired up the security app on his computer and fast-forwarded the video feed to the 12:08 mark. On the screen was a boy with disheveled, sandy-brown hair, medium length. He was wearing silver wire-rimmed glasses and a red t-shirt with a large Heinz Tomato Ketchup logo emblazoned across the front. Not something I would've worn, but who was I to judge? And he was standing at the counter with a big bowl of pink frozen yogurt.

I stood to leave. "Thanks."

"You don't want to see any more?" he asked.

"Nope. I got my suspect."

I recognized the boy in red. I didn't know his name, but we had a few classes together. At times, I'd seen him playing soccer with the guys after school. I couldn't care less about his extracurriculars. My questions had to do with his connection to the cryptic message left for Zadie in her desk.

"Why do you do it, Nacho?" he asked.

"For the money, I suppose," I said finally. I shoved my hands in my pocket. "You?"

"For the art." He was beaming. "I give each customer a frozen masterpiece. I like to think of this place as a tasty gallery of frozen art."

"It's nice to have a purpose." Porter brought me my drink, and I took a large swig. "Now that's how I like 'em."

I made for the door but stopped short when I spied a photo hanging on the back wall. "I've never noticed that before."

Dream's face had a vacant look, and his voice took on a reverent air. "It's me with two very special couples. The Hardcastles on the left. The Whiffletrees on the right. I'm sure you've met the Whiffletrees. He's the new principal at your school. That's his wife with him."

He pointed to a white, upwardly mobile couple. Principal Whiffletree was tall, at least six feet, and probably in his mid-forties. He had on a navy golf pullover and black-matte Ray Bans. His most predominant feature was a protruding forehead, made all the larger by a receding hairline. Mrs. Whiffletree was a thin woman, more than a foot shorter than her husband, with long, chestnut-brown hair parted in the middle. I judged her to be about five years younger than her husband. She had warm brown eyes, a pleasant smile, and was more than beautiful in her white sundress. I'd also heard she was loaded.

"Haven't had the pleasure of meeting him or her yet," I said.

"You'll like them. We've known each other for almost ten years," Dream continued, "They've always been very kind to me."

I pointed to the other couple. "I take it these are the Hardcastles? She looks much younger than him."

"She was. About thirty years younger, if you can imagine. They'd only been married five years when he died. They met when she was still a student at Overton. They always said it was love at first sight." His tone was low, and he pressed his lips together, as though his emotions might take control. "I suppose you've heard by now the awful thing that happened?"

I shook my head.

"He died a couple of months ago, only a few blocks from here. Foul play was suspected but never proven. As far as I know the case was never closed. Poor Mrs. Hardcastle."

I took in the Hardcastles more closely. He was at least half a foot taller than the others and looked to be in his mid-fifties. He had bushy salt-and-pepper hair that swept back away from his forehead and a matching mustache and beard. His eyes had an inviting warmth to them. Mrs. Hardcastle was clearly two feet shorter than her husband and looked to be no older than her mid-twenties. She had medium-length brunette hair and small round brown glasses perched bashfully on her nose. He had on a blue and white Hawaiian shirt and his wife wore a sundress with the identical pattern.

"Foul play, you say?" I squinted at the picture of the five. "Funny I didn't hear anything about this."

"It was Mrs. Hardcastle's wish the investigation be kept

under wraps." Mr. Dream edged down into the chair at his desk, wiping his brow and neck with a counter cloth. "He was such a dear friend. When they heard I needed some capital to get this business going they jumped right in, along with the Whiffletrees. I still can't believe he's gone. August fifteenth. I got a call from Mrs. Hardcastle about three o'clock saying he'd died under suspicious circumstances. I slumped down behind the counter. I couldn't help but think that while I was dipping sorbet, my friend was dying alone just two blocks away."

"When was this photograph taken?" I asked.

"About five years ago, the day I opened." He laughed. "We all look like lifelong friends here but really the two couples didn't even know each other. The day this picture was taken was the only time we were together as a group."

I gave the photograph one last look. Everyone seemed so happy that day. Smiling. Posing. Arms wrapped around each other like one big happy family. Their future dreams as bright as that summer day in July had been long. Now one of them was dead. And not just dead. Maybe even murdered?

I looked at the Hardcastles. Probably not the last photo of him. But still, nobody ever knew when his number was up, when a photo would be the final recording of his life.

"I gotta go, Mr. Dream. Thanks again for the 1885. And the intel."

"Anytime, Nacho. It's always on the house for you, my friend. The drinks and anything else I can do for you."

I turned toward the hallway, and headed for the door, snaking past the scattered tables and chairs in the dining room. Outside again, I slipped on the Maui Jim's to shield my eyes from the scowl of the lowering October sun.

As I headed for home, a peculiar thought passed through my brain. If Hardcastle had offed himself then he too had been dying to get out of Ten Spot. I didn't blame him for that, though that's not the way I would've done it. But if this was a case of murder, "foul play" as Dream had said, then it was somebody else who'd wanted Hardcastle out of this God-forsaken town, and the real questions became who and why. Find the answer to the second question and the answer to the first would reveal itself.

It doesn't help to have a license if you don't have a car. It's a forty-five-minute slog home from Dream's. The shortest route cuts through Castlerock Estates, a subdivision for Ten Spot's finest. I'd heard the mayor had a house in Castlerock, as did the new school principal. Once past Castlerock, I began the trek through Centennial Park.

At the old gazebo in the center of the park, I realized I had a tail. Wearing a black hoodie, he'd made every turn I had since Dream's. I began a brisk jog toward the eastern edge of the park to Ten Spot's Carnegie library, an old red brick structure with classical arches trimmed in sand-colored bricks and topped with a red, pressed-metal roof that from a distance gave the appearance of Spanish tiles. It'd been built over a hundred years ago with money from the Carnegie Foundation, and to the best of my knowledge was rarely frequented. It consisted of one large room inside, and two sets of entry points, one in the front that'd been retrofitted with sliding glass doors, and one in the back that only opened in the event of an emergency.

As I ran up the front steps and ducked through the library's automatic sliding doors, I got a good look at my shadow's reflection in the glass panes. He was thick, about six feet tall, with a reddish curly mop on his head. He also had a scraggly red beard, the patchy kind that never seems to come in evenly.

The building was a ghost town, except for old Mrs. Hazelton, the head librarian, who was too blind and too deaf and too weak to do much of anything but sit in an armchair her son had placed in a small office behind the circulation desk and wave to the few patrons who actually visited. Mrs.

Hazelton had adopted the honor system at Ten Spot Carnegie Library, which meant that with the help of a computer and hand scanner, something else Mrs. Hazelton's son had brought in, everyone was expected to check out, check in, and even reshelve their borrowed books so the head librarian didn't have to. Most did because most everyone loved old Mrs. Hazelton. Mostly though, everyone agreed, it was just a lot faster to use the computer without the help of the oldest librarian in Texas.

I gave a quick nod to Mrs. Hazelton before heading to the far wall, swinging a right at the last shelf. A small alcove held the men's restroom on the right, the women's on the left. I flung open the men's door as hard as I could and jumped back into the women's, leaving the door ajar enough to see him take the bait. As soon as the men's restroom door closed behind him, I shot out, grabbed a nearby chair, and jammed it under the knob.

"Motherfucker!" He threw his weight against the door, but the chair that incarcerated him didn't budge.

"Pipe down," I said. "Tell me why you're tailing me."

"What are you talking about? I wasn't following you. I had to take a piss." Again, he threw his weight against the door. Again, the chair held tight.

"You're a terrible liar, even worse at surveillance. A Fourth of July parade could've tailed me better. Who sent you?"

"Go fuck yourself," my prisoner suggested. "I said what I said."

"You're not getting out that way."

There was silence on the other side.

"Tick tock," I said. "The library closes in thirty minutes. It'd be an awful shame to spend the night with two porcelain thrones."

I never got my answer. The door tore open, and the chair shattered, splinters of wood exploding through the air like heavy shrapnel. The sudden eruption sent me flying backwards toward the ladies' room, sprawling across the alcove. I tried standing, but he gave me a swift kick in the ribs that sent me reeling back to the floor.

"You're like I told him," he said. "Too predictable. Do us both a favor. When the boss calls, tell him no."

He pushed open the emergency exit, setting off the alarm, and disappeared outside.

I lifted my aching body off the floor and staggered out, squinting into the bright light. My assailant was nowhere to be found.

I was still trying to make sense of what my attacker had just said and wondering how long it would take for old Mrs. Hazelton to realize the alarm was screeching from the back door, when my phone rang.

"Nacho," I answered.

"Mr. Blanco," the voice on the other end was low, even, deliberate. "I see you've met my associate, Mr. Darwood."

"If you mean the goon who assaulted me, I should have let him rot in the can all night."

"That's no way to talk about your future partner," he said.

I hobbled down the back steps to the parking lot, grimacing with each move. Somebody had to be in a car watching me.

"We will make money, my little PSI," the caller continued, "if you do as I say."

"I don't do business with assholes." There were only three cars in the lot. A Camaro, an F-150, and a Subaru. I was pretty sure none of them belonged to old Mrs. Hazelton, but they were all empty, too. "What happened to your little bootlicker? He and I have some unfinished business."

"Mr. Blanco," he said, "you're sore now. It's understandable. By morning those feelings will have passed, though I suspect the pain in your side will be more obvious than it is now. Not to worry. It happens to the best of us."

I began my walk toward home again. "If this is all you've got, the conversation is over."

"Hear me out, Mr. Blanco. I'm trying to protect you. We

wouldn't want you to come to the same fate as one very nice—albeit slightly incompetent, and extremely carnal—psychiatrist, Doctor Lincoln Hardcastle."

"Hardcastle?" I flashed back to the picture hanging on Dream's office wall. "What are you talking about?"

"My name is Finch," he said. "In short, you'll come to call me boss."

"There are a few other things I'd rather call you," I said.

"I can get you out of this shitty little town once you graduate, take you to the next level, make you a very successful and very lucrative professional private investigator."

I raised my eyebrows and my head. "Why don't you start by unloading what you know about Hardcastle. Who was he?"

"He was a psychiatrist, and you've already met one of his patients," he said. "She even showed you a blade, didn't she?"

I felt a pain in my jaw and reminded myself that grinding my teeth was bad. "What do you know about her? Stay away from Zadie."

"Trust me, Mr. Blanco, it's not Zadie I'm worried about. It's you. I need to meet with you soon. It's a matter of life or death."

"Not gonna happen," I said.

"I was hoping Mr. Darwood had misjudged you, but you're as predictable as he warned."

"What do you do, and why'd you have this Darwood guy tail me?"

A notification flashed across my screen.

"I just sent you an article from the *Austin American-Statesman*," Finch advised me. "It's dated Sunday, August sixteenth, the day after Hardcastle died. In it you'll learn they found the dear doctor sprawled out in a chair in his office with cuts on his wrists. It looked like a suicide. The police thought it a homicide. The coroner didn't have the balls to call it either way. The truth is it was a good ol' fashioned murder."

I read the three-inch headline in bold font across the top of the front page: LOCAL PSYCHIATRIST FOUND DEAD.

The headline caught me off guard. First Dream. Now Finch. Seemed as though everyone in Ten Spot knew more about the death of Hardcastle than I did. I'll admit I'm not one to watch the news much, but still it bothered me that I was just now hearing this. I retraced my movements over the past summer and remembered.

Mid-July through the third week of August my grandmother and I'd been stuck in Alvin just outside Houston with my uncle and his new girlfriend, crammed inside their two-bedroom double-wide on three and a half acres of flat grassland and sketch mesquites. Going there for five weeks hadn't been my idea, but it had meant a lot to my grandmother to be closer to her only remaining son, and I'd had done my best to make the most of it, marking time by disappearing into a stack of well-worn Ellery Queen novels I'd scored from the local library.

"What's your game in this, Finch?"

"Merely a P.I. who needs your help. And you need mine. Don't trust Miss Abernathy, Mr. Blanco. She's an evil seed. But if we work together, we can reveal her for who she really is. I need to meet with you. How about tomorrow night at seven in the gazebo at the park?"

"No thanks," I said.

"Please, Mr. Blanco, I beg you to reconsider. I want to help…"

I ended the call before he'd finished. I needed to learn more about my client, a girl who had a bad habit of cutting herself with razor blades, and maybe cutting others too.

TUESDAY

At 6:00 the next morning I got a text from Zadie with questions about her case. After my dust up with Finch and his henchman, I had some questions of my own. I texted her back. *Library 7:45*

A quick check in the mirror confirmed what I'd already suspected from the throbbing in my head. I had a dark red, egg-sized lump just above my left eye, no doubt courtesy of Mr. Darwood when he'd broken free from his library confinement. A piece of the shattered door must've smacked me good during Darwood's escape. Maybe it was his fist. Didn't matter. I hadn't noticed it prior to going to sleep, but I'd definitely felt it when I'd awakened, along with a colossal soreness in my side where my escapee had planted his foot.

I pulled on a NASA tee and the same jeans I'd worn the day before. Reaching into my pocket, I found my dad's ring. Until now I'd never wondered where Dad had gotten such cheap costume jewelry, but I also couldn't remember a time he didn't have it on, except the day his plane plunged into the Atlantic. I'd taken to wearing it when school had started up in August, mainly as a trial run for the class ring I should have already ordered by now. Jewelry wasn't my thing, and I figured if I had trouble wearing Dad's cheap black band there wouldn't be any reason for me to fork over a half a grand for some overpriced piece from Jostens. Surprisingly though, it hadn't been all that bad, wearing Dad's ring, and truthfully, I'd gotten kind of use to it. Still, trial run notwithstanding, I didn't like people prodding me with questions about it, or, worse yet, insinuating I was some chip off the ol' block, and I dropped the ring inside the drawer on the nightstand by my bed and plodded out to the kitchen for some breakfast. This day I'd go it alone.

As usual, my grandmother was waddling around the kitchen in her pink terrycloth slippers and robe, a matching set from my uncle ten Christmases ago. She was sipping coffee from a saucer because she'd once discovered that piping hot java would cool faster that way than in a typical mug. I set about pouring myself a quick bowl of Cheerios and a glass of OJ and waited for her to discover my face and the goose egg on my noggin. It wasn't long.

"*¡Dios Mio!*"

She reached up to touch the swelling above my eye but I jerked away.

"Don't touch it. It already hurts like hell!"

"Your language," she scolded, then squinted at my face as she studied the lump's discoloration. "You're on another case, aren't you?"

"It's nothing. Just a little scuffle on the way home from school yesterday." I sat down at the breakfast table and splattered the milk over my cereal, eager to change the subject. "How's Rust-Oleum?"

"*Rusti* is just fine, thank you." My grandmother popped two pieces of bread in the toaster and pressed down the lever. "She's in Dallas visiting friends. She'll be here this weekend." She sat down at the table with me and poured herself a glass of juice. "And this time she's not leaving, Nacho."

I stopped chewing and stared at her. "She's moving in?" My mouth was full of Cheerio mush and milk dribbled from the corners of my lips.

She waited until I'd swallowed. "Yes. We're very happy with each other. Plus, she can help keep an eye on you."

"I don't want her to keep an eye on me." I set the spoon down and pushed away my bowl. "I don't even want *you* keeping an eye on me. How long have you known each other? Three months. Not even? Why the sudden rush?"

She didn't answer right away, not until the toaster popped and she'd gotten up. "I can't explain it, *mijo*. When you know, you know." She gave me an impish grin. "I like being with her."

I sighed. "I just don't get it. I mean, you're a grandmother, for God's sake."

"Grandmothers fall in love too." She sat down at the table with her toast and began to butter it. "This is about your mom, isn't it?"

I narrowed my eyes at her. "What's she got to do with anything?"

"You and I are not so different, you know." She took a bite of the toast. "You don't want to lose me like you did your mom. And I don't want to lose you like I did your dad."

"Oh my God." I rolled my eyes. "I keep telling you what happened to Dad, a simple, boring, benign accountant, of all things, was an accident. It could happen to anyone! People die in Ten Spot, too, Grandma, and never leave this crap-hole a day in their lives."

She let out a long sigh and set her toast down. "Maybe. But the way your face looks this morning makes me think that day may come too soon for you."

I stood to leave. "I've got to…"

She came down hard on the tabletop with the palm of her hand. "*¡Siéntate ahora!*"

I sat back down.

"You want me to be careful, Nachito? I want *you* to be careful too. You don't know everything. You're still young. You have dreams? Good. Just make sure they're the right dreams."

I nodded.

She pointed to her cheek. "Now stand and give your *abuela* a kiss before you go to school."

I kissed her, and she hugged me.

"What am I thinking, Nachito Blanco? *Dime.*"

I smiled and tried to look away.

"*Dime.* Or you will have to spend all day with me cooking those chimichangas you love to eat."

I laughed at the thought of me and her cooking together in the school cafeteria. "That you love me."

"That is right. That I love you with every part of who I am, and nothing and nobody will ever take that away. Not your dad. Not your mom. Not Rusti." She pointed at me. "And not you either. Now go and show those teachers who you are."

I slung my backpack over my shoulder and opened the front door.

"Be careful, *mijo.*"

I turned around to see my grandmother, her arms crossed, the terry cloth robe bulging around her pudgy frame.

"Be careful what you dream for. Be very, very careful. It just might come true."

The school bus stops at Old Gnarly, a massive live oak with long knotty limbs that reach out and seemingly tries to grab anyone trolling down my grandmother's street. It's on the end of Debra Lane, my grandmother's street, where about twenty students wait every morning for their free ride to their free and public education. Conversations at this time of the day are generally nonexistent. I like it that way. Gives me time to mull things over, and this morning my mind was still on the exchange with my grandmother, the encounter with Darwood, and my new client. I had some questions for Zadie. For one, where she lived. I also wanted to hear more about her relationship with Hardcastle.

"Hey, Blanco, my boyfriend says you're a dick."

I looked up to see two emos, a girl and a guy, both about my height, standing a couple of yards away, their arms around each other. And they were matching. The tees. The hoodies. The pants. The hair. The nails. The leather straps around their necks and wrists. All black. The guy had a lip ring, the girl a pair of drumsticks in her back pocket. And they'd both shaved half their heads.

The boyfriend laughed at the nerviness of his girlfriend's humor. "Isn't that what they called a detective? A dick. Like Dick Tracy."

The girl turned to her boyfriend. "Who the fuck is Dick Tracy?"

"I don't know. Some old comic my grandpa told me about." The boy turned back to me. "You could call yourself Dick Blanco. The white dick."

There were a few chuckles and some raised eyebrows from students standing near enough to overhear. The boy smiled and nodded to everyone. The girl told her boyfriend his Spanish was brilliant.

I took a few steps toward them both. They dropped the smiles and the act, and I leaned in, staring hard at the boy, lowering my voice.

"I could beat you down right now, Emo, knock your teeth out, send you back to your momma crying, take your girl. But where would that get me? In the end, I'd be stuck with your problem: dating a girl who doesn't have the sense to know that black goes with everything but stupid."

The boy stared for a moment, shook his head, and laughed. "You crazy, Tracy!"

"Maybe. Or maybe I just know that a man who calls another man a white dick only does so because he doesn't have one at all."

I took a step back and waited. Emo studied me, then backed away, and with his arm around his girl's shoulder, walked them both to the other side of Old Gnarly.

I pulled out my phone and fired off a text to Zadie. *Library 20 min*

At 7:25 the school bus arrived, and I found a place to sit two seats from the back. The emos sat in the row directly behind me. Two minutes into the ride, a black student several seats ahead rose and approached me. Lanky, broad-shouldered, and muscular, he kept his neck bent so his head wouldn't scrape the roof. He had tiny black pupils centered in large white eyes. Long thick dreads trickled down the sides and back of his head.

Reaching over, he jarred the phone loose from my hands, causing it to hit the floor with a dead thud. "You stepped on my backpack."

I stood. "I don't remember that. But if I did, I apologize."

The murmuring began from the surrounding students. Someone yelled, "Fight!" and half the bus joined the chant.

The bus driver looked up at the mirror above him and told us both to sit. Neither of us did.

The kid put his left hand on my chest, giving me a shove, like a warning shot over a warship's bow.

I lifted my hands, feigning surrender. "Go back where you were so we can all enjoy the ride in peace."

He put his hand on my chest again, only this time I grabbed it and bent his fingers as far back as they'd go. He jerked his hand back, shaking it as though the pain might fall out.

Again, I raised both hands in a show of amity. "I don't want this."

But he did.

I wondered if he was right-handed or left. I chanced the odds and prepared for a right.

I was wrong. He came around with a left hook.

I threw my head back just in time to only feel a rush of air pass my face. The bus exploded in pandemonium, and the bus driver, still jockeying for position in rush-hour traffic, threatened to pull over and call the cops if we didn't sit down. We called his bluff, and I came around with a right, connecting with the kid's jaw, causing him to stagger from the impact. Again, the bus driver yelled for civility. Twice more I smashed the kid in the face, once with my right to his nose, a second with my left to the side of his face near his eye. The two blows sent him tripping into the laps of two girls who screamed as they scrambled to dislodge themselves from beneath him.

I stole a quick glance at the driver and saw him looking up at me in his mirror again. For a moment, I thought he might actually pull over. Instead, he put his phone to his ear and floored it, his only recourse to get to school as fast as he could.

The kid I'd socked slinked back to his seat, nursing his bloody face with the bottom of his burnt orange tee.

I settled back into my own seat and noticed the guy next to me starring.

"Can I help you?" I asked.

His mouth dropped open. "You always start your day beating down star football players?"

I gave him a blank stare.

"You don't know who that is?" he asked.

I shook my head. "Should I?"

He dropped his voice further. "That's Tobias Williams. I heard he tried to kill his mom last year." He mouthed the word *crazy*, as if to punctuate something I found hard to believe.

The boy emo leaned up and whispered in my ear. "I told you, Tracy. You crazy."

Great. Maybe Emo was right. Maybe I was crazy getting mixed up with someone like Tobias Williams. I stared at the back of his head. I'd have to monitor him for a while. News about the fight would spread and the narrative might convince Tobias of the need for a rematch.

The bus skidded to a halt at the school. I was ready to meet Zadie.

As I moved up the aisle, I noticed Tobias still sitting. He grabbed my wrist as I edged past him. "I'm coming for you."

I jerked my arm free and leaned into his bloody face. "Save

the dirty talk for your girlfriend, Tobias. Trust me. I'm not your type."

I made for the door of the bus. It was time to find my client.

Off the bus I didn't get far. It was Ms. Madrid, the Principal's secretary. She was waiting at the curb of the school's front drive, and I had a feeling I knew why.

I turned back to the bus driver.

"You fight, I call," he yelled through the door.

Tobias came down the bus steps behind me, still cursing, still using my name in vain.

A short stocky Hispanic woman, Ms. Madrid was in a long black dress cinched tight around the waist by an oversized silver belt. She'd piled her straight black hair high on top, revealing two large silver loops dangling from her ears.

I eyed my watch again. "You look lovely today, Ms. Madrid."

"It's Principal Whiffletree," she said. "He needs you both in his office ASAP."

I scowled at my watch, forced a smile to Ms. Madrid, and Tobias and I followed her through the crowded front doors of the school and into the front office. The typical consequence for fighting was a three-day stint in ISS. Even one day of In-School Suspension would hinder my progress on Zadie's case.

Ms. Madrid had Tobias sit in her office while she sent me into the principal's.

Whiffletree was waiting and motioned to a cheap black futon in his office. "Shut the door behind you." He had a severe case of Texas drawl.

I hadn't imagined my first encounter with the new principal would involve my extracurriculars on a school bus. I looked for a tell in Whiffletree's face, but the old man wasn't giving. His brown eyes, soft, inviting, were locked onto mine. A slight smile had formed across his lips. And his breathing was even and relaxed. I'd heard a few things about the new principal, most of it neither here nor there. Apparently, he'd gone to school at Tech, married well, and had no kids of his own. He had a reputation for school-hopping, which probably meant he had eyes on a superintendent prize. He wouldn't be at Milo Winkler Academy any longer than he needed to be. It was also said he handled all discipline at the school the same way he played Texas hold 'em. It was impossible to know from one moment to the next whether he was holding a royal flush or bluffing with a pair of deuces.

"The infamous Nacho Blanco," Whiffletree said when I'd gotten comfortable. He nodded to the lump on my head. "Looks like you got hold of the wrong end of the ugly stick." He pushed up the knot on a lavender tie and adjusted the cuff links at the end of a long-sleeved pinpoint white oxford. "You have any idea why I called you here?"

"You tell me and we'll both know." I peeled away the wrapper from a stick of Juicy Fruit and folded it into my mouth.

"That work you did last spring, solving the mystery of the missing PTA money."

"I see someone's been bending your ear. Where's this going?"

"From what I hear, you have a knack for that kind of thing, detective work."

I looked at my watch. "I still don't see where this is heading."

"It's my wife." A slight smirk filled in the creases in his face. "Mrs. Whiffletree has a problem, and she's personally requested to meet with you. It's a case you can't refuse."

Actually, I could. Another piddling school mystery was the last thing I wanted.

"That's too bad. I'm already at my case limit."

The tardy bell rang. I wasn't going to make it to class on time. And I wasn't going to meet with Zadie either.

Whiffletree skimmed a business card across the desk toward me. "My wife's a formidable woman with considerable wealth, not to mention powerful connections. Saying no would be a career killer in your industry. Then again, saying yes could be the thing that takes you to the next level." He tapped a pen on his forehead before pointing it at me. "Like I said, she has influence. We both do."

He leaned back in his office chair, kicked a black cherry ostrich western boot up on his desk, and laced his fingers across his chest.

"Funny," I said.

He tilted his head to the side.

"Suddenly everybody wants to take my career to the next level."

Whiffletree dropped the boot to the floor, sat up straight, and clicked a lone fingernail against the desktop. "You're gonna want to meet her."

I spat the wad of Juicy Fruit into a wastebasket next to the futon and chewed on my bottom lip. "A case I can't refuse?"

"You're damn skippy." He leaned forward and dropped his voice. "A lot better than three days of ISS, Blanco."

Damn bus driver.

He leaned back up. "Knowledge is power, kid. It's the school motto, right? So, what's it gonna be?"

I nodded. "All right. I'm down."

"Ten hundred hours tomorrow. My house." He pointed to the business card still untouched on the desk. "There's the address."

I picked up the card and slipped it into my front pocket. "I'm supposed to be in lit at that time."

"Actually, you weren't going to literature tomorrow. You were going to ISS, and I just bailed your ass out. You're welcome." He picked up a copy of *Sports Illustrated* and pointed it toward his door. "Have a great day."

I stood to go.

"One more thing," he said, catching me midstride. "Don't be late. Mrs. Whiffletree's not the kind of woman you keep waiting."

I couldn't resist. "What kind of woman is she, Principal Whiffletree?" This time I smirked.

He licked his lips and pressed them together as he pondered his response. "The classy kind, who can afford the best and leave the rest."

I nodded. "Seems to me she's made at least one exception in her life."

I opened the door and headed toward my first period class.

"Mrs. Cer, you mind if Zadie and I go to the library?"

English with Mrs. Cervantes was the only period I shared with Zadie, and it was high time I had a come-to-Jesus with her.

"Nacho Blanco," Mrs. Cer began, "why should I let you go to the library when what I need is your flash fiction from two weeks ago?"

"Nacho and I need to collaborate on the project."

Mrs. Cer and I turned to see Zadie at attention behind her desk. The red Rodeo Drive glasses had disappeared, but her long platinum hair looked the same, streaming over each shoulder. She had on a heather-grey sweatshirt and faded blue jeans rolled at the bottom of each leg just above low-cut black Converses. It was a plain ensemble, unpretentious, alluring in a soft kind of way. It suited Zadie perfectly.

"We need to collaborate on the journalism project you gave us Friday," she said. "Nacho and I are partners."

Mrs. Cer raised a brow and narrowed her eyes but said, "Be back in thirty. I'm watching the clock!"

Mrs. Cer loved the word collaborate. She also loved to watch the clock.

In the hallway, Zadie matched me step for step. "Did you solve my case?"

"Pipe down." I gave her a quick glance. "What happened to the glasses?"

She scoffed. "That was yesterday's outfit." She stopped us and stared at my face. "What the hell happened to you?"

"It's called a goose egg, and it's today's outfit. Now come on. We don't have much time."

We rounded the corner and scooted through the front door of the library, winding our way to a shelf of fiction hidden in the far back. We didn't have long, so I got right to the point, tugging my phone from my back pocket, and pulling up the article from Finch. "This look familiar?"

"He was my psychiatrist. I told you that yesterday." She smiled, her eyes wide, as if to say, "Is that it?"

"You told me he was a bad teacher. You said he died. You didn't say you were a patient of a murder victim and suspected of his killing."

"Of course I was a suspect. The police questioned and cleared me and his other four patients in Ten Spot."

"Don't you think you should have mentioned this?" I pulled the note and razor blade from my pants pocket and dropped them on a shelf. "This makes sense now. You were a suspect, and he was killed with a razor blade, which, by the way, you just happen to be so handy with."

Zadie crossed her arms over her chest, but not before wiping away a tear that had welled up and threatened to smudge her eyeliner.

I held both palms up, like scales, and weighed the possibilities before us. "The way I see it, either you're getting pranked, or you planted the note and blade yourself to throw the heat elsewhere."

"I didn't kill Dr. Hardcastle," her voice breaking. "And I didn't put the note and blade in my own desk. Why would I do that? I'd have to be batshit crazy to draw that kind of attention to myself when I'm already in the clear. If you want to drop my case, fine. Just don't go around thinking I'm some narcissistic murdering bitch. That's not me."

They say the eyes are the windows to the soul, which is why people who have something to hide look away when speaking. Zadie's eyes never left mine.

I leaned in, softening my voice. "Let's assume for the moment you had nothing to do with it. Who did?"

"Why don't you use the receipt I gave you? Find out who bought the ice cream."

"Already did."

She stood up straight, her chest out, hands to her hips. "And?"

I shook my head. "You leave that to me. Rest assured, he's on my radar."

"I see." She drew back, crossing both arms. "I tell you everything, but you tell me nothing? Aren't you the one working for me, or is it the other way around now? I'm not sure I trust you."

"You don't have to worry if you can trust me," I said. "Your problem is whether or not I trust you."

I turned to go but Zadie stopped me, grabbing my arm, pulling me toward her.

"Please don't quit on me, Nacho. Somebody's trying to frame me for a murder I didn't commit. The police were all over my ass with the cutting and all. I should've told you yesterday, but I was afraid you wouldn't believe me either." She paused to dab at a tear. "I need you."

I nodded, and she took both my hands in her own, holding them firm, steadying me with her green eyes. I felt her thumbs stroking the tops of my knuckles, brushing my skin with the lightest of touches, like a cat's tail lazily swishing back and forth. I could feel my heart rate picking up, and I hoped she couldn't see the burning in my face.

I smiled. "I won't quit."

I slipped my hands away from hers and pushed them deep into my pockets.

"But we'd better get to Mrs. Cer. She's watching that clock."

CHAPTER 4
SWEET POISON

At lunch I slammed a twenty-ounce Cool Blue Gatorade behind a chimichanga special before heading toward the outside commons area at the rear of the campus. I caught my grandmother's eyes stalking me from the kitchen on my way out the door. I slipped her a smile but that was it. I had prey of my own to stalk, the kind that eats frozen yogurt at Mr. Dream's and then goes and puts a terroristic note and a bloody razor blade in the desk of the new campus hottie. The kid didn't seem the threatening type. Sometimes, though, the most innocuous are also the most insidious.

I wound my way to the basketball courts, careful to keep an eye on my suspect. I was about to move in closer when a hand landed hard on my shoulder. I turned and found myself face-to-face with two senior athletes I'd seen on the football field but never met. It seems I wasn't the only one people-watching that day, and, by the stench, one of us should've brushed his teeth that morning.

"Who you creeping on?" said the one on my left, a white guy with a square jaw, wavy blonde hair combed to one side, and black hipster glasses that made him a lock for Clark Kent's twin. He even had a widow's peak at the center of his hairline. I wondered if he was sporting hero tights and a cape under his Cowboys jersey and blue jeans.

I let loose a sardonic laugh. "It's a bird. It's a plane…"

"Cut the shit, asshole." Clark pulled a knife from his pocket, a four-inch blade that swished open, and brandished it between our bodies. "Who are you watching, asswipe?"

"Who? Me?" I nodded over my shoulder. "I'm just passing time."

"You're out of your lane, Sherlock. Turn around and walk away."

Interesting, I thought. Why would two seniors be bothered by me scoping on the froyo kid?

"Boys, boys," I lifted my hands, "you got me all wrong. I'm not looking for drama."

Now it was the other one who spoke, the black kid, in a purple polo and a crazy blonde afro that made him look like Redfoo's kid brother. "Leave Aiden alone."

Well, at least now I knew the name of my suspect, I thought.

"Absolutely, boys," I said. "That's all I ever really wanted."

Redfoo flipped me off. "You better hope it is, smart-ass. Next time you might get something you never really wanted."

As they walked away, I made a mental note to get better acquainted with Aiden. I also needed to find out more about these two jackasses. Why were two athletes so protective of a kid who was as barney as Aiden was.

When I turned back around, Aiden was gone, so I headed toward a grove of trees near the courts to seek the sanctuary of some shade. That's when I heard my name from across the yard. It was Ms. Baxter, and the counselor was rabid in her attempts to get my attention.

"Nacho! It's your grandmother. She's on the way to the hospital!"

"Can't this buggy go faster?"

Ms. Baxter was already speeding, and it was just three miles from the school to Ten Spot's Memorial Hospital, but still.

"I'm trying, Nacho."

Within minutes, we were at the Emergency Department entrance. I slung open the door of the red Hyundai Sonata and barreled out. From the medical assistant inside I discovered my grandmother was in ICU.

"The doctor will be with you as soon as there is news." She motioned to the waiting room. "Please get comfortable."

I balanced on the edge of a chair across from Ms. Baxter. "What happened?"

"Someone found your grandmother on the floor of the cafeteria kitchen. She was slurring her words and she couldn't move, totally unaware of who or where she was." The counselor rubbed her arms with her hands to fight off the chill of the frigid waiting room. "Has your grandmother ever had a stroke?"

I bit my lip and tried to think. "Not since I've lived with her."

After thirty minutes, a young black woman in blue scrubs found us. She had her hair pulled back in a pony, a loose stethoscope dangled around her neck, and she hugged a patient chart to her chest like I'd seen the female students at Ten Spot's Overton College carry their books. She introduced herself as Dr. Cooper, and said my grandmother was in critical condition.

"Has your grandmother had any suicidal thoughts in recent days or weeks?" she asked.

I lifted my chin and narrowed my eyes at her. "What are you insinuating?"

She sat down, placing her hands over uncrossed legs. "I'm not positive, and it's only something I've heard. There was another case similar to this here in Ten Spot a few years ago. Have you ever heard of ethylene glycol?"

Ms. Baxter gave her a blank stare.

"Antifreeze," I said.

The doctor continued. "Ethylene glycol is the main ingredient found in antifreeze. It's very sweet to the taste but deadly, particularly if enough is ingested."

"Could a person die from drinking…antifreeze?" Ms. Baxter asked.

I watched the doctor wrinkle her brow as she weighed the question.

"Potentially," she said. "The body goes into cardiac arrest, the vital signs shut down, and the victim is aware but disoriented. Words may come out, but they're not audible or intelligible. The person often slips into a coma just before they die."

I stood up from the edge of the chair and squeezed the back of my neck. "You think my grandmother tried to off herself with a bottle of Prestone?"

"It's not what I think." Dr. Cooper continued to speak in soft, even tones. "It's what I'm asking. Your grandmother has the symptoms of antifreeze poisoning. We've taken her blood, and we're waiting on the results to decide how best to treat her. She's stabilized for the moment, but she's in critical condition."

I took in a deep breath and let it out. "Assuming she swallowed antifreeze, and assuming she didn't drink the stuff on purpose, that would mean somebody tried to kill her."

"I couldn't speculate on that," she said. "That would be a matter for the police."

"Or me." I swallowed the lump that'd been building in my throat and replayed in my head some of the words she'd spoken to me that morning. There were times when we were at each other's neck, each of us succumbing to the same weapons in our verbal war. Guilt and anger. Hammer one, ply the other. But then there'd been other times, like that morning, when it seemed we were more alike than different. We both knew I wanted out. She'd been working hard to change my mind. I'd been working overtime to avoid her until I could get the hell out of Ten Spot. It all just seemed easier that way.

But now, knowing I might never have the chance to talk to her again, the fact that she was secluded in some cold, sterile intensive care unit without any family by her side, her life hanging by a thread, ripped at my insides, and I bit my tongue to hold back the emotions that were climbing. This wasn't the fix I'd been vying for.

Ms. Baxter spoke up. "What can we do until the lab results come back?"

"The best thing you can do," said the doctor, placing a light hand on Ms. Baxter's arm, "is to go home and get some rest. We're going to run her through a battery of tests and watch her closely over the next twenty-four hours. I'll have a better picture of the situation then, and when I do, I'll call you."

Back in her car, Ms. Baxter was the first to speak. "I'm taking you to Tom Brockett's. I don't want you in your grandmother's house alone."

It took me a beat to remember the name of the person she'd wanted me to meet yesterday. Zadie's case. Hardcastle's warning. My grandmother's poisoning. It all rattled around in my head like mismatched marbles in a worn-out sock.

I pinched the bridge of my nose and watched the hospital disappear behind us in my side mirror. "There are some things I need from my house first. 31 Debra Lane."

"Heading there now." She made a hard left on Travis and continued past the school.

After a minute of silence I remembered something. "Will you call Rusti? She's my grandmother's new girlfriend. She should know what's happened. I've got the number, but I don't..."

"It's no problem, Nacho." She pulled up to the light at my grandmother's street and stopped. "I'm happy to talk to her."

I sat up straighter in the seat. Across the intersection, Old Gnarly snarled at me, its tenacles daring me to come closer. "My grandmother didn't try to kill herself."

"I know she didn't."

"I'm going to find whoever did this to her."

She pulled her eyes from the road to make brief eye contact with me. "I know, Nacho. I know you will."

Straight away I could tell something was off when we drew up to the house on the gravel drive. My grandmother never left her front door even a little ajar, and today it was wide open.

"Stay here," I told the counselor. "I'm gonna have a little look-see. If anyone comes barreling down the steps, throw this thing in reverse, and get the hell out."

"I don't like this, Nacho. I don't want you going in there." She plucked her phone from her purse. "I'm calling the police."

But I didn't wait for the boys in blue to show. I twisted out of the car, Ms. Baxter yelling for me to come back. Even from the sidewalk, I could tell the front door had been pried open and torn from its lock. The wood near the handle had splintered and there was a deep raw scarring where some metal object had dug in. Somebody'd been in too much of a hurry to just pick the lock, something even I could've done. And the fact that it was broad daylight said the intruder wouldn't think twice about making sure I didn't impede their escape.

I skulked up the front steps, half expecting someone to plow over me. I peeked around the corner into the living room. Nobody was inside, but they had been, and they'd given the place a good thrashing.

The doors to the antique china cabinet were open, its drawers upended on the floor. I found my grandmother's heirloom silver scattered across the dining room table, and with it, the dozen papier-mâché Easter eggs my grandfather had brought back from Frankfurt for their first wedding anniversary. The family photo albums lay open haphazardly on the coffee table. All five of them. The sofa had been tossed across the room, minus its seat cushions which now lay in a pile in the adjoining dining room. Shards of broken glass like tiny little crystals made soft crunching sounds beneath my shoes as I crept across the living room shag. And a picture of me and Dad taken when I was about eight lay on the carpet, the wooden frame splintered, the photo crumpled.

I reached for it and cut my thumb on a small piece of glass that lay undetected beneath. I winced, seizing back my hand. A drop of blood fell from the cut onto the picture below, causing a red stain to spread across my father's face. I compressed the wound against my jeans and reached down for the picture with the other hand, careful this time to avoid any glass splinters.

"Sorry, Dad." I wiped the blood on the photo across my shirt.

"That wasn't cool, Nacho."

I spun around. Ms. Baxter was in the doorway, her eyes throwing darts, her left hand clenched into a tight ball, her right with her phone smashed to her ear. Through gritted teeth and labored breathing, she was talking to someone, the 911 operator I guessed, and from what little I could infer, neither of them was happy with me.

"I *did* try to stop him," Ms. Baxter was protesting, "but he just barged right in." She took a breath to give me an evil stare. "Well, yes, I'm in here now. I couldn't just let him go alone, could I?" Her eyes scanned the room. "No, I don't think anyone else is here." A slight pause. "Yes, tell them to hurry." With that she ended the call.

I raised my eyebrows and let out a sigh as a request for unmerited sympathy.

She shook her head. "Nacho, that was stupid. Don't do that again. You didn't know who might've been here."

She waited for my acknowledgement, and I nodded. "Yes, ma'am."

Her shoulders dropped, and her head swiveled from one side of the living room to the other as she stepped into the house. "Who could've done this?"

"That's what I'd like to find out."

She made her way in, careful to step over a Tiffany table lamp that had been in the family for generations, its glass multi-colored shade shattered. "Burglars?"

"Hard to say. TV and laptops are here. So's my iPad. There's even twenty…" I counted, "…thirty-seven dollars on the breakfast table." I surveyed the room from where I stood. "They weren't looking for money or anything they could sell or pawn. This was something different."

I slipped the photo of me and Dad into my pocket and surveyed the remainder of the house. They'd pulled out a few dresser drawers in my grandmother's room. I found the same scene in my room. The kitchen was the same. Nothing overturned, nothing broken, nothing shredded. It was almost as if someone had given the rest of the house a cursory glance.

I let my eyes roam over the room piece by piece. Was the clue there, some missing piece, scrambled with the others, surreptitiously hidden beneath the mess, buried in the chaos, something that could bring this picture into focus?

I was still racking my brain when two of Ten Spot's finest arrived.

It took all of thirty minutes to dust the place for prints, which they didn't find, and fill out a report, which I suspected would go nowhere.

The cops left and Ms. Baxter inched up to me and lay a gentle hand on my shoulder. "I can come over and clean this weekend."

The mess didn't concern me. I was thinking about the timing. This wasn't some random break-in any more than my grandmother's poisoning was some run-of-the-mill suicide attempt.

"Hold on," I said, snapping my fingers. "There's something I need to check."

Ms. Baxter followed me to my room. I opened the drawer of my nightstand and there it was. Dad's ring, right where I'd left it that morning. I closed the drawer and tried to decide what to do. Finally, I opened the drawer again, snatched the ring, and dropped it into a side pocket of a small duffel. I wondered if Ms. Baxter had seen me do this but decided not to ask. Instead, I tossed some clothes into the duffel and tried to make sense of the break-in. Just one more reason to leave Ten Spot as soon as possible.

I pulled out my phone and tapped on the last incoming number.

Finch answered after one ring.

"I'll meet," I said.

Maybe Finch had something worthwhile. Maybe he didn't. I wouldn't know unless I met with him and heard him out. One thing was for certain. This situation with Ten Spot wasn't getting any better. The sooner I met with Finch, the sooner I'd know if he was the gilded detective he claimed to be.

"I hoped you'd come around, my lad," Finch said. "I have a great opportunity for you, and for me. We can talk more about it when we get together."

"When and where?" I asked.

"Tonight, at the gazebo in the old park, seven o'clock," Finch said.

"Make it seven-thirty."

CHAPTER 5

PERSON OF INTEREST

Brockett had a slight log cabin at the outskirts of town on the edge of Lipan Lake. His hair was white and thinning, and his face was lined with the creases of time and responsibility. I judged him to be about mid-seventies, though he still carried himself like a man who'd at one time been both athletic and striking. He was lanky, his face chiseled and ruddy, and his eyes were piercing blue, like the water of the lake behind his home. He had on khaki cargo pants flanked by a grey tee and black hiking boots, and he greeted us outside with a broad smile and a large right hand firm to the shake. He also greeted us with a 9mm Glock holstered to his hip.

"Welcome, Nacho. I've heard much about you." He studied the lump above my eye. "That's a nasty contusion. You want some ice for that?"

I waved him off. "Thanks, but I'm good."

We walked to the front porch and I noticed a lone eight-foot palm to my right, a solitary sentry standing guard over the entryway, and strangely out of place among the live oaks and mesquites that otherwise dotted the grounds.

"I didn't realize palms were native to central Texas."

"That's Philo," he said.

He ushered us into the cabin, and I dropped my backpack and duffel onto a brown leather sofa.

"You named your palm?"

"Me and that palm have been together for a long time," he said. "Every time I move, I take him with me. He's learned to bloom where he's planted."

I sized up the cabin at a glance. A modest living room off to the right. A sparse, white kitchenette to the left. And a small white granite bar the only line of demarcation between the two living spaces. *The Charm School* by Nelson DeMille and a big black Bible, its leather cover worn and cracking, sat next to a bowl of oranges on the bar. Two sliding glass doors led to a deck hanging over the bank of the lake. And mounted above the doors was an unassuming flat screen TV. The cabin was immaculate and devoid of the customary tchotchkes.

I pointed toward the lake, the water still, the sun's blazing likeness glaring off its polished surface. "That's quite a view."

"It's the first thing I see every morning, and the last I see at night." He considered the setting. "Every man needs a place to get re-centered."

"I have to go," Ms. Baxter said, putting her arms around Brockett's neck, kissing him on the cheek. "Thanks, Dad, for letting us come over. Call me if you need anything." She grabbed both his hands in hers, leveling her eyes on his, like a mother giving one final desperate plea to a child before shipping him off to school. "Be careful!"

"I'm always careful." He patted the 9mm, slipping her a wide grin and wink.

She tilted her head and gave him a look. "You know what I mean!" Turning to me she added, "You be careful too. Not everybody in this town is who they seem."

I gave her a three-finger Boy Scout salute and we walked her out. Settled into her car, she backed out and headed toward town.

Back inside the cabin, I discovered Brockett also had an office adjacent to the living room. He invited me in, and I slumped onto a red leather couch while he found his way behind a giant oak desk that held three large monitors.

"You're Ms. Baxter's dad?"

He reached under the desk, retrieving two bottles of Big Red from a small fridge, one of which he handed to me. "My wife and I unofficially took her in when she was three. Truthfully, I'm the only father she's ever known." He took a swig of the soda, wiping his mouth with the back of his hand. "Tell me a little about yourself, Nacho."

I offered a shrug. "Not much to tell. Just another junior at Milo Winkler Academy living with his grandmother."

"That's not the way I hear it," he said.

I gave him a curious look.

"My daughter says you've got an exceptional talent for solving mysteries. I heard what went down with last year's principal. Your grandmother called me the day it happened."

I snapped my head toward his. "She did? Why would she do that?"

"Told me she was proud of you, even though she was scared of the work you want to do."

I raised an eyebrow. "I didn't realize she even knew."

He let out a chuckle. "She knows more than you'd ever want her to know." His tenor turned serious. "I heard she's in the hospital. What happened?"

I filled in Brockett on my grandmother including the scene at her house.

"What's your theory?" He rubbed the stubble on his face with his left hand, no doubt taking in my story as well as the quality of his shave that morning.

"I don't believe it's a coincidence someone breaks into my house the same day my grandmother winds up in ICU."

He lifted his chin, drew in a deep breath, and let it out. "If you ask me, somebody's sending you a message. Got any cases you're working on?"

"One. Nothing big so far."

"Could be somebody wants you off that case. Wouldn't be the first time an investigator was *encouraged* to stop poking his nose around. Talk to anybody new in recent days?"

"Another private eye. Wants me to work for him after I graduate."

"Interesting."

I studied the label on the bottle of the Big Red. "Maybe. Maybe not."

He downed another swig. "This town isn't what it was. A lot has changed since I entered law enforcement fifty years ago."

"You grew up in Ten Spot?"

"I grew up in Austin and they recruited me right out of the police academy. They needed a new deputy in Ten Spot. I needed a job. I put in five years before landing in Quantico. I saw some shady things in those days, but I was too green to understand it."

"Still with the FBI?" I picked up a picture frame from the end table next to me. In the photo was a much younger Tom Brockett holding a young girl with short curly brown hair. Next to him was an attractive brunette in a dark blue sun dress.

"Retired. I came back seven years ago after a short stint as a consultant for the San Francisco office. I've always had a soft spot for this place." He motioned toward the photo in my hand. "My sister took that picture the day we brought Darcy home." He took another drink. "I always felt one day someone would come in and clean up Ten Spot. It's gotten seedy over the years."

I laughed. "You mean sketch?" I narrowed my eyes at his. "How so, I mean, besides being boring and old?"

He smiled. "Sketch is a good word. And I can see how it's boring for a young man like you. I'm talking about the break-ins and the drugs and the unemployment and the violent crimes. It's not that we didn't have all that back then. We just have fifty times more of it now."

"What about Ten Spot's finest? I mean, surely they are aware and doing what they can."

Brockett pursed his lips and gave me a thoughtful look. "I sometimes wonder if Ten Spot's police department isn't responsible for a lot of the delinquency this town has now." He let out a low sigh. "It has to be someone outside the system who'll come in and clean up."

"Ever think you're the one?" I drained my bottle and set it on his desk. "Looks to me like you can still handle yourself."

"Too old now. Has to be someone young, with character and grit." He stared out his office window toward the lake. "I once knew a man. I thought he was the one. He was young and bull-headed enough to not let others get the best of him. It didn't work out." He bit his bottom lip and looked to me. "You kind of remind me of him. What are your goals?"

"Simple enough. Get out of Ten Spot. The sooner, the better."

He swished his Big Red around in the bottom of the bottle, watching the rich, sugary liquid come alive to a frothy swirl. "You don't like it here."

I raised an eyebrow. "Does anyone?"

"A lot of us still feel there's hope for the town. It's a calling, I suppose, to make a difference."

I let my hands carve through my hair, holding it back, then letting it go. "You'd have to be called to want to be here."

He chuckled, then leaned back in his chair, propping one boot on the desk. "Tell me about your case."

"Not much to tell. I'm trying to figure out why someone put a threatening note and a razor blade in a girl's desk at school, a girl who also happened to be a patient of a psychiatrist who died from a few well-placed slashes on his wrists."

"Hardcastle?" He lowered his chin. "Your client was his patient?"

"Says she's being framed. Finch says otherwise."

"Who's Finch?" he asked.

"That's the private eye. He's trying to solve the murder, and my client is on his radar."

Brockett let out a low whistle. "Let me get this straight. Your client hires you to prove she's innocent in Hardcastle's death, and a private investigator wants to hire you to prove she's guilty."

"Something like that. Now my grandmother is in the hospital and someone's tossed her house. Somebody's working overtime to push me away."

"Or pull you in."

I pulled out a stick of Juicy Fruit and chewed on what Brockett had just said. "What've you heard about Hardcastle? Any suspects? Motive?"

"I have a friend who worked for the Bureau. He's retired, in Austin, but consults for Ten Spot's PD. His name is Chuck. According to him, their person of interest is an individual in a red hoodie." He made a few quick strokes on his keyboard and motioned me to come around the desk to his side.

On one monitor was security footage taken the day Hardcastle died of someone entering the dry cleaners across the street from Hardcastle's office. Three seconds later the person turns and walks out. That person wore a red hoodie, blue jeans, and a Texas Rangers ball cap turned around backwards over long red hair.

"Ten Spot PD pulled it from the dry cleaner's surveillance system," he said. "The camera caught this about the time Hardcastle was killed that Saturday in August, right across the street from his counseling office."

"I don't get it," I said, jutting out my chin and stroking my Adam's apple. "Why was it tagged?"

"On its own, probably wouldn't have been. Just another customer walking in and out. Maybe the person forgot something and had to turn around as soon as they arrived. But we have two other videos."

He opened another file and we watched the same individual,

same red hoodie, same backwards Rangers cap, walk into Book-marks, the downtown bookstore, and back out again. He opened a third file, this one from Sweet Tooth's, the local candy shop. Same red hoodie, same M.O., same careful back to the camera.

"Person of interest," I said.

"And in all three cases, about the time Hardcastle's killed, the individual walks in and out of three businesses all on the same street as Hardcastle's office. The dry cleaners, the bookstore, the candy shop, in that order." He finished his Big Red and tossed the bottle into a recycling bin.

"This person needed to get down the street," I said. "The best way to get away from Hardcastle's office on a busy Saturday afternoon was to blend in with other customers running errands that day. It also appears the individual knew exactly where not to look."

"This was no stranger," he said. "They had an intimate rela-tionship with Ten Spot."

"Any theories on motive?"

He leaned back and threw up his arms. "You've heard the saying. It's either money, sex, or revenge."

"Or all of the above. What happens after Sweet Tooth?"

"Nobody knows," he said. "Could be a driver picked him up. Could be he walked home."

"Any evidence this person of interest was actually in Hard-castle's office?"

"None. Hardcastle didn't have any cameras. At least none we know of."

I stood up to leave. "As they say, the absence of evidence isn't evidence of absence."

Brockett gave me a startled stare. "I'm impressed with your working knowledge."

"I probably watch too much *Dateline*," I confessed.

He went on. "Nacho, this town needs young men and women like you to restore it, make it whole, healthy, like it used to be. Might not hurt to get some professional training from an established PI, like this Finch fellow, regardless of where you decide to hang your shingle one day."

I slung my backpack over my shoulder and headed for the front door. "Thanks for the drink and a place to stay. I gotta go to town for a bit. It's a long walk and time's evaporating."

"Hold up a second." I turned to see Brockett reaching behind his head to massage his neck. "I probably shouldn't do this…"

There was a long pause, and I gave him a wary eye as I waited for him to finish. He bit his bottom lip, and those blue eyes took on a blank stare, as though his thoughts were miles away. At last, he licked his lips and asked, "Have you ever driven a motorcycle?"

A motorcycle? I couldn't hide the smile that slipped across my lips. "Actually, I have. Plenty."

Brockett took a deep breath and let it out slowly. "There's an old one on the side of the cabin. It's probably fifty years old now. I got it in my twenties and tore up the streets with it." He smiled as he remembered his good times. "It's a Honda Triumph." He fished from inside his pocket a shiny, silver, palm-tree key chain and removed a key from the ring, tossing it to me. "I warn you, it's not much. In fact, it's hardly anything. Honestly, I can't tell you the last time I even rode it. Darcy's been on it a few times, but I wouldn't know when. If it still runs, she'll get you around a lot faster than walking." He cocked his head to one side. "I don't suppose you have a license for driving a motorcycle?"

I grinned. "Let's just say I'm working on it."

"Well, I won't say anything if you won't."

"Deal." I stuck out my hand and we shook. "Thanks."

I found the bike waiting inside a large dark green pop-up Coleman tent on the left side of the cabin. Brockett wasn't quite right about the bike. It was a whole lot less than not much. The part of the tank that wasn't beginning to rust was half Carolina blue, half white, with deep cut marks scarred into its metal exterior. The black leather seat had cracked, and somebody'd done terrible repair work with gray duct tape. Surprisingly enough, the tires were the best thing going for this hunk of junk. They'd obviously been replaced not too long ago. Well, sometime within the last fifty years, anyway.

I looked at my watch. With the bike I had just enough time to make one stop before meeting Finch at the park. I gave the bike a swift kick, and much to my surprise it actually came to life between my legs. I hit the road that led away from Brockett's cabin back toward town, toward the old highway that led to Austin. At the highway I stopped and pulled out my phone.

"Steele. It's me. You home? Great. I'll be there in ten, and I'm in the mood to spend some money."

Thanks to the Triumph I pulled up at the home of one Steele Buchanan at a quarter past six, and this time it wasn't to keep him on retainer for my homework assignments. Back at Brockett's, an idea had seeped into my brain, and Steele was the only one I knew with the goods to make it happen.

Steele's parents were lawyers, which probably meant they were as crooked as barrel of fishhooks. I didn't care. Not today, anyway. They'd always been friendly to me, even invited me on a couple of their family trips with Steele. But more importantly, they had a son who had a knack for hooking me up with gadgets a normal teen shouldn't get his hands on. Steele's dad had a private practice near the courthouse. His mom was a poli-sci professor at Overland College across town. They were loaded, they had connections, and their son had become very adept at using both to his advantage, something I intended to put to my advantage before meeting Finch.

Steele's family lived on the outskirts of town in a yellow turn of the century Victorian home with a gray wrap-around front porch, white intricately carved gables, and tall, sweeping, angular black roofs. They called the place Stanhope, supposedly named for some small town in Jersey where his mom grew up.

From Steele, I'd learned his parents had socked some serious money into Stanhope, in the hopes that one day it'd become one of those overpriced B and Bs honeymooners flock to. The house set dead center on a well-manicured three-acre spread. A long gravel drive led up to the front of the house. Out back was an Olympic-size pool and a separate entertaining pavilion. Midway across the back of the property, just beyond a pecan grove, set an impressive navy-blue private tennis court where his mom actually liked to hold court every weekend with a bevy of tennis pros. And at the furthermost end of the property was a small taupe-colored metal shed with a black roof, a set of windows on one end, and a single automatic garage door on the other. This was "Santa's Workshop," as Steele called it, his own personal space for both business and pleasure.

He met me out front on the gravel drive. "You got wheels!" He gave the Triumph the once over. "You comin' up in the world, P.I."

I turned off the bike and dismounted. "Just trying to get around, you know."

"I hear ya." Steele looked around behind me as though someone was missing. "Where's your boo, bro?"

I rolled my eyes. "If you mean my client, I don't know. Probably wanting to know if I've solved her case yet."

Steele chuckled and gave me a broad smile. "You outkicked your coverage with that one, Iggy."

"Don't I always?"

He led me around the side of Stanhope, past the pool and through the pecan grove, to the workshop. He tapped in the password on his keyless entry and the garage door dithered open.

I looked around inside. "You been doing some remodeling?"

He laced his fingers on top of his head as we entered the shop. "Nah. Not recently. You must not've been here in a while, man."

I took the place in. He'd definitely changed things up. On

one end of the workshop were a couple of leather sofas that faced an enormous flatscreen mounted on the wall, a tangle of multi-colored wires pouring out of the side of the unit to a jumble of gaming boxes on a console below. On the other end of the room were two oversized worktables and a pair of large bookshelves on either side of the long window. Spread out across the tables was an assortment of various sizes and styles of drones.

"Let me guess," Steele began. "You need a bird."

"You'd be right." I walked over to the tables and began browsing.

"You got interested in that little birdie I was telling you about yesterday. Am I right? No bigger than a quarter. The one that can fly *and* spy? I hope you brought some serious cheddar for that one."

I stopped walking, shook my head, and let my eyes rest on the table while I thought. "I need something that will let me follow someone outside. He can't know I'm there. And I need some serious visuals. I want to be able zoom in without the drone moving in."

Steele moved to one of the bookshelves and selected a medium-sized black drone with the words Urban Scout printed across the top of the body. He sat the unit down on one of the tables and unfolded the wings. "You're gonna like this one, Iggy. This one is used by authorities for search-and-rescue operations." He turned to face me and winked. "And talk about optics! You can read a dime from fifteen hundred high."

The Scout stood on four long legs and looked to have a wingspan of about two and a half to three feet tip to tip.

"How much?"

"With one battery this bird, if you could even get it, would cost you more than five, close to six, on the open market. For you, let's call it an even five and I'll throw in an extra battery."

"You're all heart, my friend."

"That's what they call me. Steele 'All Heart' Buchanan." He

tossed the controller to me. "It's got a full tank, too. You wanna take it for a spin over some of my closest friends?"

We headed outside behind the workshop. Here, just on the other side of the fence that marked the end of the Buchanan property, the terrain sloped down toward the old Ten Spot Cemetery. I was not unfamiliar with drones. I'd acquired quite a few from Steele over the last several years, but nothing like this bird. I flicked on the system's power, doing the same for the controller. The craft came to life, lifting, hovering about six feet off the ground. With the left and right toggles, I found I could maneuver the UAV with ease and complete abandonment, and for the next five minutes I buzzed over the final resting places of two hundred of Ten Spot's most famous namesakes. Even without an audio feature the HD screen between the toggles gave me a clear panorama of the landscape below.

Then I tested out the real reason I wanted it. While the craft hovered in place about a thousand feet high, I zoomed the camera in so close I was able to read one of the markers at the base of a colossal pecan tree. Bird poop covered the unassuming granite headstone, and it appeared nobody had bothered to mow around the plot in years, but with the drone's visuals I had no trouble making out the name of the deceased. *KATIE LOVE.* For a quick moment I wondered who this had been, but the stone had none of the customary sentimentalities inscribed beneath the name, only the years marking the beginning and end of life. Steele was right. The bird had some serious optics. Using the controller, I zoomed back out and away from the marker, once again getting a more panoramic view of the cemetery. The drone had continued to hover in place the entire time. I flew it across the landscape a few more times, until at last, satisfied I had a good feel for the drone, I brought it down to preserve what juice the battery still had left.

I picked it up, folded its wings in, and pocketed the controller. "Throw in some way for me to carry it on my bike and I'll take it."

Steele slapped me on the back and let out an enthusiastic laugh. "And this why I like doing business with you, Iggy."

He gave me a small black backpack with drawstrings, and I slipped the drone inside and slung the pack over my shoulders. I slipped him five Benjamins and he walked me back to the front where the bike was waiting.

"Whatever you're doing," Steele said, "be careful." His tone was low and lacked his usual exuberance, the first time since I'd arrived.

"I'm always careful," I said. "Except when I'm not."

I mounted the Triumph, kicked it to life, and headed back down the long gravel drive away from Stanhope to the highway. Before pulling out, I checked my phone. No messages, so I called the hospital to check on my grandmother's status. The nurse on duty said she was still out cold in ICU but stable. I told her to give me a call the moment my grandmother awoke, or the moment her vitals changed, and she assured me she would.

I headed out onto the old highway to Austin and pointed the bike toward town, toward the gazebo in Centennial Park. It was time for my meeting with Finch, and time to make good use of the five C-notes I'd just given Steele.

CHAPTER 6
DOWN

A large hill rises three hundred feet above Centennial Park's southern end, a frequent locale for joggers who take the paved winding trail to its pinnacle, a brick and limestone-covered lookout with a gunmetal-gray steel covering. It was from this vantage point I set up. I pulled the drone from my backpack, along with a pair of wireless Bose headphones synced to my iPhone. I slipped the headphones over my ears, fired up the drone, and at seven twenty-five set the bird free.

I had one goal for this get-together. I wanted everything Finch had on Hardcastle and how his death related to Zadie. I also knew he had one goal. He wanted me to flip on my client so he could pin a Murder One rap on her.

At exactly seven-thirty, I caught sight of a figure trudging his way across the bridge over Centennial Lake. Using the drone's HD visuals, I zoomed in and laid eyes on a short, stocky man in his mid-forties. He was wearing a white polo, khakis, and a brown sport coat with black patches on the elbows. In his left hand he held a manilla folder. In his right, one of those disposable coffee cups with a lid. He also had on a white Western straw hat and aviators. I zoomed in tighter. On the folder's tab the initials ZA were handwritten in red marker. And on one side of the coffee cup a barista had written the word *Joe*. I smiled. *Cup of Joe*. At least Finch had a sense of humor.

Inside the gazebo, this drugstore cowboy glanced at his watch several times as he paced. He was getting pissed, and when he couldn't take it any longer, he yanked out his phone, causing mine to buzz.

"You're late, Finch," I answered.

"Late? I'm here! Where the hell are you?"

"Closer than you'll ever realize."

I jumped up on the stone retaining wall and sat down, straddling it. The lowering sun behind me warmed and softened the muscles in my back. More importantly, the sun's rays would keep Finch from spotting me through the blinding glare. Aware that his associate Darwood might be nearby, I wasn't leaving anything to chance.

He let out an expletive and stepped outside the gazebo, shading his eyes from the bright light, rotating a full 360 degrees as he scanned the park's perimeters.

"Don't worry about where I am," I said. "I thought this a safer way to meet since the last time we talked your little freak assaulted me."

Finch stepped back into the shade of the gazebo, fanning himself with his hat. "Listen, Blanco, I don't do business this way."

"If you want to do business with me, you'll do it any way I please and you'll like it. You have ten minutes unless I get offended or you get boring. Make me care, Finch, and keep it interesting."

"God damn it." He sighed. "In short, I need you to help me find out whether one Zadie Abernathy was responsible for the death of Dr. Lincoln Hardcastle."

He paused, probably wondering if I'd dash at the mention of Zadie's name.

"I'm listening," I said. "Go on."

"Hardcastle's death had all the makings of a suicide, without the note. Ten Spot PD saw it as a homicide. And the coroner, bless his heart, reported the cause of death as unknown. Now the insurance company won't settle. Whether it was a suicide or a homicide doesn't matter. They're ready to pay out. They just need it clear on the report."

He paused to catch his breath.

"I need concrete evidence, not theories, not speculation. That's where you come in. You know this town. Working for me would be very lucrative for you, not to mention a tremendous career enhancement."

"And you?" I asked. "I assume you think it's murder."

"Hell. It don't take no genius to see somebody murdered Hardcastle and then tried to make it look like hari-kari. Simple as that."

"And you think my client did it?" I asked.

"Hell yeah, I do."

Everyone is capable of murder in the right circumstance, but Zadie didn't fit the bill, and Finch was looking more and more like another washed-up cop with tunnel vision, happy to nail my client first, nail down the evidence second.

"Look, Finch," I said, "Leave Zadie out. The police cleared her."

"I'm gonna find who did this, Blanco, and you can bet your ass, if it's her, and you get in my way, I'll take you both down. Impede this investigation and the insurance company will call for charges against you as an accessory after the fact."

He was breathing heavy. He pulled a handkerchief from his back pocket and wiped his brow.

"It's your choice, kid," he said. "Work with me to find who killed Lincoln Hardcastle or get caught in the crossfire."

"And when you find she didn't do it?" I asked.

He softened his tone now, like a father trying to reason with his son about getting a job, going to college, moving out, anything that would keep the old man from playing bad cop.

"Look," he said. "I'm not gonna lie. I need your help. You

asked me and I told you. I hope it's not her. If you help me, we can find out for sure and put an end to it."

He lifted his arm, pulled back his jacket sleeve, and looked at his watch. "You got three hours to contact me. Help me help you, and maybe, if she's lucky, we can help her too."

Finch ended our call on that note and with the drone I watched him head back in the direction he'd come. It was my turn to play the role of tail, and I wouldn't be as conspicuous as Darwood had been.

I watched Finch get into an outdated blue Crown Victoria. He backed out from a row of cars and turned left onto Brookfield. A block later he took a right onto MLK, then a left onto Travis. Then he made a slow turn into the parking lot of Winkler Academy, pulled up to the curb in front of the school, and got out. At the front door, he pulled out a keyless entry badge and disappeared inside, like he owned the place.

I let the drone hover above the school. What business would Finch have inside MWA? Who could get him access to the school after hours? And most importantly, was he right about Zadie?

I didn't want to admit it, but Finch's offer was growing on me. Never had I been this close to a real solution to leaving Ten Spot.

The drone's handset chirped. The battery level was at one percent. I set the bird down across the street from the school in Mr. Dream's parking lot, gathered up my gear, and hopped on the Triumph. I had a drone to retrieve. I needed an ice cold 1885. And I had to figure out how to tell Zadie I was dropping her case so I could investigate her for murder.

The drone was waiting for me in the middle of Dream's parking lot. The place looked dead, and I went inside and found Mr. Dream sitting behind the counter looking at his phone. Not another soul in sight.

"Slow night?" I asked as the door closed behind me.

He looked up when he saw me, and his face brightened. "My good friend! What brings you out tonight?"

"Just a little investigative work." I popped a fiver on the counter. "Give me the usual and make it a large."

"Your money's no good here," he said when he handed me the drink.

"My money's better here than any other place." I looked around at the empty dining room. "Must be kinda tough…"

His phone rang, stopping me midsentence, and he moved around the corner at the far end of the counter to answer it. His voice was low and muffled but I managed to catch two words: "I know!" Within a few seconds, Mr. Dream turned back to me, pocketed the phone, and said, "I'm sorry, Nacho. I have to close up. I have a slight emergency I must attend to."

I desperately wanted to ask him about the nature of the call, but I didn't. I told him I understood and helped myself out the front door. I sat on the Triumph to finish the drink and watched as Dream locked up and sped off in his car.

I was still thinking about Dream's untimely phone call when my phone rang.

"Blanco," I answered.

"Mr. Blanco," the caller began, "this is Regina Waters, your grandmother's nurse at the hospital." She had one of those slow, syrupy, southern drawls.

"I'm glad you called," I said. "I've been waiting for some news about her."

"She's still in ICU, Mr. Blanco, but she's in stable condition. We're still running some tests and I hope to tell you more tomorrow. I do think the worst is behind her, though."

"That's great. I appreciate your call."

Nurse Waters hesitated. "There is one other thing I thought you should know."

I narrowed my eyes and pushed the phone closer to my ear.

"Your grandmother received some flowers today. They were

dropped off at the nurse's station. Anyway, I think you might want to call the florist."

"Why should I do that, Ms. Waters?" I asked.

"Well, you see," she said, her words as thick as maple syrup on a six-inch stack of flapjacks, "there was an envelope that came with the flowers. You know how they put the envelope on that little stick to let you know who sent the flowers?"

"I'm familiar. Tell me about the envelope." I took another large gulp of 1885.

"Well, that's just it, Mr. Blanco. Inside the envelope where they put the little card there wasn't a card. Instead there was a razor blade. That's all there was. A razor blade. Can you believe that?"

I choked on the 1885, threw the drink to the ground, and pulled the phone away from my ear so Ms. Waters wouldn't hear my hacking. When I'd finally pulled myself together, I wiped my mouth with the back of my hand and put the phone up to my face only to realize Ms. Waters hadn't skipped a beat.

"…it's one thing to be sent up the wrong flowers, I mean that happens all the time. But I mean really this is quite inexcusable and…"

"Ms. Waters!" I didn't mean to say her name as forcefully as it came out.

"Mr. Blanco? Are you okay?" Her voice still had its southern syrupiness, but the tone was guarded now, like a genteel woman who knew she'd been offended but refused to say so.

"I'm sorry, Ms. Waters. I just need you to slow down." I was gesturing with my free hand now, like a cop waving someone to pump the breaks in a school zone. "Tell me again what you just said."

She let out a deep sigh. "Well, Mr. Blanco, I think the florist ought to hear they made a mistake. Somebody could've got hurt on that. I was the one that opened it, but luckily I did it, you know, kind of slow-like so I didn't get cut."

"Good thing you played it safe," I said. "Would you take a

picture of that razor blade and text it to me? And save it for me. Place it in that envelope and put it where nobody else can get to it until I get there. You're right. I need to talk to the florist."

She agreed to hold the blade for me and sent me the picture too. It was the same kind Zadie found in her desk, a flat, silver, single-edge blade. A Merkur Super. Somebody wanted my attention, and somebody had it.

I kickstarted the bike and high-tailed it to Brockett's cabin. He was standing in the kitchen pouring himself a generous glass of milk as I entered.

"How goes it?" he asked, settling himself onto a stool at the kitchen bar.

I took the seat next to him and filled him in on the evening's developments, the meeting with Finch, and the discovery of another blade. He found my use of the drone impressive, and I pulled it from the backpack and went over some its more technical aspects. I didn't tell him of my growing concern with Zadie.

He took a drink. "Where's all that leave you?"

I ticked the points off using my fingers. "Who put a razor blade in Zadie's desk? Who put my grandmother in the hospital? Who trashed her house? What do I do about Finch?" I looked around the kitchen and wondered if Brockett had any Dr. Pepper. I also wondered if he had some chocolate syrup. "What would you have done when you were my age if a P.I. offered you a job?"

"I would've been tempted to take it," he said, and there wasn't the least bit of hesitancy in his voice. "Iron sharpens iron." He patted the black Bible sitting on the bar in front of him. "Success is never a one-man operation. Finch might be the thing you need. You might be the thing Finch needs too. Works both ways."

I pinched my bottom lip and rubbed it with the thumb. "That's what he said."

"But be careful. Do your homework on him. You just met

him. He's probably who he says he is, but it still wouldn't hurt to investigate the investigator." He stood, downed the last of his milk, and washed out his glass in the sink. "I believe you'll make the right decision."

He headed back to his office, leaving me alone with the thoughts swirling around in my head.

I pulled my laptop out of the duffle and powered it up. Logging onto Newspapers.com, I typed in the words "Hardcastle" and "Ten Spot" in the search engine. The next page loaded with ten separate entries, most from the *Austin American-Statesman*. All had to do with the doctor's death.

They found the psychiatrist on the afternoon of Saturday, August fifteenth, when a teenager came to his office around four that day. According to the articles, upon finding the body, she'd run out of the office across the street to the dry cleaners. The proprietor of the cleaners called Ten Spot PD, who arrived within minutes.

The medical examiner stated that rigor mortis had not set in when he'd examined Hardcastle's body. That meant he'd died within hours of being found, putting his time of death around two that day. The cause of death had been blood loss from the cutting of both wrists. He would've lost consciousness while bleeding out before succumbing to the injuries. The manner in which he'd died had not been determined at the time of the initial investigation, that is, whether the wounds were self-inflicted or inflicted by some unknown assailant. No suicide note was found. And the articles stated that Hardcastle, although residing in Austin, had been working in Ten Spot as a private counselor for teens. The police had investigated each of his patients and cleared them. For HIPAA reasons, none of the articles mentioned the students by name.

Some articles also mentioned that Hardcastle had received many awards for his community work and his innovative methods in psychotherapy. He was survived by a wife. They had no children.

Next I googled Zadie and checked her social media accounts. The only unusual thing I saw was a picture she'd posted on Instagram, a photo of her and Hardcastle standing in front of a tree with a large trunk. Her in a yellow, sleeveless sundress. Him in a Hawaiian button down and a pair of gray slacks. Odd, I thought, that she'd post a photo of her and her psychiatrist together. I tried to glean her thoughts from her face. What did her eyes say? Her hands were clasped in front of her, relaxed like, the fingers just barely hooked into each other. I bit my bottom lip and let my gaze trail over to Hardcastle. He looked at ease, too, towering next to her, his left arm casually draped behind her neck, his left hand not even touching her shoulder. He was being careful. And they looked happy, both of them standing there for some candid shot, smiling, laughing almost it seemed. I wonder who'd taken the photo. Mrs. Hardcastle, perhaps? The longer I studied the photo, the more I felt one of them would surely say something to me. But neither did. They just stood there smiling. At last, I looked at the date of the posting. Exactly one week before he died. Interesting.

I stood and began rummaging around the kitchen until I found a half-used bottle of Nesquik chocolate syrup in the pantry. From the fridge I discovered a Dr. Pepper two-liter and filled a tall glass. I added five shots of the syrup, then decided on five more. It'd been quite a day, and it wasn't over yet.

1885 in hand, I slid back in front of the laptop and began a search on Finch. There wasn't much, but what I did find checked out. He was a licensed investigator in the state of Texas, and he had an office in Austin. There was even a small article in the *American-Statesman* concerning his volunteer work with disadvantaged students in the Austin area. Cool.

I closed the laptop and pulled the picture of me and Dad from my back pocket. It was the last one taken of the two of us together before he died nine years ago. I was in the second grade. He had his arm around me, and I could see the ring on his finger, the ring he'd given me the morning he disappeared over the Atlantic, the same ring I now had in the pocket of my duffel.

"What would you have done, Dad?" I wondered aloud, and then reminded myself that he probably would've told me to play it safe and go to college to be an accountant.

I dropped the picture into my duffle, downed the last bit of the 1885, and picked up my phone.

Finch answered right away. "Well?"

"I'm down."

"Great news," he said. "Listen. Mr. Darwood will be around in fifteen to pick you up. We have a lot to do and not a lot of time to get it done. Be ready."

He ended the call without asking for my address. Something told me he didn't need it.

I didn't like the idea of double-crossing Zadie. I'd be working for her to help Finch nail her for the murder of her psychiatrist. But I could walk away from Finch at any time.

I could also walk away from Zadie, and I wondered if I'd already done that.

Just one last case in Ten Spot. After that, I'd walk away from it all.

Ten minutes later, the same blue Crown Victoria I'd seen Finch driving pulled up in front of the cabin. I was ready. I opened the passenger side door and slid in. Darwood was behind the wheel, and he was fuming.

"I told you to say no."

"You did," I said.

His eyes stared into the empty darkness ahead, his nostrils flaring. "Motherfucker!" he spat out.

He slammed the car into reverse, backed out to the main road, and gunned it toward Ten Spot.

CHAPTER 7

INSIDE MAN

Darwood pushed the Crown Victoria faster, whipping up dirt and rocks behind us, before narrowly missing another car in the oncoming lane as we erupted onto Highway 12.

Five minutes later, we were at the Apple Blossom Motor Court, not one of Ten Spot's finest attractions. Most came to the Apple Blossom for one of two reasons – to make money or to spend it. Either way, the services were the same.

Darwood gave a hard rap on the door of room 54. Face to face, Finch was even shorter, stockier, and more balding than he'd appeared on the drone at the park. He was rounded too, all over. His head. His body. On his face he wore a cheap pair of black reader cheaters. And he had the bushiest eyebrows I'd ever seen. They connected in the middle and curled up on the ends, reminding me of Mr. Dream's mustache, only higher up the face.

"Finch." He stuck out five stubby little fingers for a handshake.

I reciprocated, and he pulled us both into the small room, slamming the door behind us. I watched Darwood go over to a small refrigerator and retrieve a glass bottle of Sprite. He knocked off the cap against the top of the room's dresser and kicked back onto one of the unmade beds.

Finch motioned for me to take a seat on the other side while he slid into the room's lone chair. "Let me get right to the point. I don't think it's an accident someone poisoned your grandmother today."

I narrowed my eyes at him.

He grinned and leaned back in the straining chair with his legs spread wide. "I make it my job to stay informed."

He opened the refrigerator and pulled out a beer, offered one to me, which I declined, then reached for a bottle opener on the dresser and popped the top. After a long, satisfied gulp, he wiped his mouth with the back of his hand and continued.

"Seems to me whoever did it also had access to the school."

I stared at him. "You have access to the school."

He lowered his head and eyed me over the top of his readers. A slow smile curled around his thin lips. Then he cut loose a booming laugh, pointing one of those stubby little fingers at Darwood. "I told you this kid was worth his rocks! He does his homework." He took another swig and twisted back to me. "Wasn't me. But you have a big problem on your hands with your client."

"I doubt that," I said.

Darwood made a snorting noise behind me.

Finch continued. "She's hired you for a case involving a note and a razor blade she found in her desk. She's toying with you. The first murder is always the hardest, and she's crossed that line. She's serial, and I'm convinced you're on her list." He took another large gulp of beer and smacked his lips. "Which is why I need you on my team."

"Let me get this straight," I said. "You want to hire me as bait to catch your killer."

He leaned forward, shifting his weight in the chair. "You have the makings of a fine P.I. With some mentoring and guidance, you could become a real asset in the business. Mr. Darwood, I'm sorry to say, doesn't share my enthusiasm for you. Says he doesn't trust you."

"Damn right I don't trust the little motherfucker!" Darwood sat up with such a start I thought for a moment he might spring at me. "First chance he gets, he'll double-cross us for that murdering bitch."

Finch smoothed the air with his fat hands. "Duly noted, Mr. Darwood. Duly noted." He turned to me. "As I was saying, I believe you can become an excellent investigator, but you must prove Mr. Darwood wrong."

Finch downed the rest of his beer and placed the bottle on the dresser before continuing.

"I need evidence that would kick this case in one direction or another. Let me show you something I obtained from the school earlier today after my meeting with you."

Finch opened a small laptop sitting on the writing table in front of him and started a video. The footage was grainy, but it was clear enough to see we were looking at the school cafeteria. There were no students. The timestamp said 12:52, which would have been right after my lunch period.

Finch pointed to the monitor. "Pay attention. There's gonna be a test."

We watched a figure enter the cafeteria from the outside doors, someone with long blonde hair, a blue skirt, pink leggings, and a pair of red shoes.

"The school's surveillance system shot this video about twenty minutes before one of the front office personnel found your grandmother lying on the floor in the back of the kitchen," said Finch. "I'll admit the video is a little hard to see. But if I was a betting man, and I'm not, I'd say this is your client, and that would make her most likely the one who poisoned your grandmother."

Darwood slammed his empty Sprite bottle down on the nightstand. "Case closed."

Finch gave me a pained look. "Mrs. Hardcastle's a patient woman, but she deserves justice, and she deserves indemnification by the insurance company. Until someone fully resolves this case, the insurance company may withhold any and all payments."

"May?"

Finch raised his bushy eyebrows. "Will."

"How much are we talking about?" I asked.

"How does a cool five million grab ya?" he chortled.

I jerked my head back. "Mrs. Hardcastle had a five-million-dollar life insurance policy on her husband?" I looked over at Darwood, then back to Finch, wondering if I was the only one in the room who saw the elephant. "This one's easy, Finch. Follow the money."

Finch dropped his head and put a finger to his bottom lip before cutting his eyes up to me. "Not that simple." His voice was quiet, slow, rhythmic. "They took out those policies as soon as they got married, when they were still in the throes of their honeymoon, four years ago. They each had one for the same amount. And it was *his* idea, not hers."

I still wasn't convinced, but for the moment I let it slide, and leaned back on the bed with arms crossed. "What do you want from me?"

"I want you to solve the mystery of the murder of Dr. Lincoln Hardcastle. Mr. Darwood will be your associate. You'll be assisting each other every step of the way. This is your opportunity to become a full-fledged private eye and get the hell out of this tin-star town."

I stared at him.

He smiled knowingly. "I did my homework on you." He took a handkerchief from his back pocket and blew his nose. "It's up to you how you wanna play it."

"My role is to stay close to Zadie and report back?" I asked.

"She trusts you, Mr. Blanco," he said, "and Miss Zadie Abernathy doesn't trust many. Consider yourself our inside man."

He picked up a photo and handed it to me. It was an eight-by-ten color glossy of Zadie wearing the same yellow strapless sundress she'd had on in the photo with Hardcastle.

"Not bad, huh?" Finch said. "This assignment may have some perks for you. I wouldn't mind being the inside man myself, if you get what I mean."

I looked up at Finch. "Isn't she underage?"

He smirked. "Couldn't tell from this picture."

I jumped up and headed for the door without another word. I had my hand on the knob when Finch's words arrested me.

"You'll get the same as Mr. Darwood," he called after me. "A thousand a week, plus expenses."

I stopped and turned. Finch's offer was sound, ten times what I made now, and that on a good week. Still, boundaries needed to be set.

"I do all the face-to-face with Zadie. Not you, and not him either," I said, throwing a glare at Darwood. "Otherwise I walk. Agreed?"

Finch scoffed. "Of course, kid. I was only horsing around. Trust me, she's all yours."

I looked at Darwood again. "Don't you have another case for him? I can handle this on my own."

Darwood bolted up in the bed again. "Bullshit! You can't do fuck without me."

Once again Finch smoothed out the disturbances in the air. "Our investigative work is always done with a partner, Mr. Blanco. It's safer that way, and more effective."

"Who do you work for?" I asked. "Who are the three of us working for?"

Finch smiled and nodded approvingly. "The insurance company hired me to investigate Hardcastle's death. I soon realized they were fine dragging their heels while poor Mrs. Hardcastle wasted away in abject poverty."

Somehow, I doubted the widowed wife of a prominent psychiatrist was skipping meals. Or pedicures, for that matter.

"After meeting Mrs. Hardcastle, I realized my services were better suited for her needs than the insurance company. We work for her, and she wants this matter solved ASAP. It's not about the money, mind you. It's about justice for her late husband and his enduring legacy."

I raised my brow and lowered my chin slightly. "What about Mrs. Hardcastle? What's her story?"

Finch drew back his head and scrunched up his chubby face. "Mrs. Hardcastle? Not a chance. She was in Austin and had a whole house full of church gals over serving tea and those tiny little cakes. I checked out her alibi and she's as clean as a whistle. Plus, she's a sweetheart. Wouldn't hurt a fly."

"All right, she wouldn't," I said, "but somebody she hired might."

He pulled back his shoulders and pointed one of those little round fingers at me. "Drop it, Blanco! She's squeaky clean. We're not investigating our client."

"You mean we're not investigating *your* client. It seems we are investigating mine."

"Look, kid, nobody's twisting your arm." He held both of his hands in front of him, palms up, weighing the options. "You got two choices: Take it or leave it. It's up to you."

I stood and took a few steps over to the little refrigerator, opening it. "I don't like your choices."

"What?" he asked.

"Beer or Sprite." I said, closing the fridge. "I don't like either."

"Oh, I thought you meant…"

"I'm in," I said. "But only if you stock this thing with Dr. Pepper. I'm gonna need a bottle of chocolate syrup too."

Darwood exploded behind me. "Are you fucking kidding me? This little ass thinks…"

"Come now, Mr. Darwood." Finch's voice was soothing and calm. "If our newest investigator works better with a little Dr. Pepper and some syrup, I don't see why we can't be accommodating. Take some petty cash from the drawer tomorrow, Mr. Darwood, and get Mr. Blanco his beverage of choice."

Mr. Darwood let loose another string of expletives, then shut the hell up, which suited me just fine.

Finch yawned and stretched. "It's getting late, Mr. Blanco. It's time for my beauty rest. Mr. Darwood will take you home."

Darwood and I headed for the door.

"Funny story about Mrs. Hardcastle," Finch said after us. "The first time I met her she almost accidentally killed me."

I stopped and turned around. Darwood continued on outside.

Finch went on. "I visited her at that gorgeous house where she and the doctor lived, and she offers me a piece of chocolate cake. I look at it because I'm allergic to all nuts except almonds and I don't see any nuts in it, so I eat it. It was damn good. It was also damn full of ground up nuts. All kinds of nuts. And I had an allergic reaction like you wouldn't believe." He let out a loud howl of a laugh.

I raised my eyebrows. "You didn't think to ask if there were nuts in it?"

"Hell yeah, I did." Finch had on a big grin. "But she was in such a tizzy that day with her lady friends coming over for some social they were having that when she said the word *no*, I thought she was talking to me. Come to find out, she wasn't talking to me. She was talking to her damn housekeeper who'd just asked her a question about setting out flowers in vases or some shit like that." He released a long sigh. "It's a miracle I survived."

"Sounds like the devil's own luck."

Finch continued, still grinning. "You should've seen her face. Mortified, I tell you. After that she vowed to never put ground nuts in bread. What you see in her bread is what you get. I tell you, she's the sweetest thing you'll ever meet."

"I'm sure she's the bee's knees," I said.

I opened the door and we stepped outside. The temperature had dropped a few degrees, and I stuffed my hands inside my coat pockets.

"Go home and get some sleep, Mr. Blanco," said Finch. "You're gonna need it. We start tomorrow."

Finch closed the door to room 54, and I slipped into the passenger side of the Crown Victoria, ready for another wild ride with my new partner.

"Get out," he said.

I stared at him with eyes wide. "You're not taking me back to the lake house?"

"Get out, motherfucker."

Mr. Darwood was starting off our investigative partnership by leaving me five miles from Brockett's cabin at the Apple Blossom no-tell motel on Highway 12 at eleven-twenty-three at night.

I stepped out into the cool air and began the long trek back to the lake.

In the distance, I heard the roar of the blue sedan as Darwood gunned it onto the highway and headed off in the opposite direction.

I could've called Brockett to pick me up, but I didn't relish the thought of asking someone to rescue me before I'd even had a chance to begin the investigation. It already felt like I'd been given one of those junior fire marshal badges they pass out in elementary school to make you feel more responsible than you really are. Plus, the walk home and the cool air would give me time to think.

Finch and Brockett had both been right. This was a good opportunity for me, a chance to prove my mettle as a real detective pursuing a real crime for a change. Show myself competent, a team player, a problem solver, an investigator with a knack of getting answers from people who tended to clam up, and I could punch my ticket to the big stage in Austin just as soon as I graduated from MWA. And, in the process, I'd be exonerating my client at the same time. For sure, this was the chance of a lifetime for me.

I just had to convince my new partner to see it that way too.

WEDNESDAY

It took me a moment to realize where I was the next morning when the alarm sounded. Thanks to Finch and that little prick Darwood I'd gotten two measly hours of sleep. I was dead, and I thought about skipping classes, but didn't want to give Whiffletree any more solids for throwing my behind in ISS. I tugged on a pair of khaki chinos and a black tee, grabbed a bottle of Diet Coke from Brockett's fridge, and headed to school on the Triumph.

I slept through most of first period. Wasn't the first time. The girl next to me prodded me when it was time to switch classes. On my way to Mr. Calishaw's American History, I ran into Whiffletree who jabbed at his watch and mouthed the words "don't forget." I gave him the two-finger salute as I whipped past him. Rounding the corner just outside the gym, I saw Aiden hanging by the door to the guy's locker room. That got me curious, so I pulled up and filtered my way through the passing crowd to a small alcove near the stairs. I jerked out my phone as though I was checking messages and watched Aiden pace back and forth. Every now and then, he'd stop at the water fountain and take a drink.

Within a few minutes, several athletes burst out of the locker room, including the two who'd accosted me the day before while

I'd been pulling surveillance on Aiden. The one who doubled as Clark Kent stopped cold when he saw Aiden and said something to him, but I couldn't make it out. Aiden's eyes got wide, and he shook his head. Clark put both his hands on Aiden's shoulders and shoved him, causing Aiden to stumble into the water fountain. Redfoo's kid brother breathed something in Clark's ear who nodded and took a step back. I wished to God I could read lips, but from the looks of it, Clark didn't look happy with my prime suspect. I wondered if the topic of razor blades had come up.

Then Redfoo saw me, and when he said something to the other two, all three pounded my way. I pocketed the phone and skinned through the crowd up the stairs, two at a time. I took the first hall to the left even though it was in the opposite direction of American History. I weaved past every classroom and hung a right to double back to second period. That's when I ran into Steele coming from the opposite direction.

"Don't go that way." He grabbed my arm and nodded back over his shoulder. "Tobias Williams is looking for you."

"Damn." I ducked into the teacher's lounge and headed for the door on the opposite side.

Mrs. Cer was sitting on a sofa chatting it up with another teacher when she saw me. "Students are not allowed in teacher break rooms, Ignacio Blanco."

I was already out the other door before she had a chance to squawk about anything else. Back in the main hall, I fought my way through the rushing students and skated into Mr. Calishaw's as the tardy bell rang. I spent the fifty minutes of class time replaying in my mind the scene I'd witnessed downstairs. I wondered why Clark had been so upset with Aiden. Was it about the razor blade? Maybe Clark had put Aiden up to it and was tying up the loose ends that would lead back to him. None of it made sense, and when class ended, I tripped down the stairs at the back of the hall, slipped out a door, and made my way around to the parking lot where the bike was waiting. I had to put the whole thing out of my mind because I needed to make a couple of quick calls before my ten o'clock with Principal Whiffletree's wife.

First, I called the hospital to check on my grandmother. Her condition hadn't changed, said Ms. Waters, and she assured me that when she had something new, she'd let me know. She also still had that razor blade waiting for me to pick up.

Next, I called the florist that had delivered the flowers to my grandmother. After a brief discussion with the owner, I learned that they hadn't made any deliveries to the hospital on Tuesday. Not only that, but they didn't use razor blades in the preparation of floral arrangements. All of this left me with only one thought. It was no accident my grandmother had been sent that blade.

I started to pocket the phone when I saw a message from Zadie. She wanted to meet. My guess was she wanted to know if I'd figured out who'd dropped her that blade and note. I started to ignore her, then thought again. I was on Finch's payroll now too. Maybe a face-to-face with my client wouldn't be such a bad thing after all.

I texted her back.

Dirty Diva after school

I put the phone away, pulled out the business card Whiffletree had given me, and aimed the bike toward Castlerock Estates.

I couldn't even imagine what Mrs. Whiffletree needed from me. No doubt she'd heard the tale concerning the previous principal and the sting operation I'd run on him. Maybe the principal's wife was afraid I'd try the same with her husband and wanted to bring me into the fold right from the start.

Most of Ten Spot's old money is banked in Castlerock Estates, and it's not moving, which made it all the more surprising that a young couple from Austin like the Whiffletrees could acquire one of its exquisite homes. At least one of them must have inherited significant capital, and the scuttlebutt around town pointed to her. I'd heard Mrs. Whiffletree's family was diversified, owning shares of high-end restaurants, real estate holdings, and sundry other lucrative investments. Add to their portfolio the house I now stood in front of—a manor really—French Country with large, manicured hedges on both sides that complemented the pink-and-gray brick exterior and its dignified symmetry. I stepped up to its grand entrance and rang the bell.

A strange-looking little old lady greeted me at the door. Her silvery hair was pulled back and she wore a thick pair of orange horned-rimmed glasses with a silver chain that ran down both sides of her face and disappeared somewhere beneath the collar of an unremarkable blue house dress. A white apron cinched her small waist.

"Nacho Blanco," I said. "Mrs. Whiffletree asked to meet with me."

"Of course," she replied. I'd imagined her to have one of those high, lilting, proper voices characteristic of little old ladies fastidious about life's accoutrements. Hers was soft, gravely, and low. "Right this way."

She ushered me into an impressive living room with white walls and an ebony-colored, hand-scraped hardwood floor. A single white Benetti's Italian perlite sofa trimmed in gold sat in the middle of the room on an oversized white shag rug. A curving staircase to my right led to an upstairs landing. To my left was an immense fireplace, quiet since it was only early October. The entire room dripped with money, power, and drama. And it reeked of cigar smoke.

She showed me into a side room which had more of an early American theme that didn't quite seem to match the main living space. The walls were painted blue. An empty antique pie chest stood in one corner. A small stone fireplace adorned the opposite wall. And in the center were matching red leather loveseats that faced each other, separated by a glass coffee table trimmed in black wrought iron.

"Mrs. Whiffletree will be with you momentarily." My host gave a slight bow. "May I offer you anything to drink? Perhaps some fresh juice?"

"Water'll do."

She lowered her head and scurried away.

A moment later, Mrs. Whiffletree entered. Just like the picture I'd seen in Mr. Dream's office, her hair was a soft chestnut, silky and long, down past her shoulders and parted in the middle. She was a thin woman, but not scrawny, the kind who enjoys green smoothies for breakfast and a bowl of goji berries and kale for dinner. I imagined her to be the active sort, with a full calendar of social gatherings and private golf lessons for which she paid some lucky schmuck handsomely. She wore a black, tight-fitting, pleated sweater dress, and her presence seemed to fill up the room all at once when she entered.

"Nacho." With both hands she reached eagerly for one of mine. "I'm so glad to meet you. I've heard amazing stories about Winkler Academy's very own private eye."

Her voice was soft and sweet and kinda breathy, like it couldn't decide whether to be properly heard or shared in secret, and I strained to hear her.

I slipped my hand from her grasp, and we sat down, her on one of the red loveseats, me on the other, the coffee table resting between us like a carping nun between two inexperienced teenagers on a first date.

"Please excuse the mess," she said, "and the smell. Your new principal is a cigar aficionado. He loves him some cigars. Cubans. He smokes one every night and the smell has permeated every nook and cranny. It's a stinky habit, and a costly one."

I leaned toward her and lowered my voice, as though the walls were bugged. "Aren't those kinda hard to come by? Last I checked it was still illegal to sell them in this country."

"Let's just say my husband knows a guy who knows a guy." She raised her shoulders and squinted her eyes the way innocent little kids do when they're not so innocent.

I threw a glance around the room and gave it several nods. "Nice place you have here, Mrs. Whiffletree."

"I've been fortunate," she said. "And I'm reminded of it every year on my birthday."

I gave her a questioning look.

"April fifteenth," she explained. "Tax Day. Every year my husband bakes me a cake to celebrate and every year it seems the government helps itself to the biggest slice!"

I gave her the obligatory chuckle. "I find it curious you called me instead of Ten Spot PD."

She placed a hand over her heart. "Oh my, now that is funny. You won't think it's curious once I share my dilemma."

"What exactly is your dilemma, Mrs. Whiffletree?"

"Please, Nacho, call me Story." She pulled both legs up to her chest before crossing them yoga style beneath her, allowing the dress to loft freely over the edge of the sofa.

"Okay, Mrs. Whiffletree," I said.

"Story," she said, raising one brow. "I insist."

"Okay, Story, what's your dilemma?"

The housekeeper returned with my glass of water.

Mrs. Whiffletree gestured toward me. "Rachel, this is the P.I. I told you about."

"PSI," I said. "Problem Solver Investigator." I threw back a quick shot of water. "I'll save the dangerous stuff for the real P.I.s."

Mrs. Whiffletree waved me off. "I think you will be a godsend to me." She turned to Rachel. "Will you bring us some lemonade and some of those yummy brownies you made yesterday?"

Rachel bowed her head again.

"And one more thing, please," said Mrs. Whiffletree. "Would you turn on the Sonos? I'm in the mood for some Ben Webster."

"Yes, ma'am," said the housekeeper.

Mrs. Whiffletree and I turned our attention toward each other again. Blue eyes. High cheek bones. Full natural lips. She was a beautiful woman.

"I just love her," she said. "We moved in a few months ago

and Rachel has been a tremendous help unpacking everything. Plus, between you and me, I can't cook worth a dime. Isn't that funny? A restaurateur who can't cook or bake. Oh well, *c'est la vie.*"

"Hilarious." I crossed my arms and stole a quick glance at my watch. "Tell me why I'm here."

She sat up, folding her hands in her lap. "Does the number 420 mean anything to you?"

"Depends on who's saying it."

She lowered her voice, and her bottom lip. "What if I were saying it?"

"Mrs. Whiffletree...Story...surely you're not referring to weed, are you?"

The sultry sounds of jazz interrupted us, purring from speakers embedded in the walls of the room. The music was hot, muggy, and sensual, and stuck to me like a sweaty shirt on a humid day in the French Quarter.

Mrs. Whiffletree leaned back and closed her eyes, breathing in the light trickles of a piano, the improvisations of a soulful sax, and the steady beat of a deep bass.

"Do you like Ben Webster?" Her eyes remained closed, and her head swayed with the mood of the music.

"Never heard of him," I said. "But I like the sound."

She opened her eyes. They were dreamy, like the song. "It's from the album *Music for Loving*. I love *love*. Don't you?"

"I suppose everybody loves something."

She breathed out a smile, a warm and satisfied kind of smile. "What do you love, Nacho?"

"Right now, I'd love to know why I'm here."

She paused to study me, her eyes narrowing, her lips forming a thin smile. Then she blurted out a nervous laugh. "You are a hoot, Nacho Blanco!" She sat up straighter, tucked loose threads of her hair behind her ears, and focused her gaze onto mine. "I'm a vegetarian, but I'm also an herbalist. I believe all good things come from the ground, things our bodies need to be healthy and whole."

"Your dilemma is whether or not the principal's wife should smoke weed?" I asked.

She paused her narrative as Rachel returned and placed a pitcher of lemonade and a plate of brownies on the table between us. Mrs. Whiffletree reached over for the lemonade, filled both glasses, offering one to me.

I pointed to the brownies. "Should I be worried?"

She laughed. "Just brownies. Delicious, but boring."

The housekeeper left the room and we tried our snack.

I toasted Mrs. Whiffletree with my glass. "My compliments to Chef Rachel."

She lifted her glass. "I will pass on your regards." Lowering her voice again, she continued. "I grow it, Nacho."

"You grow weed?" I asked.

"I have a secret crop of cannabis. It's in the greenhouse around back, hidden from plain sight. And every day, at four-twenty in the afternoon I smoke a little, for the health benefits, mind you." She took another bite of the brownie.

"I see your dilemma," I said. "It's bad optics for the wife of the new principal of Milo Winkler Academy to be growing marijuana at her house in Castlerock Estates."

She waved off my assessment with a dismissive hand. "I'm not worried about the police."

"What are you worried about?"

"About a week ago, I noticed someone had been in my greenhouse. I noticed it again yesterday. Each time someone pilfered my stash. I don't want to involve the police because, let's face it, what are they going to do? Right? But I need someone to find out who's been stealing my cannabis."

"And that's where I come in?"

"I need you to investigate this, off the record, off the radar. I want the person who's been taking my marijuana caught."

I picked up my glass of lemonade and downed it. "Pardon me for saying so, Mrs. Whiffletree…"

"Story." She cocked her head and smiled.

"Story. It's also a crime to grow marijuana in Texas."

She raised a brow again and pursed her lips. "It's not my ass I need protected, Nacho. It's my assets."

I unwrapped a stick of Juicy Fruit and folded it in my mouth. "I don't think I'm the one for this job."

I watched as she unfolded her legs, stood and moved around the glass coffee table in front of me. Sitting on the edge of the table, she reached for both my hands, holding them in hers, like moms do when they need a child to focus.

"Nacho, I need you to investigate this."

I tried to pull my hands away from her, but she resisted and held firm.

"Mrs. Whiffletree…Story…"

"I won't accept no for an answer." Her voice was calm and steady. "My husband and I may be new to the community, but we're not new to the people who run this town. I have a lot of influence in Ten Spot, even more in Austin. Trust me, you want me as a friend."

She loosened her grip and I slipped my hands free.

She took a deep cleansing breath and smiled. "You help me, I help you. This world isn't about who you know, Nacho. It's about who knows you, and it wouldn't hurt for my friends to become your friends." She stood, smoothing out the pleats in her dress in front of me.

I looked at my watch. I had five minutes before the start of my lunch period.

"Okay, Story Whiffletree, I'll take your case. Give me a few days and I'll see what I can dig up."

"Perfect!" She made for the door. "How much do you need to get started? I need to get my purse."

I put up a hand to stop her. "We'll tally it up at the end. I know where you live."

I stood up to leave as the housekeeper came back into the room. "Is there anything else I can get, Mrs. Whiffletree?" she asked.

"No, thank you, Rachel."

As I moved around the twin red sofas, I noticed a small unframed photo on the fireplace mantle, similar to the one in Mr. Dream's office. Mr. Dream stood in the middle with Dr. Hardcastle on his right and Mr. and Mrs. Whiffletree on his left.

I picked up the photo and held it closer. "Y'all were good friends, I take it."

"Actually, we'd only met them just that one time five years ago when the photo was taken," Mrs. Whiffletree replied. There was a somber tone to her voice now. "It's so sad about Lincoln. We never imagine the pain some go through."

I studied the picture closely. "This is the second time I've seen this photo."

"That's interesting," she said. "Where else have you seen it?"

I shook my head. "Never mind, it's not the same. But it's similar."

Mrs. Whiffletree opened her mouth, as though she were going to say something, the lines in her forehead wrinkling. But she didn't, and instead, she closed her lips, and I laid the photo back on the mantle.

"Where were you when you heard Dr. Hardcastle had died?" I asked.

Mrs. Whiffletree dropped to the red loveseat in front of us. "I was at the church volunteering. We were cleaning up from the fall carnival that day. The carnival had worn me out, and I wanted to collapse by the time I got home. It was around seven that night. Could've been a little later. Mrs. Hardcastle called me because she guessed I'd want to hear it from her first. Poor thing, hysterical, inconsolable, and I didn't have the words to say to her. It was all so…tragic."

I offered her my hand and she stood and walked me to the front door but stopped short of opening it.

"I just remembered," she said. "I'm having a party tonight for the school board, the faculty members of Winkler Academy, and a number of community leaders. Please won't you come? I must insist you do."

"I have a feeling I don't have a choice, do I?"

She rested her hands on her hips in a faux commanding fashion. "You will find, Mr. Nacho Blanco, I get what I want."

"I'll be here."

"Thank you. And thank you for taking my case. I owe you one."

"Yes, you do, Mrs. Whiffletree."

"Story," she corrected.

I shook my head. "Your name suits you."

She squeezed my hand with both of hers. "Bad choices make great stories."

I laughed. "But can a bad Story still make a good choice?"

She smiled. "Touché."

CHAPTER 9

THE DIRTY DIVA

"**Y**ou want the regular, Nacho?"

Miss Fitts stood behind the counter, order pad in hand, as I stepped through the door of The Dirty Diva.

After leaving the Whiffletrees that morning, I'd started back to school. I never made it. At the corner of Travis and Conroe, I banged a U-ey and drove back to Brockett's to make a sandwich and kill some time. I knew trying to finish out my last few classes would be a wash out. I was exhausted from the night before. My mind was too preoccupied with the conversation I'd witnessed between Aiden and Clark. And I also didn't want to take the chance of getting into a fight with Tobias. So, I ate. I slept. And at two-thirty, I drove to the Dirty Diva to wait on my client and hopefully get the answers to the questions that were bugging me.

"Yeah, but don't put it in yet. I'm waiting on someone."

"Is she business or personal?" she asked.

"When you find out, let me know." I slid into one of the booths next to the front window facing the courthouse square. "How are things with my favorite misfit?"

"Same soup, different bowl." She turned to wait on another couple who'd arrived.

I knew more about Amy Sue Fitts than most, mainly because The Dirty Diva's heavy-set proprietor, with the tangled strawberry blonde hair and the pallid skin, didn't mind sharing with me more of herself than I wanted to know. I'd learned she was somewhere in her fifties, had worked at the diner since her twenties, bought it in her thirties, and had four kids, three of whom she raised as a single mom, two of which had gone to Ten Spot's Overton College. She was a nosy Nellie, but she also worked hard, and that put her on the top shelf in my book.

In less than a minute, she'd placed an 1885 on the table in front of me.

"Let me know when she arrives," she said with a wink, "and I'll warn her away."

I nursed the drink while I waited for my date and watched the hustle from the lunch rush wind down. The diner itself was small, with only a dozen black booths and one long white counter accommodating half a dozen red stools. The black-and-white checkered floor had long since lost its shine, but not its traffic. Customers came in and out of The Dirty Diva all day, some for Miss Fitts's World Famous Cup of Joe, some for a square meal, and some just to catch up on the town gossip. There was an old jukebox playing in the corner, but I couldn't make out the tune over the sounds of dull metal cutlery scratching across white melamine plates and the midday buzz of locals' conversations.

A little after three, I saw Zadie across the street. She still had on the grey hoodie, jeans, Converses, but she'd pulled her hair into a pony and covered her eyes with a pair of aviators. Her look suited her, and that suited me. Then I sighed as I remembered the video Finch had shown me of the school cafeteria.

"Cool it, Blanco," I chastised myself. "She's just your client."

I watched her start across the street before turning to an elderly woman on a bus bench. She knelt and spoke with the woman, then took a seat beside her when the two laughed. Their time was brief, less than a minute, before Zadie gave the woman a hug and made her way to the diner. The bell above the door announced her arrival and I waved her over.

"Waiting long?" Her voice was sunny.

"Just got here." I nodded toward the window. "Who's your friend?"

She slipped her petite frame into the booth across from me, dropping the Ray-Bans on the table. "I'd never met her before. But she looked so sweet and lonely." She let her gaze linger a moment on me, smiled, and picked up the laminated menu. "I've never been here. What's good?"

"The Dirty Special," I said. "It's a grilled cheese sandwich layered with smoked brisket and onion rings."

She licked her lips. "Hmm! Sounds amazing!"

I introduced her to Miss Fitts, and we ordered two of the house specials and a glass of water for Zadie.

Miss Fitts laid a couple of cloth rollups on the table and looked at Zadie. "Honey, if this fellow gives you any trouble, just remember something my divorce attorney said: Men are like dessert. They're good to have every now and then, but sometimes the calories they carry with them just isn't worth the trouble. I'm pretty sure she stole that from Cher, but good advice nevertheless."

I looked up and gave Miss Fitts the stink eye. "You're not helping, you know."

"You be good to this one, Nacho Blanco."

She turned away, and I turned to Zadie who was smiling. "Now don't you start, too."

"I like her!" She put her elbows on the table and rested her chin in her hands. "I wonder what kind of dessert you'd be?" She began to tap her lips with her finger. "Maybe a pecan pie because you're kinda nutty."

She laughed at her own joke, and that made me smile.

"I'm more like this 1885." I took a long drink. "An acquired taste for sure."

She snatched the drink from my hand and tried it. "Not bad.

Kinda weird, but not bad." She thought for a second. "Yeah, you're definitely like this 1885!" She took another drink before sliding it back across the table to me. "How's your grandmother?"

I looked at her and smiled. "That's a curious question."

"I'm a curious girl."

I took another drink. "What I mean is how'd you know about my grandmother?"

"I heard my foster parents talking about her this morning." She stole a glance outside the window before returning her eyes to me. "What happened?"

"Antifreeze," I said. "The doctor suspects someone tried to poison her with antifreeze. They're running tests." In light of Finch's video, I was curious to see her response.

Her mouth dropped open. "That's terrible! How would you even get someone to drink it?"

"Antifreeze is very sweet and can blend in with anything—sweet tea for example, which my grandmother drinks regularly. The real question isn't how but why?"

"That's awful." She broke eye contact with me and used the camera on her phone to check her make up. "How's my case coming?"

I smiled. No follow-up questions. No segue. In my experience, people who don't ask questions usually have the answers.

"Let's just say I'm working out some of the leads. What I need is some background about you, your family, your relationship with Hardcastle." I took a sip of my drink. "What brought you to Ten Spot in the first place?"

"I was born in Austin. My mother ran off with another man when I was three and my father killed himself when I was five."

"That's a rough way to start a life. No kid deserves that."

She rested her elbows on the table again, letting her chin drop into praying hands, and continued.

"He hung himself in the garage. I was the one who found him. I kept looking at him, wondering how he could float like that. His head had flopped over to one side and his face was purple. And there was shit running down the side of his leg inside his pants, dripping on the floor below. The next thing I remember I'm screaming and running to the neighbor's house."

I watched her dab the corner of each eye with her ring fingers.

"I never went inside that house again. After that, I started living with one foster family after another. The excuses were always different. I had too much baggage. I had an authority problem. Or the man of the house had a wandering eye. Whatever it was, the result was always the same. Nobody wanted me."

"Is that what led to the cutting?"

"I guess. I started doing it when I was seven. My counselor told me I had PTSD and had numbed my emotions for survival. He said I was cutting myself to feel something, anything. That's why I wear these rubber bands. It takes the place of the cutting." She popped a pink band around her right wrist and smiled.

"Hardcastle told you that?" I asked.

"My first counselor, the one who cared."

"You didn't like Hardcastle?"

She leaned across the table and lowered her voice. "I'm glad he's gone. We all are."

Miss Fitts walked up with our plates, the buttery, smoky aroma wafting from the stacked sandwiches. A generous amount of cheese had melted down the sides, and the large portion of brisket and onion rings, too much even for the Texas toast, seemed poised to tumble onto the plate.

Zadie sized up the enormity of the meal in front of her. "Thank you."

"You're welcome, darling," Miss Fitts replied. "And pay no attention to Nacho. He may come across like a junkyard dog, but he's as soft as a pussycat."

Miss Fitts winked at Zadie and walked away.

Zadie cut her sandwich into manageable pieces. "About a year ago, the Hardcastles took me in."

I looked up from my plate. "You never told me that."

"You never asked." She stabbed at a bite of the sandwich with her fork and stuffed it into her mouth. "Oh my God! This is the best thing I've ever put in my mouth!" She closed her eyes while she chewed, moaning. "This is orgasmic!"

Her revelation explained the photo I'd come across on her Instagram account. I wondered if Finch knew Zadie had lived with the Hardcastles, and if so, why he hadn't bothered telling me. And why was she living with her counselor in the first place? That situation wasn't just irregular. It had red flags planted all over it, and I wondered that nobody who'd known at the time had thought to say something about it.

I steered us back on course. "Let's go back to Hardcastle's other patients."

She swallowed and took a drink of water. "Like I said, nobody liked him."

"They told you that?"

"There were five of us, and he would meet with each one of us for an hour every Saturday morning, one right after the other."

"What are their names?" I asked.

"Besides me there was a girl named Holiday Le, another girl named Price Patterson, a boy named Tobias Williams, and another boy named Aiden Dixon."

"I recently met Tobias. Interesting cat." I took a bite of my sandwich. "Price I know. Another rich white girl. Holiday? Isn't she in Mrs. Cer's class?"

"Yes. Her family's from Vietnam. They moved here just a few years ago. She's sweet."

The bell above the door rang and Zadie leaned her head toward it, her eyes wide, her eyebrows raised. "Speak of the devil."

I turned and saw the two guys who had challenged me after lunch. With them, the one I had under surveillance.

"That's your Aiden?" I asked.

"The one and only. But he's not mine." She grimaced. "He creeps me out!"

All three guys sat down in a booth across the diner. The one who looked like Clark Kent waved Miss Fitts off when she headed over to get their orders. Something told me they weren't here for The Dirty Special.

Zadie continued, "Everyone cheered when he died, including Aiden. Go ask him for yourself. He'll tell you the same thing."

I wiped my mouth with the cloth napkin and rested my arms on the table between us. "Tell me again about your relationship with the Hardcastles. They became your foster parents?"

She rolled her eyes and groaned. "There's more. About six months into it, they said they wanted to adopt me, which was great because Mrs. Hardcastle and I got along swimmingly. Then the touching began. Not her. Him."

"Your psychiatrist who wanted to adopt you started touching you?" I raised an eyebrow. "How did he touch you?"

She took in a deep breath and slowly let it out. "He started by putting his hand on my leg when we were in the car together. I did nothing at first because I thought he was just being overly friendly, even though it was kinda creepy. From there he started moving his hand up my leg and under my skirts. He would ask me what color panties I was wearing and if I ever free-buffed. He even suggested we go shopping at Victoria's Secret together. He assured me it was all normal and that this is what parents did for their kids."

"Did you ever tell Mrs. Hardcastle?" I asked.

"Yes, and she said she would talk to him, and I guess she did, but it didn't help. I was thinking about talking to my high school counselor in Austin when suddenly Dr. Hardcastle died. I guess somebody else didn't like him touching her panties either."

I looked over at the table across the diner. The three boys had gotten some water and were talking.

"And you and Mrs. Hardcastle got along fine?" I asked.

"We got along great! She was so sweet and kind. We did all kinds of things together. We'd get our nails done. We'd go see movies. She's about my size, and I found tons of nice clothes to wear in her closet. She didn't mind at all. And she has the best perfume! In fact, I think I'm wearing some of it now."

I could smell it. Rose petals and sweet almond milk.

"Why come back to Ten Spot after Hardcastle died?" I asked. "Seems like this is the last place in the world you'd want to live considering what happened here."

"I never wanted to come back here. But Mrs. Hardcastle had a nervous breakdown after her husband's death. She knew this nice couple in Ten Spot, the Allens, and they took me in and that's where I am now."

I nodded and turned to stare through the diner's front window, digesting The Dirty Special and the trauma Zadie had been through.

Zadie was the first to break the silence. "What about you, Nacho? What's your story?"

I took my last bite and pushed the plate aside. "Not so different from you, I suppose," I said. "My mother disappeared when I was six, and my father died in a plane crash over the Atlantic when I was in second grade. I've been living with my grandmother for nine years. Not a day goes by I don't wish I was out of this town."

"Where did your mom go?" she asked.

"One day she was here, the next she wasn't. I figured there was another man."

Zadie stuck out her bottom lip and gave me puppy dog eyes to let me know she understood.

Then she pointed behind me. "Looks like we have visitors."

I turned to see Aiden and his two friends walking toward us.

"We need to talk," said the one who looked like Clark Kent.

"I'm kinda busy," I said. "You three boys run on home and practice your piano lessons."

The one with the blonde afro put his hand under my arm to lift me up.

I pulled back from him. "You don't want to do that."

Clark Kent leaned over the table, his knife popping open in my face. "You need to get up." He looked over at Zadie. "I'd hate for blood to get on your little girlfriend."

Zadie let out an audible gasp. "Oh my God."

I turned my head toward her. Her eyes were wide, and they were staring at the blade in Clark's hand.

She didn't need this kind of drama, and neither did Miss Fitts, so I decided to take it outside.

I stood and looked at Zadie. "Be right back. Me and the boys are gonna have a little chat."

The four of us walked toward the back of the diner, past the restrooms, and out the back door into a blind alley. Outside, I turned to face them. They had closed ranks around me, Aiden to my left, Clark Kent to my right, and the blonde afro kid in the middle. I closed my right fist and brought it around in front of me as hard and as fast as I could.

It felt as though a thousand tiny bones in my hand had splintered all at once. But I'd connected, and the brunt force of my right fist popping Clark Kent in the jaw had caused him to stumble into his counterpart who, after taking a few steps back, was now out of range of my left hook. Aiden hadn't moved, and now the other two stared motionless, no doubt sizing up their chances with me. Notice had been served. This would be a slugfest.

The blonde afro was the first to approach. He took a swing at my head with his right. I dodged the hit but couldn't move away in time from a left hook to my solar plexus, which doubled me over as I gasped for air. As I tried standing, Clark got in two rapid punches to the face. They closed the gap and I sent my right flying, followed by my left, each connecting only with the air in front of me. The next thing I felt was a fist on the left side of my face, the impact so hard it sent me flailing hard to the asphalt. I looked up, but everything was awash and swirling.

Clark Kent knelt beside me, and I felt cold metal against my cheek.

"What you think, BroFly?" Clark pressed the flat part of the blade into my already bruising cheek. "You think our friend here needs a little reminder to stay in his own lane?" He looked up at the other two boys and laughed. "I can't believe this asshole threw a punch at me!"

He hadn't realized it, but he was squatting over my right hand. I curled my fingers into a fist and brought it up hard and fast into his groin. He dropped the knife, grabbing his junk with both hands, rolling onto the street moaning. I tried getting up, but BroFly caught me in the side with a swift kick, and I doubled over in pain.

Then the white kid was back on me. I felt a quick slice on my cheek, a sudden sting, and a warm trickle seeping down my face.

"Stop!"

The four of us turned to see Zadie running from the back door of the diner. She had one of Miss Fitts checkered napkins in her hand. She knelt beside me on the ground and pressed the napkin against my cheek to stop the bleeding.

"What are you doing to him, Trip?" she screamed.

Trip. So that was his name. Trip, BroFly, and Aiden.

"He threw the first punch. Right, Bro?" Trip looked from face to face, nodding his head repeatedly like one of those cheap, plastic bobble head dolls you get at Cowboy games.

Zadie's eyebrows folded inward, and her nose crinkled. "So you cut him?" She turned to Aiden. "Is this what you want? Tell your little friends to back off or I swear to God I'll spill every dirty little secret about you!"

I didn't know what she had on Aiden, but it wasn't too hard to see the fear rising in his eyes as they cut back and forth between Zadie and the rest of us.

"Tell them, Aiden, or I swear I'll tell everyone what you do with your fingers when nobody is around!"

Bless his heart. She had him by the balls, and she wasn't letting go.

"This isn't what I wanted." His voice was soft and trembling. "I thought you were the one who put that box of razor blades in my backpack."

I took the checkered napkin from Zadie and boosted myself

into a sitting position. "I didn't put any razor blades in your backpack. Who's to say you didn't make up that story to throw the heat off yourself?"

Aiden raised his eyebrows and gave me one of those "you must be crazy" looks. "Why would I do that?"

Trip stepped forward, the switchblade still in hand. "Blanco, you pathetic little piece of shit! I found the box. He said you planted it in his backpack to prove you'd solved your little girlfriend's mystery."

I stood, careful not to go too fast, and Zadie reached under my arm to brace my efforts. Good thing, too. The cut on my face, minor as it was, stung like a thousand tiny bees. I felt lightheaded, and for a moment, I thought I might actually puke from the putrid odor of rotting garbage and frying grease.

I swallowed the surging bile and pointed to Aiden. "I think whoever planted that box is trying to frame you, or at least implicate you in the death of Dr. Hardcastle, like somebody has already done to Zadie."

"You think the same person is trying to frame Zadie and Aiden for the murder of Dr. Hardcastle?" asked BroFly.

"Zadie got one. So did my grandmother. Aiden got a whole box. A psychiatrist died by one. Looks to me like somebody's trying to pin Hardcastle's murder on his five clients." I turned to Aiden. "When did you first notice the box?"

Trip slapped the knife closed, shoving it in his pocket. "Like I said, I found it when Aiden told me to get a game out of his backpack."

"What time was that?" I asked.

"It was during Analytical Geometry," said Aiden. "So it must've been around ten-thirty."

"How did you and Dr. Hardcastle get along?" I asked him.

Aiden glared, and there was a visible tightness in his jaw and neck. "You think I did it?"

"Aiden didn't kill nobody," BroFly insisted.

"I didn't say that. I asked how the two of them got along." I looked at Aiden, waiting. "What about it?"

"I hated him," he said at last. "We all hated him, and we all talked about killing him."

"Told you," Zadie said, in a sing-song kind of way.

"Why?" I asked Aiden.

"He said I was worse than a girl. Made me wear a dress one time in one of my sessions."

"How were you guys gonna kill him?" I asked.

Aiden lifted his shoulders and scrunched up his face. "We weren't. It was just talk. Shit you say because you're mad." He paused and swallowed hard. "I'm glad he's gone."

"Where were you when Hardcastle died on that Saturday after your last appointment with him?"

"He was with us," said Trip.

"I'm asking him," I said.

"It's okay." Aiden looked at me. "He's right. I was with them. My appointment was always at noon. I left at twelve-fifty and walked home. Then I walked to the theater and met Trip and BroFly to watch a movie."

"What time was that?" I dropped the napkin from my face and felt the cut. The wound had clotted.

"The movie started at two forty-five, but I got to the theater at two."

"What time did you leave?" I asked

"After the movie, which would've been…" He stopped, trying to go back over the day in his mind. "After four, I guess?"

"The medical examiner said Hardcastle died between two and three that day. Somebody found him at four. You never left the theater from two o'clock on?" I asked.

"Actually, Aiden, you did leave once," said BroFly, and everyone turned to him. "You got there, but you didn't have your wallet. You left to get some money and came back."

I looked at Aiden. "Is that right?"

"I forgot. I left at two-fifteen and ran home to get money for the ticket and concessions. I came back fifteen or twenty minutes later."

"What time did you get back?" I asked.

"Right before the movie started. That's right. I remember now because Trip and BroFly were mad because they had to wait so long."

"I hate missing the previews," Trip admitted.

Zadie grabbed Trip's arm. "Me too! I mean, I always think that's a part of the show I paid for."

I gave Zadie a look and she mouthed the word "sorry" to me and pretended to zip her lips with her fingers.

I went on. "Did anybody see you, Aiden?"

Aiden shrugged.

"Did you go to Hardcastle's office on your way home?" I asked.

"You mean did I kill him before watching a movie? I'm glad the son of a bitch is dead, but I didn't do it."

"Did you put that note and razor blade in Zadie's desk Monday morning?"

Aiden shook his head, annoyed. "I wasn't even at school Monday!"

"He didn't kill him, and he didn't put no damn razor blade in Zadie's desk," Trip buffed. "The end!" He turned to BroFly and Aiden. "Come on, let's go."

The three boys turned and walked down the alley toward Main.

Trip turned back to me. "Sorry about your face, man."

I lifted my hand and waved it off. "I am curious about one thing."

He narrowed his eyes at me and took a few steps back.

"What's the deal with you and BroFly and Aiden?"

He gave me a confused look. "What do you mean?"

"Yesterday and today, you and BroFly took offense to me watching Aiden at school, but you didn't find the blades in his backpack until afterwards. What was all that about?"

Trip relaxed his shoulders and took a step closer, lowering his voice. "He's my cousin and new to Ten Spot. And, just between you and me, he's got some problems. Got kicked out of his last school in Austin for threatening students and teachers. When he enrolled this year, my mom told me to keep an eye on him."

I nodded slowly. "I get it. Keep the bullies away."

Trip hesitated. "More like making sure Aiden doesn't go off the deep end again." He pursed his lips thoughtfully. "Like I said, he's a special kid."

With that, he turned and jogged to where his cousin and BroFly were waiting at the end of the alley.

Alone again, Zadie stood beside me, stroking the cut on my face with a gentle thumb.

"Are you okay?" she asked.

"Just another day on the job." I put a hand to my cheek to test the wound. I was lucky Trip's knife had only nicked me.

She stood on tiptoes, stretching toward me, placing soft lips on mine. The kiss was light and quick, and surprised me, but her lips felt good. She pulled back to note my response. I put my hands on either side of her waist and pulled her close. The kiss was longer this time, deeper, and for a moment I felt the slightest bit of tongue slip between my lips.

She stepped back and adjusted her shirt. "Thank you, Nacho, for helping me."

"Thanks for coming out when you did," I said.

She slipped on her Ray-Bans and began walking up the alley toward Main. "Call me!"

I liked the way she walked. I liked the way she felt in my hands, and the way she smelled. And I liked the way she kissed. The problem was I shouldn't like any of it. She'd been a suspect in the death of her psychiatrist, and the video Finch had shown me of Zadie slipping into the cafeteria just before my grandmother's poisoning was still tripping me. There are reasons why an investigator should never get emotionally involved with his client. On top of it all, I knew this business with Zadie would get ugly if she found out I was on Finch's payroll too.

I would just need to keep her from finding out.

"Zadie!" I called, when she was halfway up the alley.

She stopped and spun, both hands on her hips.

"You got an hour to spare?" I asked.

She lifted the Ray-Bans to her forehead. "I have few strings and sharp scissors, Nacho Blanco."

"Perfect," I said. "I think it's time you and I paid a little visit to the scene of the crime."

CHAPTER 11

SCENE OF THE CRIME

With her arms tight around my waist, Zadie pressed her chest into my back as I guided the Triumph to Hardcastle's former counseling office on the corner of Sumner and Leon, one block over and a few blocks down from Mr. Dream's Ice Cream and Milo Winkler Academy. Hardcastle's office was on the end of an unattractive strip with five suites, and I parked the bike in front of it. I tried the handle on the front door. It was locked.

"You thought it would open?" Zadie asked.

"Sometimes the path to least resistance is the only one that works." I scanned the street. "Let's go around back."

We found the small undeveloped property behind the strip of store fronts overgrown with weeds and littered with debris trapped in the grassy undertow. A few scraggly mesquites stuck out across the back-property line, and it was to one of these Zadie headed.

"It's missing," she said, fumbling with one of the taller branches.

I gave her a quizzical look.

"The backdoor key." She looked back up to the tree limb

I flexed my hands and wiggled my fingers. "We don't need a key."

I pulled a small leather case from my backpack and studied the lock before selecting one of the picks. Then I slipped the flat, stainless-steel instrument into the lock and jimmied it up and down until I felt the lock release inside the handle.

"How do you know how to do that?" Zadie asked.

"Got a lock-picking kit off Amazon. Even came with a stop-watch." I pushed open the door. "Come on. Let's go."

To my surprise, the lights came on when I flipped the switch by the door. The room we'd entered was small and lined on the one side with white plastic utility shelving and on the other with four identical gunmetal-gray filing cabinets. Zadie and I passed through this room into the waiting area where someone had assembled a half-dozen chairs next to an opaque window and the front door.

She pointed to another room on the left and made a disgusted face. "That's his office, where we met with him."

The dark musty office reeked of mold and mildew. There was no window and no overhead light, but I discovered a cheap floor lamp with a yellowing shade and jerked its chain. A wooden executive desk sat off to one side and two chairs, one brown, one blue, faced each other in the middle of the room. An old credenza stood behind the desk, its laminate curling, leaving the wood beneath bare.

"What are we looking for?" she asked.

"Anything the police might've missed." I opened each of the drawers on the desk but came up empty.

"That's where they found him," she pointed to the brown high back leather chair with tufted buttons that faced the smaller terry cloth blue one, "sprawled out, both his wrists cut."

A large brown stain covered the carpet beneath the chair.

Zadie drifted around the room, her hands caressing each piece of furniture. I could tell she was back there again, remembering all that had gone on in this place. She stopped in front of the credenza, closing her eyes.

"Tell me what you see," I said.

She swallowed and crossed her arms tightly in front of her. "He had a hidden camera on these shelves, and he would record us while in session. He sat in that chair, the leather one, and I always sat in the blue one that faced him. He would stop the session and play back the video of what had happened on a monitor, making comments on what I'd said, what I was wearing, my posture, even my figure."

She opened her eyes and began again her tour of the room.

"One time he asked me if I'd ever considered an enhancement. A boob job. Can you believe that? He even said he would pay for it! How fucking generous of him. I guess he thought it would flatter me."

The room was stifling, the air unmoving, and there was a gnawing pain behind my eyes, like someone had wrapped a band around the top of my head and was slowly twisting the screws. "What were the therapy sessions like?"

Zadie moved to the center of the room and sat down in the blue chair. She crossed her legs, folded her hands in her lap, and shut her eyes tight. A frown formed itself across the wrinkles in her forehead.

"He would ask me questions and I would answer them. At first it was your basic garden variety counselor type, like how was my week and how did I feel about a certain thing that had happened. But those were prelude to what he really wanted. Sometimes he would put on seductive music and tell me to get up and act out through dance what the music suggested."

"Did you?" I asked.

She opened her eyes and stared into the empty space in front of her. "At first. Later, I was like fuck this and stopped. He said he could break through a lot of my past pain, but he would need to use some innovative techniques."

"Like having you dance in front of him?" I walked over to the brown, leather high back and sat down, facing Zadie.

"Like dancing," she said. "And with something he called touch therapy."

"Touch therapy?"

She drew in a long deep breath and exhaled. "He said touch therapy was a way for my body and my emotions to get reconnected. He'd lay a blanket on the floor and I would lie on it, and he would lie next to me and touch me and ask questions, make comments."

"Like what?"

"Comments about my body, what I liked most about it, what he liked most about it. He said I needed positive affirmations to raise my self-esteem. He would ask if I enjoyed having certain parts of me rubbed." She paused and dabbed at the tears that had collected beneath her eyes. "At first he just rubbed my back. Then he was touching my ass. Then he had his hands under my shirt or inside my panties. Each week it was something new, like he was on a quest to go further, conquer new territory, with each session."

"Did you ever tell him not to touch you?" I asked.

She dabbed the corner of her eyes again. "I was afraid he would send me away like everyone else had."

"Did he do this with all his patients?" I asked.

"With all the girls. We talked about it in the waiting room. One girl called him Dr. Hard-On. So we began calling him that, only not to his face."

She let out another breath and pulled on her bottom lip. "One of the girls had heard he'd try to do the same thing in Austin, but parents complained and he closed up his practice. After that he began a new counseling group in Ten Spot. Lucky us."

I looked at the credenza. "I wonder where that camera is, or at least the video."

She stood and walked over to the door of the office. "It didn't look like a camera. It looked like an owl, but it had a secret lens in one eye. Mrs. Hardcastle probably threw it out. After he died, and after the police investigation, she drove down from Austin and cleaned out anything that reminded her of her husband. She said the memories were more than she could bear. I bet she never realized the secrets that little owl was keeping."

We made our way back to the storage room. I opened one of the metal filing cabinets and found it empty except for a small notepad Ten Spot investigators had left behind. It was upside down. There was no writing on it, but when I held it up to the light, I could tell somebody had written on the previous page and left an imprint of letters and numbers on the top page. I took out a pencil and made light brush strokes across the paper, illuminating the indentions.

"What is it?" she asked.

There was one word and one number.

DREAM $30,000.

"I've heard the Hardcastles helped get Mr. Dream started in his business, as did the Whiffletrees," I said. "Could be he was in the red to Hardcastle for quite a bit of dough."

"You don't think Mr. Dream would kill someone?" she asked.

"Doesn't seem likely." I folded the paper and slipped it into my pocket.

"Speaking of owing money," Zadie said, "I still can't pay you, at least not yet. But I have something for you." She reached into her pocket and pulled out a ring, dropping it into my hand.

It was a man's signet ring, silver with a flat onyx adorning the top. There were no symbols on the stone and no inscriptions inside the band.

"Where'd this come from?" I asked.

She put a finger between her lips and smirked. "It was Hardcastle's pinky ring. It was in his nightstand. I saw it and took it. I meant to pawn it, but he died, and I forgot all about it until the other day."

I laughed out loud. "You're giving me the pinky ring of a predatory murder victim?"

Zadie's face turned a pale rose. "Okay, it's stupid. I don't know. I thought you would want it, like a talisman, to help you find the killer."

"You think if I wear it Hardcastle will tell me from the grave who sliced him open?" I slipped the ring on my right pinky and held it up for her to see. "Not bad, huh?"

I looked into the waiting area and raised a hand, stopping us. Through the opaque glass in the front window I could see silhouettes moving about, and I placed a finger to Zadie's lips. I crept into the waiting room and heard two men talking outside the front door.

"It's locked," one said.

"Of course, it is, dumbass," said a second. "Stand back. I'll kick it open."

"Wait," said the first, "let me check the back."

I stole back into the storage room, pulled Zadie into a closet with me, and closed the door behind us. I heard the back door open.

"I'm in! Hold on! I'm coming!"

The intruder passed through the storage room to open the front door for his partner.

"You think somebody's here?" one of them asked.

"Duh! There's a bike out front and the back door is unlocked. Do you have shit for brains today?"

Zadie leaned over. "Burglars?"

"Be quiet," I whispered in her ear.

The closet door swung open and a blast of intense LED light hit us in the face. I squinted and raised my hand to fend off the sudden glare and saw two men, their pistols drawn.

"You two, out," said one.

We stepped out of the closet. Both men wore identical black suits, white button-down shirts, with matching solid black ties. And both had FBI badges clamped to their lapels.

They lowered their firearms, sliding them into holsters beneath their coats.

The shorter one spoke first. "I'm FBI Special Agent Lance Atkins. This is my partner, FBI Special Agent Roger McKee."

His partner gave us the obligatory fed nod. "What are you two doing here?"

I squinted at their badges and played the dumb teen routine. "We were just looking for some place to get high, man. That's all. We weren't trying to steal nothing. I mean, there's nothing to steal in here anyway. We thought you guys were burglars."

"We're investigating the death of Dr. Hardcastle. This is an active crime scene. You shouldn't be here."

Zadie walked around the agents. "We were just leaving."

The one who called himself Atkins stopped her, pushing her back into me. "Not so fast, missy." He turned to his partner. "Let's take 'em down to police headquarters and make their parents pick 'em up."

This was going south fast.

"Officer…um, Special Agent Atkins…can't you just give us a warning this time? We promised our parents we would make changes and get serious about school and college." I looked at Zadie and she nodded with large doe eyes. "My grades are getting better and I have my first college visit to UT this weekend."

Zadie stepped forward and placed a light hand on McKee's arm. "Please, sir? I promise, this won't happen again."

McKee looked at Atkins, then jerked his head toward the door. "You two get out of here and get home."

Zadie and I tripped over each other getting to the front door.

I didn't look back. "Thank you, sir. And have a nice day."

Outside, we jumped on Brockett's bike which roared to life with one quick kick. We took off down Sumner, Zadie plastered to my back.

Back at the Allens's house, she slipped off the bike, flashing me a smile. "That was fun, Nacho. I like doing detective work with you."

"Be careful," I said. "Something's off, even by Ten Spot's standards."

She blew me a kiss. "You be careful too."

As I waited for her to step inside her house, I felt a buzzing in my back pocket. I pulled out my phone. It was a message from Mr. Dream.

NEED TO C U ASAP

CHAPTER 12

SWINGING SNAKE

I had two phone calls to make before meeting Dream, and I made them both sitting on the bike in his parking lot.

The first was to Ten Spot's lead detective in the Lincoln Hardcastle investigation. I figured it wouldn't hurt for him to learn about the note I'd found concerning the $30,000 Dream owed the victim. In return, I hoped to find out why the FBI was working the case. The dispatcher transferred my call to a Detective Larry Books, and he was less than thrilled to hear my voice.

"Listen, kid, stay away from my case. You're poison."

"Good afternoon to you, too, Detective," I said. "This is Nacho Blanco. I may have…"

"I know who you are, and I don't want you anywhere near this fucking case, Blanco. Got it?"

I cleared my throat. "Let me ask you something, Detective. Did you have problems playing with others when you were a kid too?"

He didn't mince his words. "You got a big mouth, runt, and you run it too damn much. You haven't been shy about letting everyone know you want out of Ten Spot. If this thing ever goes to court, the defense will shoot down any evidence I bring to the DA's office with your name attached on the grounds you got your own damn motive. It's Mark Fuhrman all over again.

They'll assume you're just looking for a way out and a way up. Do us both a favor – stay the hell away from my case and stick to your little schoolhouse mysteries."

I never got the chance to ask about the FBI's business in Ten Spot. He ended the call and left me holding my phone in the air like a jackass. I guess I *had* run my mouth a few too many times.

The next call was to Brockett. I gave him a quick rundown on my late-night meeting with Finch, the lunch with Zadie, and the discovery of Hardcastle's note in the empty filing cabinet. I left out the parts involving Mrs. Whiffletree's proclivity toward weed and the fact that Zadie and I had run into two armed feds. No sense getting the old man's blood pressure up too high, I thought.

Then I spotted him the reason for my call. "The doctor attending my grandmother mentioned a situation here in Ten Spot a few years back in which a person died from ethylene glycol poisoning. You heard anything about that?"

"It was five years ago," he said. "Her name was Stephanie Sullivan. Twenty-one-year-old junior at Overton College. They found her body in a field outside town. A toxicology report revealed somebody had given her ethylene glycol, but that wasn't what killed her."

"How'd she die?"

"Strangled, with a thirty-two-inch sterling silver chain necklace from Tiffany and Company wrapped three times around her neck. The necklace even had that little heart that says 'Return to Tiffany' still attached. The killer didn't even bother to take the chain with him."

"That's an expensive way to ice someone," I said. "No prints, I suppose."

"None. But look at this. I'm sending you a photo of the necklace."

I looked down at my phone as a photo from Brockett came through. It was an evidence photo of the chain still wrapped around Stephanie Sullivan's neck. The signature Tiffany and

Company heart was flipped over but clearly visible against the girl's ashen skin. And on the backside of the heart pendant were three words engraved: *Act as if.*

I read the words aloud. "What do you think it means?"

"Pop psychology?" Brockett ventured. "I don't know. But the killer wasn't acting when he strangled Sullivan."

"Why the ethylene glycol?"

"I'm guessing they used the antifreeze to disorient, incapacitate her ability to fight back while being choked."

I lifted myself off the bike and dropped its kickstand. "And the motive?"

"The rumor around the Agency was this girl was deep cover for CIA."

"CIA?" I asked. "What would a twenty-one-year-old spy be doing in Ten Spot?"

"That I can't answer. Investigators I talked to figured someone had blown her cover and silenced her to hide whatever Agent Sullivan had unearthed."

"Was an arrest made?" I asked.

"Nope. The locals believed it was her misfortune to cross paths with a drifter. Wrong place at the wrong time. I think it's a lot more than that."

"What do you mean?"

"What was CIA even doing in Ten Spot? CIA operatives don't spy on American citizens on our own soil. That's the FBI's business."

"Somebody was running a covert operation in Ten Spot?" I suggested.

"That's what I'm thinking. At least until Sullivan got killed."

"What do you think happened to her?"

"For sure that wasn't her necklace, and I'm not buying the drifter angle. How many transients have you met shopping at Tiffany and Company?"

"Can't say I've ever shopped at Tiffany's." I looked up and chanced to see Dream standing in his dining area staring at me through the window. He caught himself and looked away, but I wondered if he'd been there a while. He looked back at me again and I raised a finger as if to say, "One moment."

"In all my years of law enforcement," Brockett continued, "more often than not, the perp knew the victim. Chances are the last thing Agent Sullivan saw was a family member or friend of hers wrapping a thousand-dollar chain around her throat."

I thanked him for the information, pocketed the phone, and made my way inside Dream's.

Dream turned when he heard the door and motioned with frantic hands for me to follow him down the back hall to his office. Inside, he collapsed in his chair, turned on his monitor, and cued up a security feed.

As I stood over his desk, I watched him scroll the video forward, the same footage from a few days earlier.

"We've seen this," I said.

He rubbed the back of his neck and looked me in the eye. "There's more."

He clicked play and the feed started. There was Aiden in his red Heinz Ketchup t-shirt, ordering a bowl of pink yogurt. There was Porter giving Aiden his receipt. But, as Aiden turned away from the counter, the receipt fell from his hands onto the floor. At that moment another customer walked into the frame. It was Zadie. She picked up the receipt, slipped it into her pocket, then walked out of the camera's frame.

Dream stopped the video and offered a pained look. "I'm sorry. I thought you'd want to see."

"You're right. Unfortunately." I moved for the door but stopped short. "Can I ask you a question, Mr. Dream?" This would be awkward, but the most difficult questions shared between friends often are.

He looked at me, eyes wide.

"Did Hardcastle demand his $30,000 back from you?"

He folded his hands in his lap and smiled. "Am I a suspect now, old friend?"

I rubbed my chin. "Some might say $30,000 is motive enough for murder, especially if you can't pay it back."

Dream didn't respond but twisted his chair toward the monitor and began a new search. I had a hunch what he was looking for, and I figured he'd find it. But I didn't stop him. Something was troubling me about Dream. It wasn't proof of his innocence I was looking for. It was proof of his complicity, and I was hoping I didn't find it.

I stood looking over his shoulder as he tried to locate the video, an embarrassed reticence filling the small space between us. Calling a man you call a friend a liar is hard to do. Calling him a loser at the thing he's sunk his heart and hard-earned bacon into, not to mention someone else's bankroll, is a quick way to lose that friend. I'd just called him out on both, and Dream looked desperate to show me otherwise. Mr. Dream's Ice Cream wasn't doing well and lying is always the last resort of a man who can't stop the losing.

He fast-forwarded to the noon hour of August fifteenth, the day Hardcastle died, then put the video in fast-play mode. We watched Dream in the front lobby, serving ice cream, waiting on customers, wiping down tables, taking phone calls. It took all of two minutes for three hours of footage to stream by. At the three o'clock hour he stopped it and looked up.

"I never left the front lobby or counter the entire time."

He paused, waiting for me to acknowledge his blamelessness. I didn't. I kept my mouth shut. It was the only way I figured I could keep his running.

"I was here the entire day." He dropped his chin to his chest, his eyes settling on the floor. "I couldn't have killed Lincoln. He was my friend. Sure, I owed him $30,000 but I also owe that much to the Whiffletrees. Yes, he wanted the money back, said he'd made a big mistake loaning it to me. I told him to go to hell because I didn't have it. Four days later, he was dead." He pointed to the photo of him and the Hardcastles with the Whiffletrees. "Every morning I walk into this place I'm reminded of our last words to each other, and how I wish those words would've been different."

The silence between us was palpable. Mr. Dream and I had entered a new chapter in our relationship, one which neither of us appeared to know quite how to handle. I stared at the photo of Scout taped to his computer's monitor. He rested his eyes on the issue of *Reader's Digest* lying on his desk. At last, when he spoke, his voice was low and soft and had taken on a determined edge.

"I think it's best you left."

He didn't look at me, he didn't stand, and I ushered myself back out of the store.

I was about to mount the Triumph again when I heard a screeching of tires behind me. I whirled to see a blue Crown Victoria sliding my way. The car missed me but not the bike, hitting its fender, sending the machine hurtling to the asphalt.

The driver side window came down. It was Darwood. "Get in, motherfucker!"

I righted the bike back to a standing position. Other than a cracked left side mirror the Triumph still looked operational. I threw a leg over the saddle and brought it to life.

"I'm not asking again!" He pulled a 9mm Glock and aimed it at me.

"You gonna shoot me here in the parking lot of Mr. Dream's?" I kicked the stand on the bike and pushed it back a few feet.

I felt the pop from Darwood's Glock before I heard the sound. At first, I thought he'd shot me. But the bullet slashed through the front fender on the bike and sent it reeling to one side, wrenching the handlebars from my hands, sending me and the bike down hard.

I turned off the Triumph and untangled myself from the pile of metal. "You're a freaking psycho!"

"Get in," he ordered, "or the next one goes through your kneecap."

I righted the bike a second time and got into Darwood's piece of crap car. True to form, he squealed out of the parking lot, turning right onto MLK as we headed toward the northern end of downtown.

"You and Finch are paying for that damage," I said. "Jesus Christ! You're crazier than the murderer we're looking for! We *are* on the same team, you know!"

Darwood didn't say a word.

"You wanna tell me where we're going?" I asked.

Still, he didn't reply, and we continued on for several blocks before taking a left onto Highway 12. Just past the city limits sign he gunned it, and the car shimmied under the torque of the straining engine. I watched the yellow hash marks down the center of the road whip by at a dizzying rate while a three-inch gold metallic snake swung faster and faster on a leather cord wrapped around the base of the rear-view mirror, striking left and right, back and forth, like a Texas copperhead.

"You almost got your ass handed to you at The Dirty Diva today, until that little murderer stepped in." He laughed, flashing a full set of bright teeth, the first time I'd seen something that wasn't a scowl on his face. "You need to get something straight. She's suspect numero uno. You need to stop sticking your tongue down her throat."

I felt the heat rising in my face.

"That's right." He shot me a quick glance, then resettled his eyes back on the road. "I saw you two swapping spit in the alley. I'm tracking everything you do and everywhere you go."

He let up on the accelerator, allowing the car to coast down to the speed limit.

"You want to date a murder suspect, that's your business. But when she goes down, I will make it my fucking business that you do too. I suggest you pull your head out and stop tonguing the slut."

Maybe it was the fact that Darwood had been spying on me, or maybe I was mad at myself for disregarding a lot of unsettled feelings for Zadie. Could've been some of both. Either way, I didn't stop to think. My left fist struck Darwood's jaw, snapping his head to the left. It wasn't as hard as I'd wanted, but it was my non-dominant hand, and he *was* driving the car I was in.

Despite the blow to his face, Darwood didn't utter a sound, and the car never veered from its lane. He rotated his head to face me, reached inside his jacket, and pulled out the Glock, pressing the muzzle against my forehead.

"I'll blow your fucking head off if you ever do that again." He holstered the weapon and pointed to the back seat. "See that file? Get it."

I stretched back and picked up a manila folder. The file had the initials ZA on the tab, handwritten in red. Same file I'd seen Finch holding at the gazebo. Inside I found the official Ten Spot police report on the murder of Dr. Hardcastle.

"How'd you get this?" I asked.

"By doing my damn job! Read it!"

I flipped through the file. It was a typical police report detailing the evidence discovered regarding Hardcastle's death. There were also photographs of the crime scene. In one Hardcastle's body was spread-eagled in that brown leather high back, a pool of blood beneath him, his arms slung over both sides of the chair. Other pictures showed the slice marks on his wrists. The cuts were the same on both, from top left to bottom right. And there was also a photo of the razor blade, dropped, as it were, from Hardcastle's right hand to the floor, swimming in his blood. It was a gruesome scene. I took out my phone and snapped a shot of every graphic photo.

"Read the summary at the bottom," he said.

I turned to the last page of the report and let my eyes scan down. The police had interviewed all five of Hardcastle's teenage clients in Ten Spot. All had alibis. But there was an asterisk by Zadie's name, and a footnote below it. The evidence at the scene looked staged and that convinced Ten Spot's investigators Hardcastle's death was a homicide, not a suicide. Zadie

Abernathy was their prime suspect, not because of her history of self-harm, but because as his foster child, she had a closer association with him than the others. It also noted there had been no sustainable proof to justify a continual investigation of her nor anyone else.

I closed the file and let it slip to the floorboard between my feet. The Ten Spot police detectives were following a well-worn path when it came to investigating homicides. Start with the victim's family and work out from there. About the closest thing to family Hardcastle had that I knew of was his wife and Zadie. No wonder Zadie was on the radar right from the start. But I wondered why the police hadn't mentioned Mrs. Hardcastle as a possible suspect. And I wondered where she was in all of this right now.

Darwood stopped the car next to a guard rail. "Get out."

This time I didn't even argue.

Standing on the gravel shoulder, I watched Darwood make a U-turn and beat it back to Ten Spot. Then I started walking.

I needed to get the bike from Mr. Dream's. I needed to get to the hospital to check on my grandmother. And I needed to figure out where I stood with Zadie. In my heart, I didn't want to believe it was possible for her to kill someone in cold blood, especially after I'd seen the way she was with the old lady on the bench. But my mind had a lot of questions. Why hadn't she told me right from the start she'd been living with the Hardcastles when he died? Of all places, why'd Mrs. Hardcastle find a new foster home for Zadie right back in the same town where she'd already suffered so much sexual abuse? And what *was* Zadie doing in that cafeteria the day my grandmother had been found on the floor?

I started walking. The sooner I got back to Ten Spot, the sooner I could wrap up this mystery and put this town in my rearview mirror once and for all.

CHAPTER 13

SPECIAL OPS

I t took twenty minutes to get back to Ten Spot. It would've taken longer if it hadn't been for a silver hair with a need for speed.

I'd walked at least a mile when a lone, black Mercedes coupe, top down, pulled up alongside me, the radio belting out some old song from the '80s.

The driver turned down the music and pointed to the passenger side door. "Need a lift?"

She didn't have to ask me twice. I skimmed onto the soft black leather seat next to her and she put the car back onto the blacktop and floored it.

"Where to?" she asked.

"Ten Spot Memorial. Thanks for the ride."

My driver was clearly cut from a fine cloth. She had short white hair with a dramatic flip up that gave her the look of someone who frequented expensive salons. Her lips were bright red, as were her nails, and she wore two large metallic earrings that could've easily passed for a pair of antique Spanish doubloons. Beneath a large V-neck black sweater was a white, oversized button-down Oxford with French cuffs clamped by a pair of black onyx cufflinks. A pair of tight black pants covered her legs. Oversized black cat-eye sunglasses hid her eyes.

She gave me a quick glance. "Girl trouble?"

"Something like that," I said.

"There's always a girl involved when somebody strands a young man in the middle of nowhere." She checked the rearview mirror. "The name's Vega."

"Nacho," I said. "Nacho Blanco."

"Yes, you are," she said matter-of-factly. "I've seen your picture in the paper. You're the young sleuth who solved the case of the missing PTA money at Milo Winkler Academy last spring."

"I guess word gets around."

"Seems to have a way of doing that," she said, her eyes glued to the road, her hands steady at ten and two.

She turned up the music and we rode the rest of the way without a word. At the hospital, she swung the Mercedes into the emergency drive like we were coming in for a tire change on our last lap at the Texas Motor Speedway.

"It was nice meeting you," I said, easing out of the car.

"You take care, Nacho Blanco."

I gave her a curious nod, but she didn't wait for it. She floored it again and I watched her drive off until she was out of the parking lot and out of sight.

Inside the hospital, I found the elevators and stabbed at the up button. I dug my phone from my back pocket and called Price Patterson.

She answered right away, and I asked to come over.

"I'm looking into the murder of Dr. Hardcastle," I explained. "I have some questions for you."

"You can talk to Holiday too. She's with me. She also saw Dr. Hard-On."

I groaned at the euphemism. "I'll be there in thirty."

A half-hour would give me enough time to check on my grandmother, retrieve the bike from Dream's, and get over to Price's.

On the second floor, I introduced myself to Ms. Waters at the ICU nurses' station.

"Would you like to see your grandmother, Mr. Blanco?" she asked, carefully enunciating every syllable with southern charm.

"How is she?" I asked, steadying myself for her answer.

"Much better today, I would say." She leaned in closer to me and smiled. "She's been asking about you."

She led me over to a room completely encased by glass walls and opened the door. I found my grandmother sitting up, a nasal cannula attached to her nose, an IV drip attached to the back of her hand, and some kind of tube protruding from the side of her neck. Her eyes were halfway open, and she gave me a weak smile as we entered.

"I'll leave you two alone," said the nurse. "But just a short visit, mind you."

My grandmother and I stared at each other for a moment. The previous morning I'd tried to slip by her on the way to school without a word. Now, having almost lost her, I struggled to find just the right way to begin. It pained me to see her there, knowing what she'd been through, the fear she must've had waking up in the hospital alone. She lifted her hand and gave me a little wave of her fingers.

"*Mijo.*" Her voice was low, weak.

I inched over to her and gingerly took her hand in mine, careful not to bump the IV. "Hi, Grandma. You look good."

She laughed, coughed, then winced, and readjusted herself on the pillow behind her back as best as she could. "Thanks. I put on my best outfit for you."

We both looked down at the blue hospital gown she had on.

"You're rocking that new uni."

She smiled and stopped herself from laughing. "Doctor Cooper says I was probably poisoned."

I nodded. "I'm gonna find out who did this to you."

She lifted her hand from mine and pointed a finger at me. "You be careful."

"I know. I know. I will."

There was a pause in our conversation before she continued. "What am I thinking, *mijo?*"

Before I could give her the answer, the door opened and Nurse Waters entered the room. "Mr. Blanco, I think we better let your grandmother rest. She's still got a lot of recovering to do."

I forced a smile at my grandmother and followed Ms. Waters back to the nurses' station where she handed me an envelope.

"Here's that razor blade you asked me to keep for you," she said.

I folded the envelope and shoved it into the pocket of my coat. "Somebody told my grandmother she'd been poisoned."

"When she started coming around this morning, she asked why she was here, so we told her. We're still waiting on the lab results. That can often take several days in these cases. In the meantime, we've been using hemodialysis to treat her, and the results have been positive."

"Hemodialysis?"

"It's similar to dialysis for people whose kidneys have stopped working properly. Waste is cleansed from your blood. The difference is the doctor had to attach her to something called a dialyzer. That's why there's a tube protruding from her neck now. The dialyzer cleans all of the ethylene glycol from her blood. As you can see it seems to be making a difference. We'll know for sure in a couple of days when the lab results return, but Dr. Cooper is ninety-five percent certain it was ethylene glycol poisoning."

I thanked Ms. Waters for the care she was giving my grandmother, made my way to the elevators, and pushed the ground floor button. The video Finch had shown me of Zadie walking through the cafeteria kept playing on a loop in my head. Wouldn't Zadie have known the school is full of cameras recording everything that goes on in every corner of the building?

Actually, she would know, I thought. *Everybody knows.*

When the elevator doors opened, I took a step forward, and found myself face to face with two government-issued feds.

"Come with us," said Special Agent McKee.

He gripped my arm like a vice and, and he and Special Agent Atkins walked us away from the elevator toward the exit. Outside they led me to an unmarked black SUV.

"Twice in one day," I said.

"What's twice?" asked Atkins.

"It's the second time today somebody's forced me to take a ride. I must be getting real popular in this town."

"Shut the fuck up," McKee barked. "Atkins, put some cuffs on this smart-ass."

Something about this whole thing wasn't adding up, and I decided right quick I wasn't going to stick around and do the math.

McKee pulled away from my side as he opened the SUV's back door, and I stole my chance. I came around with a right hook to McKee's face, causing him to stagger backwards against the vehicle. Free now, I looked to make a mad dash across the parking lot.

That's when I felt a bolt of lightning in my side. The shock paralyzed every motor skill and I collapsed to the ground. I tried to talk, but the words wouldn't come. I tried to stand, but my legs wouldn't move. I could see, and I could hear, but that was all, and I didn't like the thought of what was coming next.

Atkins leaned over me and checked my pulse. "You still alive, kid? Damn. That must've hurt like a sum'bitch." He looked up at his partner. "You ever taken a stun gun to the side?"

They laughed as they threw me into the back seat. McKee slipped behind the wheel. Atkins shuffled in next to me.

"I gotta hand it to you, kid," said Atkins. "You got some balls."

"What's the moral of the story?" asked McKee. "Don't fucking mess with the F.B. fucking I."

He slipped a black bag over my head and the SUV took off.

My head was foggy from the electrical shot I'd taken to the side, and I couldn't keep straight all the turns we were making. After a while, the SUV came to a stop and I heard the doors open. With the bag over my head, I half-stumbled and was half-dragged out of the vehicle, across a gravel drive, and into some kind of building. One of them shoved me into a chair and whipped off the hood.

It was a warehouse. That much I could tell. Constructed of brick and tin, it was dark and damp with only a little light seeping through several wide, painted-over windows about forty feet off the ground. A floor light five feet away came on, blinding me, and lit up a small space like a tiny island floating in the middle of a giant black ocean, with me right in the center.

Atkins stepped out of the darkness from behind the light. In one hand, he held a small utility rope. In the other, his firearm.

McKee followed him into the light. "We have some questions for you, Blanco, and if you answer them to our satisfaction, you'll be free to go. No harm, no foul."

He took the rope from Atkins, tied each of my hands to the armrests of the chair, and placed an iPhone in my face.

"We're ready," he said.

"Nacho Blanco," said a woman's voice on the phone, "this is Second Deputy Attorney General Renee Howard. My apologies for the inconvenience to you today. I hope you're more comfortable now."

"It's not the Waldorf Astoria," I said, playing along, "but I'm getting used to it."

She continued. "My agents picked you up because we've gotten word you're working a case that's of utmost concern for the security and welfare of the United States. Of particular interest is a photo that has classified information in it. It's a photo of Dr. Lincoln Hardcastle and his wife and some friends of theirs. Inside this particular photo is a hidden microchip with highly sensitive, highly classified intel." She took a deep breath, and continued, her tone even more serious. "We need that photo, and we have good reason to believe you have it or have access to it."

"Why would you think that?" I asked.

"Do you, Mr. Blanco?" she asked.

In the background, from somewhere behind the caller, I heard the faint sound of chimes, and they were playing that annoying little Disney tune "It's a Small World."

"No," I said.

"No what?" asked the caller. "No, you don't have it, or no, you don't know where it is?"

"No, I'm not going to help you." I said.

There was an irritated pause in our conversation.

"Here's what we'll do, Mr. Blanco. We'll play hangman's noose until you tell me where the photo is. Only, instead of getting a body part for each wrong answer, we'll take one of yours."

I heard the swishing sound and looked to see Atkins brandishing a five-inch blade in his hand.

"Where's the photo?" asked the woman on the phone. "Your life is about to get very exciting, Mr. Blanco."

"That's all I ever really wanted."

"Take a finger from the little smart-ass," she said.

I swallowed hard. "Come on, man. You don't need to do that. I mean, you're seriously going to cut off one of my fingers?" I strained against the ropes around my wrists, but they didn't budge.

Atkins placed the edge of the blade against my left middle finger, and I looked away, bracing for the pain.

The cut never came.

A loud pop echoed across the warehouse, and Atkins and McKee hit the deck, whipping out 9mm Barettas as they did.

"Gun!" McKee yelled out.

"Don't move," said a low, husky voice from the darkness behind me.

McKee raised his pistol toward the sound and squeezed off several rapid rounds into the darkness.

Another shot sang out behind me, the bullet whizzing close enough to McKee that he ducked.

"FBI! Identify yourself!" Atkins yelled.

"Toss those weapons toward the kid or I'll put a slug in the center of that red dot on each of your mugs," said the voice from the dark.

Atkins and McKee turned to each other and confirmed a red laser dot on each other's head, and then skidded their weapons toward me.

The figure stepped out of the shadows behind me. He had on full black tactical gear, a black mask over his face, night vision goggles covering his eyes, and a semi-automatic in each gloved hand, each with a laser sight. He scooped up the knife Atkins had dropped and cut me free from the chair. Then he placed a hand under my arm and helped me stand, all the while keeping his weapon trained on the two agents.

"Can you walk?" he asked.

I nodded. "Who are you?"

"Special ops," he said. "Let's go."

We walked backwards toward the exit, the man in black firing off two more rounds in the general direction of McKee and Atkins for good measure. Outside, I hobbled my way into a waiting black van, "special ops" closing the door behind us. Inside, I saw another man at the wheel, black, with a large white toothy smile. He had on a black leather jacket and a black ballcap pulled down low over his head.

"Nacho Blanco," he said, his voice thick with a Jamaican accent, "I'm Chuck."

I looked at the one in the tactile gear and guessed. He stripped off the night vision and his mask and flung them into the back of the van.

"Didn't Darcy tell you to be careful?" asked Brockett. He turned to the driver. "Hit it!"

Chuck put the van in gear and jammed the accelerator to the floor. The tires scratched into the gravel as they struggled to grip enough traction to propel us forward. Through one of the van's side windows I saw the door of the warehouse burst open and the two kidnappers stumble out. They fired a dozen rounds at us, the sound of their bullets ricocheting off the side of the van like pebbles in a tin can. We raced across the gravel lot, slid onto the two-lane highway, and sped off.

Finally, away from imminent danger, I turned to Brockett. "Special ops, huh?"

He rocked his head back and forth. "I've had some training."

"How'd you find me?"

"I was leaving the hospital when I saw those two jump you." With one of his gloved hands, Brockett began wiping away the sweat from his face. "Couldn't let you have all that fun by yourself."

I noticed we'd left the main highway and now bumped along a dirt road that led through an open field.

Chuck looked at me in the rear-view mirror. "Tom Brockett is the best in the business."

"Chuck's the retired agent I was telling you about and the consultant for Ten Spot PD," Brockett explained. "I told him what was going on, asked him to meet me at the safe house, and we mounted up." He turned to his old friend. "Nothing like reliving the glory days, right? I appreciate your help on this one."

Chuck waved his hand and kept the van bouncing along further and further into open country. "Wherever I'm needed, that's where I'll be."

"By the way," said Brockett, "those guys aren't FBI."

"I sorta figured that one out."

I looked out the front windshield and saw a weathered gray cabin with its windows boarded and a front porch begging to cave in. The road we were on ended there.

"This is the safe house," Brockett explained. "One of them. I have twenty scattered around the country. Each one has a vehicle and an arsenal of weapons. That cabin may not look like much, but that's the idea. Trust me, she's tighter than Fort Knox on the inside."

"Can one of you get me the toxicology report on Hardcastle?" I asked.

"I can swing that for you," said Chuck. "I'll talk to the boys at Ten Spot PD."

I pulled the blade Zadie had found in her desk from my pocket. "Can you have this analyzed also? I'd like to know if that's blood on it."

He gave me a thumbs-up.

From my jacket, I pulled the envelope given to me by Ms. Waters at the hospital. "There's another one in here. Would you mind checking that one too?"

"I'm on it," he said.

We pulled up to the cabin and piled out. I waited on the front porch while the two men headed inside to dispose of their tactical gear and heavy weaponry. Five minutes later, they were back outside in their civvies.

Chuck handed me his card. "Call me. Anytime. A friend of Tom's is a friend of mine."

I took the card. "Thanks. And thanks for saving my behind back there. You think I could ask one more favor of you guys?"

"Fire away," said Brockett.

"I need a ride to Mr. Dream's."

"I'm sure we can do that."

"Let's roll," said Chuck.

"By the way," I said to Brockett as I climbed into the back seat of the van. "Your Triumph took a bullet from my new investigative partner. I'll see to it he pays for the repairs."

"Only in Ten Spot," said Brockett, as the van shot away from the cabin and headed back toward town.

CHAPTER 14

FAIT ACCOMPLI

"What the fuck happened to you?"

After picking up the bike at Dream's, I'd made a beeline to the home of Price Patterson, a large red brick house that looked more old Williamsburg than old Lone Star. The house faced Overton's iconic quadrangle. I wasn't sure, but I'd heard Price's father was a tenured professor at Overton, economics or business, or something.

"What do you mean?" I asked.

"Have you seen yourself?" She jerked me inside, positioning me in front of the foyer's full-length mirror.

She was right. My hair was a broken bird nest. The lump above my eye was darkening. The cut Trip had given me looked like someone had started sewing up my cheek and then stopped. There was a brown smear across my forehead and both cheeks. And my black t-shirt had a rip across the left shoulder.

She grabbed a wet paper towel from the foyer bathroom and wiped down my face. "OMG! Did you get mugged?"

"Nah. I just got friends who play rough," I said.

"I have a shirt you can wear. Strip." She reached for the bottom of my tee, stood on tip toes, and pulled it up over my head.

I followed her through an immaculate kitchen to an oversized laundry where she located a blue Superman tee. I didn't know much about Price except that she was smart and beautiful, having inherited her father's academic pedigree and her mother's model-like looks. I also knew she suffered from an acute case of misappropriated high self-esteem.

I looked back toward the kitchen. "Holiday still here?"

Price, wearing a black racerback yoga top and matching pants, her auburn hair in a high pony, reached for my hand and dragged me through the kitchen to a casual living area off the foyer. Holiday sat on a brown leather couch, her legs crossed beneath her, Bose headphones perched atop a bouncing head, her own ponytail marking time to the song in her ears. She was cute sitting there in her olive drab tee and cut off jean shorts, eyes closed, absorbed by the music. She looked up from her iPhone startled as we entered the room, and let the headphones slide down around her neck.

"This won't take long," I said. "A private investigative firm has hired me to look into the murder of Dr. Hardcastle."

"You mean, Dr. Hard-On?" Price scoffed then turned to Holiday. "Speaking of hard-ons, Dirk is coming over."

Holiday smiled but said nothing. I hadn't heard much about Holiday, except that she'd been in the U.S. for only a few years, and she lived with her parents and three little brothers on the other side of town in a small apartment. How she'd gotten hooked up with Price was beyond me. Maybe Price saw Holiday as a project, her personal fixer-upper. Maybe Holiday saw Price as an opportunity, her personal ticket to bigger and better things.

"What did you think about Dr. Hardcastle?" I asked Price.

Price dropped herself in an oversized purple bean bag and crossed her legs beneath her. "Hated him. Glad he's dead. He deserved everything he got, and more."

"Why's that?"

"Wouldn't you if he was constantly telling you what a dirty girl you were?" Her phone chimed and she responded to a text.

I stood next to a small entertainment center with a large flat screen. "He called you dirty?"

The front door flew open, and in unison, the three of us turned toward the foyer. A tall, thick guy with long, black hair walked into the room and rushed over to Price. He wore a black Winkler Cougars Football tee with the sleeves cut off and dark brown chinos. She jumped up and wrapped her legs around his waist, and he grabbed her backside and slapped it.

They kissed, then he put her down and pulled a small silver bracelet from his pocket and handed it to her. "Here, babe, I got you something."

Price squealed with delight and plopped down beside Holiday to study the gift, a small silver bracelet with charms that dangled from its links. While she tried on the bracelet, the new dude marched over to the bar and helped himself to a drink.

"Nacho, this is my boyfriend, Dirk." Price turned to the boyfriend. "Put the bottles back like my parents left them! The last time you were here they got suspicious and started blaming me for drinking their booze." She turned back to me again. "What did you ask me?"

"You said Hardcastle called you dirty."

I stole a glance at Holiday. She still hadn't moved, nor had she said anything.

"He said the way I talked and the way I dressed and the way I carried myself was very dirty, overly provocative," said Price. "Only he didn't say it in a condemning way, like my mom or dad. He said it like he liked it."

"I don't think you dress sexy enough," said Dirk, downing his first drink. He looked over at me. "Hey, asshole, is that my shirt?"

I looked down at the Superman tee I was wearing. "Price let me wear it. Somebody trashed mine."

Dirk absently let out another expletive and then poured himself another drink.

"What about you, Holiday?" I asked. "How was your relationship with Hardcastle?"

Holiday cut her eyes to Price and didn't say anything. Her left leg, still folded beneath her, began to tremble.

"She hated him too," Price said. "She even wrote about killing Dr. Hard-On in her journal. He found out, took the journal, and wouldn't give it back."

"In case someone tried to hurt him."

I turned to Holiday. It was the first time I'd heard her speak. Ever. She had a soft, silty voice that suited her. Her English was good but slow, not bad for someone who'd only recently immigrated. Somehow that only made her more credible, less threatening, and easy to like.

"In case someone tried to hurt him?" I asked.

Her leg continued to shake. "That's what he said. He kept it so the police would find the killer. Me, I guess."

"You hated him," I said to Holiday.

Price jumped in again. "We all hated him. He fed us a bunch of touch therapy bullshit."

"Go on," I said.

Price rolled her eyes. "He said touch therapy would get us in tune with our feelings so we would be free to take charge of our lives. Fucking pervert."

"Hey, Price, can I be your counselor now? I'm an expert at touch therapy," said Dirk as he poured himself another shot, his third. I thought it was his third. I was losing count, and I was pretty sure Dirk was too.

"This is serious, Dirk!" Price looked at her phone. "Holy fuck! My parents will be home in fifteen minutes! Put those bottles back the way you found them!"

I heard Dirk say something under his breath and help himself to another drink.

"Can I ask both of you something?" I closed my eyes and rubbed the cut Trip had gifted me earlier. It didn't feel too bad, but my face was sore from the punches he and BroFly had thrown. "Where were you when Dr. Hardcastle died on that Saturday afternoon?"

Price said nothing, but her eyes shifted from me to Dirk to Holiday.

"Church," Holiday said. "We had the carnival. Mrs. Whiffletree was there too. You can ask her. She saw me."

I turned to Price. "Where were you on the afternoon of August fifteenth?"

Price unfolded herself from the couch and walked over to the bar where she took an untouched drink from Dirk's hand and swallowed it whole. "You know where I was?"

I lifted my chin.

"I was at none of your fucking business."

Dirk laughed out loud and poured himself another drink to replace the one his girlfriend had pinched.

I shot a glance over at Holiday who remained motionless, but now gripped a throw pillow in front of her like a shield.

I walked to the bar and stood next to Price. "You can tell me what you told the police, can't you?" I picked up the bottle and took a whiff. Jack Daniel's.

She belched. "I'll tell you the same thing my daddy's lawyer told them. It's none of your fucking business."

Dirk laughed again and downed another drink.

I let my fingers wrap around the neck of the Jack Daniel's.

Price continued. "You know what else, Mr. Nacho Blanco? What do you call yourself, a PFI?"

I didn't correct her.

"I was the one who found his dead body. Isn't that some crazy-ass shit? How many people can say that? He was laid out in his chair, blood running down his arms, dripping all over the carpet. I mean, talk about a priceless experience!" She looked around the room. "Get it? Priceless?"

I looked at Holiday and Dirk. I was pretty sure neither of them got it, but for different reasons.

Price snatched the bottle from my hand, took a long swig,

and set it down firm on the bar's counter. "You wanna hear what I did then?"

I waited.

"I laughed my ass off." She gave me an exaggerated nod, as if to reinforce the fact. "I did. I swear to God. First time I ever saw a dead body and I laughed when I saw him bleeding out like some stuck pig all over that floor, the same floor where earlier that morning, he had tried his fucking touch therapy on me."

"Being with a dead body didn't bother you?" I asked.

She crossed her arms. "Whoever killed Dr. Hard-On did everybody a favor. And if that person hadn't done it, somebody else would've. He was a dead man walking. We all wanted his ass dead. Even Dirk wanted to kill him because of what he was doing to me. Who knows? I might've done it if nobody else had. It was just a matter of time."

"Which way did you go into the office that day when you found him?" I asked.

Her eyebrows knit together, and her forehead furrowed into deep lines. "Through the front door." Her words were slurring now. "Which was strange, because we always used the back door."

"Always?" I turned to Holiday, who agreed.

"Always," Price said. "I tried to get the key from the tree, but somebody had taken it. So I walked back around to the front and that door was open."

"Why did you go back to his office, anyway?" I asked. "I mean, your counseling time was over. You didn't normally go back to his office on Saturday afternoons, did you?"

She held out her phone. "I'd left my phone."

"Did you use the back door earlier that morning for your appointment?" I asked.

She nodded eagerly, like a kid trying to convince her mom she used soap in the bath. "But I guess somebody didn't put the key back."

I reached out my hand and placed it on Price's. "Where were you before you headed back for your phone?"

She snorted. "Like I said, nun ya…"

She picked up the Jack Daniel's bottle again, now empty, and laid it on its side. She gave it a good spin and when the bottle stopped, it pointed toward Dirk.

"You win, Dirk!" She leaned over the bar and gave him a kiss. Turning to me, she said, "Sorry, Nacho. I would've told you where I was and given you a kiss if the bottle had pointed to you."

"Like hell you would!" Dirk opened a second bottle of Jack Daniel's and drank from it.

"I was kidding. I only kiss you, baby," said Price.

"I need an alibi from you, one I can follow up on," I said, ignoring the accelerating theatrics. "I don't understand how you got cleared by the police if you told them what you're telling me."

Price took two steps toward me, put a hand on either side of my face, and pressed her lips onto mine. They were full and moist, and she had the distinct taste of Jack Daniel's on her tongue.

She pulled away, beaming. "That's how I got cleared."

"Did you just fucking kiss my girlfriend?"

I turned in time to see Dirk jumping over the bar. He placed both hands on my shoulders and gave me a hard shove. I stumbled back but caught myself.

"She kissed me," I said, "and don't touch me again."

I scanned the room. Price, who now seemed to be cognizant of the unfolding consequences of her impulsivity, faded toward the brown leather sofa. Holiday, still holding the pillow shield, stood, as though readying herself for an escape. And Dirk was rushing toward me again.

I swiped the empty Jack Daniel's bottle from the bar and brought it crashing down across the right side of Dirk's forehead as he closed in on me. His eyes rolled back, and his limp body smashed to the floor in a heap. Blood poured from a deep gash above his right eye.

Price screamed.

Dirk lay motionless.

And Holiday stood staring, still clutching the pillow.

"Get out!" Price screamed again. "Get out!"

I looked at Holiday.

"Get out!" Price ran to the foyer bathroom and came back with a wad of wet paper towels, dropping to her knees to aid her fallen, inebriated boyfriend. "Oh, baby! Can you hear me? Talk to me, baby!"

I reached down and put two fingers on the side of Dirk's throat. He was out cold, but he had a pulse. In the morning his head would hurt like the devil, not from the butterfly stitches he'd need, but from the massive headache he'd have from his self-administered alcohol poisoning.

I set the Jack Daniel's bottle on the top of the bar. "Thanks for the shirt."

Price remained bent over her fallen protector, her hands cradling his face as I left.

Relieved to be outside, I kicked the Triumph to life and pulled out of the circle drive. I pointed the bike toward Castlerock Estates. I could've used a serious shower. I could've used a fresh change of clothes. I also could've used some rest. But I had a party to get to, and I hoped I wouldn't look like the trash heap I felt. All I had to do at this party was make an appearance, get in and get out, without my appearance making a scene.

Cars lined both sides of almost every street in Castlerock Estates. Lucky for me, I found the Triumph a small opening along the curb by the Whiffletree's circle drive. A gangly teen about my age with thick red hair and an unfortunate case of severe acne was organizing keys behind a valet kiosk.

The spacious grand living room was now crowded with Ten Spot's pillars of the community. The mayor was chasing a tray with rosé champagne. The police chief and Ten Spot's fire marshal stood off to the side chatting. Mr. and Mrs. Whiffletree, him in a trim black tuxedo and her in a floor-length black gown with a low neckline and a string of pearls draped around her exposed neck, held court in the center of the room in front of the white Benetti, chatting, smiling, stopping to pose for selfies with fellow revelers. Dream was there too—in full tuxedo no less—talking about his new role on the school board and handing out BOGO cards to prospective customers. We were across the room from each other when our eyes met. He smiled, then turned away.

I felt a hand on my shoulder. It was Finch, and quite surprisingly he'd exchanged the cowboy look for his own black tux.

"Glad you could make it, my boy."

"I didn't realize you'd be here." I looked over his shoulder wondering if boy wonder was in tow.

"What matters is I knew you'd be here." He took a deep breath and let out a pleased sigh. "It's nice to have both my operatives working alongside me tonight."

I followed his gaze to the second-floor landing that jutted out over the room below. There was Darwood in a black suit, clenching the bannister, glaring.

Finch took a step closer and, looking over my shoulder, dropped his voice to a whisper. "In a setting like this, somebody who is protecting something could let it slip. The urge to drink, the urge to one-up the important jackass to their left...People talk, and I needed to be in this room tonight along with my two operatives to scoop up whatever information someone divulges that might help us crack the Hardcastle case. These are the movers and shakers, the ones who always know more than you think." He took a step back and winked. "Keep your ears on."

I started to mention the bullet Darwood had fired at me only hours earlier, but Finch waved to someone across the room. "Excuse me. I believe I'm being summoned." With a hearty slap on my back, he began to weave his way through the crowd.

Brockett and Ms. Baxter sidled up alongside me. He looked dapper in his black formal wear. She looked lovely in her long black dress.

"You ever been here, Nacho?" Brockett asked.

"This morning. Mrs. Whiffletree asked me to take a job."

It was then I picked up on the low music playing in the background. Mr. Whiffletree had his cigars. Mrs. Whiffletree had her jazz.

"What kind of work?" Brockett asked.

I hedged my answer a bit. "She's had trouble with teen trespassers and asked if I would check into it."

Ms. Baxter slipped off her coat and handed it to her father. "What did you say?"

I leaned toward them, raising my brow. "She made a very

convincing case." They chuckled, and I added, "Plus, she has connections and the extra bread is nice. Either of you been here?"

Ms. Baxter shook her head.

"First time," said Brockett.

The counselor smiled at the opulence of the setting. "I want to explore."

Our first stop was the early American drawing room with the antique pie chest. It looked as it did earlier that morning except the photograph with Mr. Dream on the fireplace mantel was missing.

We returned to the main room, almost running into Finch.

"Albert Finch." He pushed out a hand to Brockett.

"Tom Brockett."

They shook.

"What do you think about this place, Mr. Finch?" Brockett asked.

"Fantastic!" He looked around and spied metal folding chairs in a far corner. "Let's grab those before we lose our opportunity."

Brockett checked his and his daughter's jackets in the coat room, and the four of us staked our claim to the empty chairs. Rachel, the housekeeper, zeroed in on our quartet. "Can I get any of you a drink?" She had on a modest yet fashionable black-and-white tuxedo dress. She still had the silver hair pulled back, but the orange glasses had been replaced by black.

Brockett asked if she had Perrier. She did. Ms. Baxter asked for some lemon water.

"I'll take a Dr. Pepper with a shot of chocolate syrup if you've got it," I said.

Ms. Baxter gave me a skeptical stare with one eyebrow arched. "Is that good?"

"He calls it an 1885," said Brockett.

I felt my face flush and adjusted my weight in the chair. "My dad used to make it for me when I was a kid."

"What do you do, Mr. Finch?" Brockett asked.

"I'm a private investigator. I'm looking into the death of Dr. Hardcastle. The insurance company won't release any money to his widow until they figure out whether it was a suicide or homicide. I have my suspicions, but Nacho is helping me with the case and I'm tickled pink to have him on my team."

"It's a gracious offer you've given him," said Brockett, slipping me a wink.

Finch had no trouble obliging the flattery. "He reminds me so much of myself at his age. I'm hopeful with his expertise of this town we can wrap up this case and get back to Austin. I'd love to have him join me once he graduates. There are a lot of opportunities in Austin, and he'd be a good fit for the work there."

"Let me get a photo of everyone."

We looked up to see Steele with a large Nikon slung around his neck.

I introduced him to the group.

"What are you doing here?" I asked.

"Copping photos for the school paper," he said. "Everyone squish together, and I'll be sure you make it to press."

Steele took about ten shots in rapid succession. "That should do it."

I pointed a finger gun at him. "Make sure I get one."

"For sure." He turned to hunt for more prey.

Upon her return, Rachel served everyone their drinks. Brockett took his Perrier. Ms. Baxter got a glass of water with lemons. Finch received a dark brown glass. And I got my 1885.

We paused the conversation to try out our drinks.

Finch smacked his lips. "Nothing better than the old bartender's drink. Bourbon and cola. How's that Dr. Pepper with chocolate, Nacho?"

I nodded while I took another swig.

Finch. Never at a loss for words, even when they weren't warranted.

I rose. "Will you excuse me?"

Everyone nodded, and I tracked my way through the crowd.

On the far end of the grand living room were two dark mahogany doors. Through the stained-glass windows that adorned the top of each door I could see the room was darkened, closed to the night's guests. But curiosity had gotten the better of me when I'd spied them earlier and I began to serpentine my way across the room toward them. I had gone only a few yards when a familiar voice halted my impulsive exploration.

"You made it!"

I spun to see Mrs. Whiffletree gliding toward me with her husband and the housekeeper trailing behind.

I spread my arms, embracing the grandeur of their majestic setting. "Mrs. Whiffletree, you put on a great party."

She curtsied, holding out the sides of the black dress as she bent, the pearls drooping low over her now exposed cleavage. "*Mille mercis.* And please, call me Story."

I cupped a hand to my ear. "Ben Webster?"

She placed both hands over her chest. "I'm impressed!"

I held my hands out toward her, palms up. "You've heard what they say. When the student is ready the teacher will appear."

"I believe that." She cocked her head toward the ceiling, inspecting the sound of the music. "I'm not sure the sound fits this crowd, but oh, well. I was in the mood."

I thanked the housekeeper as she handed me a fresh 1885.

Principal Whiffletree pointed to the Superman shirt I was wearing. "You clean up nicely."

His wife elbowed him and gave him the look. "Phil, leave him alone. You can't expect your students to have tuxedos hanging in their closets."

He gave me a light punch on the arm. "Just jokes. Right, Nacho?" He leaned toward me, whispering in my ear. "You skipped half your classes today. I'm gonna let that slide as long as you solve my wife's problem by this time tomorrow." He leaned up and patted me squarely on the shoulder. "We need more young men like you, Nacho Blanco." He studied my face. "You keep getting the wrong end of that ugly stick!"

Mrs. Whiffletree chided her husband. "Phil, seriously, you're too much!" She turned to me. "I can't take him anywhere, not even to his own party!"

I waved them off in a show of modesty. "A man can say whatever he wants in his own castle. He can even take a piss on his own carpet. But what really sets a man apart from the average Joe is when he's willing to take a piss on another man's carpet. I may just throw a little shindig at my house, and when I do, Principal Whiffletree, you're the first one I'm inviting."

The three stared at me, Mrs. Whiffletree's mouth frozen in a slight smile.

I leaned in a little closer. "I have a question."

Mrs. Whiffletree's eyes were wide now, expecting.

"The picture." I leaned my head toward the drawing room. "The one of Mr. Dream I saw earlier. I'd love to get a copy, but it's gone."

I watched as the Whiffletrees and their housekeeper juggled quizzical looks.

The principal shook his head. "I'm afraid I don't have the foggiest idea what you're talking about."

"It's that photo of us with Dream," Mrs. Whiffletree explained to her husband. She turned to me. "Maybe a guest has it and is showing it around. If I find it, I'll holler for you."

I snapped my fingers as though I'd remembered something. "Never mind, I'll ask Mr. Dream. He has a similar one in his office. I'll get a copy from him."

Mr. Whiffletree looked at his wife. "I didn't realize he had a copy."

I pretended to look over their shoulders. "Will you excuse me? I think I'm being summoned."

They nodded and I weaved my way to the room with the double mahogany doors. I placed a hand on one of the knobs and turned it. With one quick glance over my shoulder, I slithered into the darkened room, patting the door closed behind me. I flipped the switch on the wall illuminating the room at once, hoping the light wouldn't attract the attention of the other guests.

Like its doors, the room was dark mahogany, floor to ceiling. There were shelves on every wall, and I would've guessed this to be the library except the shelves were devoid of books. Two oversized leather chairs sat in the middle of the room, a finely crafted, ornate wooden table between them. On the table, two empty glasses and a half full crystal decanter, along with what seemed to me to be a high-end chestnut leather humidor. Across from the chairs sat a brown leather Chesterfield sofa with rolled arms and dotted with deep tufted buttons, the kind of sofa they used in those old black-and-white film noir flicks. It was obvious to me this room was ground zero for the scent of grass and leaves and rain-soaked soil that permeated the house. I took it for granted this was where the good principal donned his night cap and his nightly stogie. I had the sensation of being in one of those nondescript smoky bars in south Austin where men with money go to escape and women who want to escape go for money.

I was about to leave when something stopped me cold.

It was chimes. They were coming from a large grandfather clock to the left of a double set of French doors that led to a patio, and they were playing "It's a Small World." It was the same tune I'd heard with two 9mm Barettas pointing at me in an old warehouse outside town. Was Whiffletree's personal cigar lounge the same room from where that phone call had been made?

I bolted through the twin mahogany doors and streaked my way through the crowd to where Brockett and Ms. Baxter were sitting.

"We have to go." I looked around. Everyone seemed preoccupied in their own conversations. "Where's Finch?"

"He went to the restroom," Ms. Baxter said.

"We have to leave."

"How do you mean?" Brockett asked.

"I'll explain outside."

I shoved my arm through Ms. Baxter's and pressed her along with me toward the front door.

"You two go," Brockett said, "I'll get mine and Darcy's jackets from the coat room."

I laced Ms. Baxter and myself through the crowd. At the front door, I stopped us to wait on Brockett. Above the noisy din of the happy partygoers came a high-pitched scream that brought the entire room to a sudden stop. A woman was pointing at Brockett. He was stumbling toward the center of the room and the crowd seemed to be parting for him as he passed, like the Red Sea parting for Moses.

"Somebody stabbed him!" a man nearby yelled.

Brockett collapsed to the ground, and everyone surged toward him.

"Dad!" Ms. Baxter pulled away from me and I followed her to where Brockett lay crumpled.

A long carving knife with a wooden handle, the kind my grandfather would use on Thanksgiving to carve the honey-baked-ham after the family prayer, was sticking out of Brockett's back.

"Stand back!" I yelled to the crowd.

A short balding man in a grey tuxedo clamored his way through the group and knelt beside Brockett. "I'm a doctor. Somebody call 911!" He looked down at Brockett but spoke to us. "The knife has to stay in. I understand it hurts like hell, but if I take it out, he'll bleed out before we get him to the hospital."

I leaned over Brockett's ear. His head lay sideways toward me. His eyes were open but glazed.

Ms. Baxter was weeping and stroking the top of her father's head.

"Who did this?" I whispered to him.

His voice was strained, weak. "Get out, Nacho." Blood was

bubbling up around the blade now, pooling on the white shag beneath us.

I put my hand on his arm. "Who was with you? Did you see them?"

"I made a mistake." He was struggling for every breath. "Get out of Ten Spot. It's too late."

The whine of a siren grew louder, and moments later four paramedics hurried through the front door with a stretcher and several medical backpacks.

"Let them through!" somebody yelled.

The doctor identified himself and the paramedics took over, inserting an IV into Brockett's arm. They slipped an oxygen mask over his face and lifted him onto the stretcher face down. A paramedic searched his pockets and handed me a ball point pen and the set of keys with the silver palm tree.

"Get these to his family," he said.

"I'm his family!" Ms. Baxter asserted. She swiped at the tears running down her face.

"We're taking him to Ten Spot Memorial," one of the paramedics said. He leaned into a mic strapped to the top of his shirt. "I've got an impalement. Knife wound to the back. We are loading and heading your way."

"Affirmative. Standing by for your arrival," came the reply.

Ms. Baxter stumbled to her feet. "I'm going too!"

With the stretcher in its rolling position, the paramedics wheeled Brockett from the house and loaded him into the ambulance. Ms. Baxter and I followed behind. She climbed into the back of the ambulance and they closed the doors behind her. The siren wailed as they sped off.

I stood in the middle of the circle drive and watched as the guests poured out of the front doors like yellow kittens running from a Cane Corso. Three police cars pulled up and half a dozen of Ten Spot's finest passed me into the house. Somebody had stabbed a guest at the home of Milo Winkler Academy's new principal during a party. There would be an investigation tonight. This would be a long night for the Whiffletrees. I wondered if the cops would find who'd tried to kill Brockett. Or if they'd be pissed that almost everyone had fled an active crime scene. Or if they'd care there was pot growing in the greenhouse.

I realized I was still holding the ballpoint pen and Brockett's palm tree key chain. I slipped the pen into my pocket and held the mirrored palm tree to my face. Whiffletree had been right. I looked like hell. I had dark circles under my eyes. My hair still looked like a rat's nest. And my face looked like it had taken a second pounding from the wrong end of that ugly stick.

"You okay, bro?"

I looked up. It was Steele. His face was grim, strained, and the camera hung limp around his neck.

"This is my fault," I said.

He gave me a puzzled look. "What do you mean?"

"Somebody's trying to teach me a lesson." I slipped the key chain into my pocket and turned toward the bike.

"Use it against them," said Steele.

I stopped. "What'd you say?"

"You say they're trying to teach you a lesson? Use the lesson against them. Hidden leverage, man. They'll never see it coming."

Use what they're giving me against them? Like what? And how?

"I gotta go, Steele."

"Be careful, Iggy."

I straddled the Triumph, kicked it to life, and got the hell out of Castlerock Estates.

From the Whiffletrees, I rushed to the hospital to check on Brockett and hopefully to see my grandmother again, despite the hour. Too many people I cared about had ended up in ICU. My grandmother was asleep, but the nurse on duty said she was continuing to improve. So far, the medical tests had shown no permanent damage to her brain. As far as Brockett, the doctors had removed the knife and he was doing well also. I left Ms. Baxter surrounded by half a dozen teachers from the Academy and set off on the bike. By two-thirty Thursday morning, I was at Dream's. I pulled the bike around to the back alley and killed the motor. Pitch black. Not a soul in sight.

Mr. Dream always kept a key hidden in a small, rusty tin with a magnet on the back that snapped to the top of the metal frame of the back door. As far as I was aware, I was the only one he'd ever shown it to. "In case of an emergency," he'd once told me. If tonight didn't fit the bill, I didn't know what would.

I slipped on a pair of latex gloves I'd confiscated from the hospital, felt my way to the back, and located the key. I unlocked the door, tucked the tin with the key inside my pants pocket, and made my way into the back hall. It took my eyes a moment to adjust to the semi-darkness, the only light coming from the dim glow of a few security lights in the kitchen. The alarm keypad at the back door began chirping, counting down its one-minute delay. I punched in the word *SCOUT*, the password Dream had given me, and waited for the system to go into standby mode.

It didn't. The red light continued to flash, the keypad continued to chirp, and the one-minute I had to disarm the system continued to drain.

I tried the code again. Still nothing.

I typed in the word *DREAM*. No dice.

I typed in the words ICE and ICECREAM, even HARDCAS-TLE. Nada.

Three things were certain. One, I had to get into Dream's office, and I knew I wouldn't get a second crack at it after what I had planned for tonight. In fact, the success of the case was riding on it. Second, I had to forget the alarm. This whole operation was about to get loud and sloppy. And third, once the alarm tripped, I had less than two minutes before the police showed up with weapons drawn. A lot of people were about to visit Mr. Dream's in the middle of the night, many of the same ones who'd just wrapped up a crime scene in Castlerock Estates. They wouldn't be too excited about fielding another late-night run, especially if they caught my mug in both places.

I took the five steps to Dream's office and tried the door handle. Locked. And another keypad, without the accompanying key slot. My locksmith set wasn't going to help me here. I typed in the word *SCOUT* and tried the door. The lock didn't budge. Then the alarm went off, sending a piercing siren through every cell in my body. I looked down the hall to make sure it was still clear. I took a step back and kicked open the door.

Inside the small office, I flicked on the light and snapped several shots of the picture of Mr. Dream, the Whiffletrees, and the Hard-castles with my phone. I wasn't buying the crap about a microchip implanted inside the photo, especially since it was a couple of fake feds who'd threatened to confiscate my fingers. All I needed was a copy of the picture which I suspected would be gone by sunrise. Mission accomplished, I cut the lights and headed down the hall.

The alarm was deafening. I covered my ears and skimmed out the back door, closing it behind me. The faint sound of police sirens ground away in the distance. In a matter of seconds, the place would be swarming. I kicked the bike to life and roared off through the back alley before turning right onto Travis. In the side mirrors, I could see the red glowing strobe of police lights from the other side of Dream's. I took another right onto Wheatley before stopping at a light at Knight Avenue.

That's when I realized my right pocket was still bulging. In all of the excitement I'd forgotten to put the key back. It wouldn't take much for Dream to figure who'd been inside his business. I made a U-turn and headed back.

I glided to a police cruiser with its lights still on and killed the motor. An officer held up a hand and told me to turn around.

Dream was standing in the doorway to the shop. He still had on the black tux, but he'd taken off the cummerbund and the bow tie. "Let him in," he said.

The officer gave me the go-ahead and I dismounted the bike.

"What's going on?" I asked.

"Break-in," he said. "We're still trying to figure out if they took anything. It looks like they got in through the back door."

"You mind if I look?" I asked.

"Come on." Dream excused himself and we made our way to the back.

"Anybody see anything?" I gave him a wary eye.

"I got here just before you did. I was still at the Hardcastles'. Oh, God, can you believe what happened over there? It's awful." He stopped and stared at me, like a man who'd just awakened from a dream. "Why are you here?"

The most believable lies aren't total fabrications. They're annotations. They don't tell a new story. They tell the real story, leaving out the parts that would implicate.

"I was at the hospital checking on Brockett and my grandmother. Heard the sirens and hightailed it over here."

Dream was quiet, his eyes fixed on some invisible position in the distance.

I pushed on. "They're both in stable condition, by the way."

He had a blank look on his face and blinked at me for several seconds, like a man who'd suddenly disappeared from one place only to reappear in another. "What?"

"Brockett and my grandmother," I said. "They're going to make it."

He nodded, catching up to speed. "That's good."

"How do you figure they got in?" I asked. "The burglars."

Fully back with me, he shrugged. "It makes sense that they would use the back door, but there's no sign of forced entry."

Dream turned on his phone's flashlight so we could navigate through the inky blackness. I pulled the box with the key out of my pants. Cupping it with my right hand, I reached for the top of the door frame, the darkness that enveloped us hiding my deception.

"You had a key up here." My hand reached the top of the door frame and I eased the tin box back into place, careful not to let the magnetic force snap the box onto the metal frame.

"I already checked," he said. "It's not there."

"Did it fall off?" I pulled the tin off the frame and dropped to one knee, my hand feeling around in the grass as though searching.

"I looked," he said.

I dropped the box into the grass next to the building as Dream passed the light over the grass in front of me.

"Shine that back over here!" I said. "Over to my right."

He did and the light lit up the dingy tin lying unobstructed on top of the weeds.

I reached for it and handed it to him. "Here it is."

Dream took the tin, opened it, and dropped the key into his

palm. "That was nice of them to put the key back inside the box."

I bit my bottom lip. "A thief won't take the time to put the key back in the box. He would just toss the key and the box into the grass."

I studied his face. He was doing the same to me.

"But you already figured that," I said. "I'm guessing at some point the key box fell off of the door frame on its own. Could be the wind, or the jarring of the door. Could've fallen some time ago."

"If they didn't use the key, how'd they get in?"

I turned away from Mr. Dream, making every effort to avoid eye contact with him. It's not so easy to just straight up lie to someone you care about. And I had a feeling he was still stinging from my questions regarding the thirty thousand.

We stood and walked in silence back around to the front of the building.

"I guess," said Mr. Dream.

I rubbed the back of my neck. "You guess what?"

But Mr. Dream didn't say anything else. He just kept flipping the key box over and over in his hand.

I decided not to say anything either. I'd said too much already.

As we made our way to the front door an officer strode over to us. "I've got good news and bad for you, Dream."

"The bad?" he asked.

"The bad is that the intruder didn't leave a shred of evidence behind. Other than busting your office door, it doesn't look like they took or touched anything."

That was good, I thought.

"And the good?" asked Dream.

"The good is that there's a camera mounted on the lamppost behind your store. The business owners behind you placed it there a few months ago and it takes a three-hundred-and-sixty-degree video of everything going on around it. Once we get hold of that video in the next few days, and if there's enough light back there, we'll see who busted into your store."

That was bad.

I drew in a deep breath and settled myself on the bike, kicking it started.

"You should leave," he said, throwing his voice above the sound of the bike's motor.

"What?" I twisted the throttle and revved up the motor.

"You should leave!" he shouted. "You should leave Ten Spot!"

"Why?" I yelled back.

But Mr. Dream didn't answer. And he didn't smile. And with a slight shiver, I noticed he was holding a gun in his right hand down by his leg.

I pointed the bike toward Travis Avenue and headed back to Brockett's cabin. I wondered if Dream had bought my story of why I'd been in the area at the same time his store had been broken into. I wondered if I would've bought it if the situation was the other way around.

Not a chance.

THURSDAY

CHAPTER 17
BLACK WIDOW

I'd already decided when my head finally hit the pillow at four in the morning I would not be going to school on Thursday, Principal Whiffletree be hanged. I doubted he had time to keep track of my butt when his own was on the line now. But two hours later Zadie called.

"I need to see you."

I looked at my watch. "Most men love it when a woman calls and tells him she needs him, especially at six in the morning. So don't take this wrong when I say I've only had…"

"It's about my case." She hesitated. "There's been a new development."

I cursed under my breath. "Okay, fine. I can be at school in an hour. Where?"

"In the covered breezeway behind the gym," she said. "And let's make it seven-thirty. I need time to do my hair."

After a quick shower, I slipped into a clean pair of Levi's and a blue Mizzen+Main button-down. The lump above my eye was starting to diminish but the bruising was ugly. And the cut Trip had given my cheek had started to heal and had a fresh pink look to it. I grabbed a Clif Bar and a Dr. Pepper on the way out of the door, and by seven-thirty I was face-to-face with my client.

Despite the lack of sleep, I actually felt alive. Part of it was the caffeine I'd slugged. Part of it was the outfit Zadie was wearing.

She had on a short black skirt, knee-high black leather boots, and a tight black turtleneck sweater molded around her. In her hair was a jet-black headband, which, with the sweater and boots, made her look like one of those Bond girls from the sixties, the kind that would either kill to love you or love to kill you, and make you enjoy it either way.

"I'm waiting for an explanation." She took a seat on a metal bench, tugging at the skirt as she did.

"Pick a topic."

She held up her phone to show me the display. There was a message from an unknown number.

"Somebody texted me last night to say you're working for a detective who's trying to find evidence that would blame me for Hardcastle's murder."

Darwood. It had to be him. I wondered what Finch would think about this.

"It's not like that," I fumbled out.

Several students walked by us. Zadie stood and began following them.

"Stop!"

Everyone stopped. Zadie spun around to face me, both hands on her hips. I waved the other students on.

"I'm working for a private eye named Finch. I met him after I met you. The family of Dr. Hardcastle hired him to find out what happened. The insurance company won't release the money until they get a definitive answer on how he died, whether it was suicide or homicide. Finch hired me to help him with the case. The problem is you're his only suspect, and now he wants the evidence."

"So it's true." She lifted her eyes to the roof of the breezeway, shaking her head. "God, I can't believe I trusted you." She leveled her gaze on me again. "What's in it for you?"

"I find who killed Lincoln Hardcastle and he makes me a full-time member of his P.I. firm in Austin."

"You manufacture evidence to pin the murder on me and you get to leave this dumpy little shit hole like you've always wanted." She gave me a fake smile. "That works out for you, Mr. PSI. Never mind the problems you create for someone else, as long as Nacho Blanco gets what he fucking wants! God, I was so stupid."

I stood up, closing the gap between us. "I'm looking for evidence to show someone else was the murderer."

She opened her mouth to say something, but I put up a hand to stop her. Over her shoulder, I could see two guys heading toward us. I'd assumed the encounter in the alley behind the diner the day before had put things straight. That's what I get for assuming.

"What's this?" I asked. "Round two?"

"We didn't come here to fight, Sherlock," said Trip.

"I invited them," said Zadie. She tilted her head and smirked.

I threw up my hands. "What? Why?"

"I called them this morning after getting that text. It was getting kinda hard to trust the players."

"We're doing this for Zadie and for Aiden," said BroFly.

I pointed at both of them. "You could've thrown a rock in the middle of the cafeteria and hit anybody better than these two chuckleheads."

Trip and BroFly flanked her sides.

"This is my team, Nacho. If you want to help me, you get on my team. It's your choice. Plus, they've already discovered something."

I narrowed my eyes at her. "I'm listening."

She wagged a long slender finger at me. "Members only. New terms, mister. Join us and we work together."

I didn't relish working with a couple of nanny guards, but I also figured it wouldn't be near as bad as working with my partner, Mr. Psycho. Still, this whole thing made me nervous.

"I'm in," I said. "But let's get one thing straight. I'm the lead. You three take orders from me, not the other way around. And if you find something, report it. Got it?"

The guys looked to Zadie, who gave them a quick nod.

"Another thing," I said. "This isn't pretend, like a game of cops and robbers. People are getting poisoned, stabbed, and kidnapped at gunpoint. Yesterday I took a stun gun in the side by some fake FBI agents."

Zadie's mouth flew open. "You saw those guys again? They're not real?"

I pulled up my shirt to show them the two "bite marks" the stun gun had made.

"Damn, dude, it looks like Dracula got you!" said Trip.

"They'll be happy to do the same to you. We need to be careful. This whole mess is deeper than some lousy shrink getting knocked off. I think Hardcastle discovered something, something that somebody in Ten Spot wanted covered up. And that something cost him his life."

They all nodded.

Zadie leaned in so only I could hear. "Don't you double cross me, Nacho Blanco. Don't you dare fabricate any evidence against me to get your ass out of town. Remember, I'm from Texas. I don't get mad. I get even."

I gave her a sarcastic salute, then turned back to the guys. "Here's where we stand. About two months ago, somebody knocked off Hardcastle. As far as motive goes, there are a few possibilities. We know he was putting pressure on Mr. Dream to repay a loan that Dream would never be able to repay. We also know he was a pedophile who preyed on teenage girls. And there could be a whole different reason someone might've wanted him dead. I think there probably was one. Whatever the motive, somebody tried to make it look like a suicide. Unfortunately for the killer, neither the police, the insurance company, nor the private eye the family hired has bought into that. I don't buy it either. I think that's why somebody planted a blade in

Zadie's desk, and a whole box of them in Aiden's backpack. If we hadn't started poking around, Tobias, Price, and Holiday might've had blades planted on them too. At any rate, somebody's not too happy with me because they sent those fake agents to pick me up."

"We should've guessed those cops were fake," said Zadie.

"And they promised to cut off my fingers if I didn't tell them where a certain photograph was."

"What photograph?" BroFly asked.

"It's a picture of Dream with the Whiffletrees and the Hardcastles."

"Why would somebody want that?" Zadie asked.

"Supposedly it's hiding government intel," I said. "More likely that was just a ruse to get me to tell them where it was."

"You know where it is?" Trip asked.

"I did last night. Probably not anymore."

"How does the photograph play into the murder of Hardcastle?" Zadie asked.

"Maybe that's why they killed him," BroFly suggested.

"You might have something there," I said. "It's possible Hardcastle found the photo, stashed it, and somebody killed him when he didn't turn it over. The murderer began covering his tracks by making it look like one of his patients killed him."

"What do we need to do?" asked Trip.

"First," I said, "How about you guys tell me what you discovered."

"Tell him, Tre'von," said Zadie. "You were the one who figured it out."

BroFly gestured with his hands as he spoke. "I was googling and popped in the words *Hardcastle* and *Ten Spot* and *married* and I came across the Hardcastles' wedding announcement. I discovered her maiden name was Burton. Gloria Burton."

"Which makes sense because she often signed forms as Gloria B. Hardcastle," Zadie added.

BroFly went on. "Then I searched for the key words *Ten Spot* and *Burton* and you'll never guess what I found!" He paused for effect. "Before she and Hardcastle hooked up, Gloria Burton was a student at Overton University right here in Ten Spot. A theater major. In her junior year, the police found her roommate dead in an abandoned field. Murdered."

I stopped him. "Are you sure about this? Hardcastle's wife was the college roommate of a murder victim? Then she marries a man who is also a murder victim?"

"Talk about a black widow," said Trip.

"Was the roommate's name Stephanie Sullivan?" I asked.

"Damn!" BroFly exclaimed. "The brother's like psychic or something! How you know that?"

"Lucky guess," I said. "Go on."

"That was five years ago," he said. "Shortly afterwards Hardcastle meets and marries Gloria Burton."

"Okay, here's what I want you to do," I said to the two guys. "I want you to keep tabs on a detective named Finch. There's something about him that's tripping me up. I don't know. Maybe it's nothing. He's in room 54 at the Apple Blossom. If he leaves, follow him and see where he goes. Trip, you got your dad's truck?"

He pulled the F150's keys from his pocket and dangled them for us to see. "It's in the parking lot."

"Check him out after school." I pulled on my bottom lip, thinking. "If you can, keep tabs on our new principal too. There's something off about him. I can't put my finger on it."

The first bell rang and the two guys headed to their first period, leaving me and Zadie alone under the breezeway.

"What are we gonna do?" Zadie asked.

"You mean, what am I gonna do," I corrected. "You're going to your first class. I'm about to pay a little early morning visit to the Whiffletrees. I've got a little snooping around to do."

"I'm coming with you," she said.

I let out a listless laugh. "No way. The best thing you can do is stay here and wait for me to get back. I'll update you at lunch."

"Nacho, I'm going with you," she said again. "You can't stop me. If you try, I'll go there by myself. Do you want that, or do you want to keep an eye on me?"

I pressed my lips together and squinted my eyes. "Has anybody ever told you you're a sassy little blackmailer?"

She smiled, proud of herself.

"Fine."

"Yay!" she cheered, clapping her hands.

I sighed. "Can we go?"

"Almost," she said.

She took a step toward me, and standing on tiptoes, pressed her body into mine. Our lips melted together. My hands reached for her waist and I pulled her in. Her body fell into mine. I could feel the heat beneath the black turtleneck. Her hands slid up the side of my neck and folded into the back of my hair. And I could smell the sweetness of rose petals and almond milk rising from her slender neck. Our lips released, and she dropped from her toes. I let my hands slip from her petite waist and she took a step back.

"Now I'm ready," she said.

CHAPTER 18

HAUTE BOHÈME

"Wow! Now that's impressive!"

Zadie took in the full measure of the pink-and-gray brick French country manor that stood before us.

I knocked down the Triumph's kickstand and we both dismounted in the circle drive of 123 Castlerock.

She pointed to the fender with the bullet hole. "What the fuck? Did somebody shoot at you?"

I laughed. "He was only trying to scare me." I leaned my head over to her. "Stick close to me. Something dark is going on in this place. I can feel it."

I rang the bell expecting the little old housekeeper. This time it was Mrs. Whiffletree.

"Nacho, do come in." She closed the door behind us and pointed to the blue room off to the side. "Rachel is not here at the moment and she left something in the wash I have to get out. You and your friend make yourself at home. I'll be right back."

Zadie took in a deep whiff as we settled onto one of the red facing loveseats. "God, it smells heavenly in here."

I chuckled. "Smells like they're baking this morning." Staccato-like footsteps outside the room arrested our attention. "Let me do the talking."

Mrs. Whiffletree entered wearing a pearl-white dress that cleaved to her figure. Her hair, tied in a modest pony, lacked the luster I'd seen only twenty-four hours earlier. No doubt it had been a difficult night for her. She looked tired and worn, like a university student who'd just pulled an all-nighter cramming for an exam she had no business passing.

She carried a silver tray with a small loaf of bread wrapped in cellophane and set it on the glass table as she settled herself across from us. She crossed her legs and I watched an expensive-looking pair of white pumps dangle from the toe of one foot.

"Good morning, Nacho," Mrs. Whiffletree looked at her phone. "Aren't you supposed to be in school?"

"Let's just say your husband has made your predicament my priority." I cocked my head to the side and raised a brow. "White after Labor Day, Mrs. Whiffletree? What *will* the neighbors say?"

She rolled her eyes. "If you haven't guessed, I don't give a fuck what the neighbors say or think, nor this whole goddamn town for that matter." She pointed to the tray with the loaf. "This is for you. Rachel made a dozen loaves this morning for the front office staff at the Academy. That's where she is, delivering them to the school. She's an amazing cook." Mrs. Whiffletree's voice was flat, fatigued, and lacked the playfulness of my previous visit.

I pointed toward the fireplace mantel. "The photograph. I guess it never showed."

She gave a curious tilt of the head, then looked at Zadie. "I'm sorry," she said, extending a hand. "I'm Mrs. Whiffletree. Call me Story."

"I'm Zadie." Zadie stood, smoothing out the short black skirt. "Do you mind if I use the little girl's room? I may have had a little too much orange juice this morning."

Mrs. Whiffletree yawned, quickly covering her mouth with a hand. "Excuse me." She pointed nonchalantly toward the door. "The closest one is down that hall to the right."

Zadie exited and we turned our attention toward each other.

"I take it the police were here late last night?" I asked.

"Too long," she said. "I'm so tired I didn't even go to my barre workout this morning."

"And your little farm out back? Still intact?"

She cocked her head to the side and gave me a quizzical look. "You mean the weed?"

I nodded.

She shrugged it off. "It's fine. I'm sure they're aware. They have bigger fish to fry than my little patch of Mary Jane."

"Like attempted murder in your kitchen?"

She perked up straighter now, more alert. "You haven't heard?"

I turned my head slightly to listen better, eyes wide.

"The police determined Mr. Brockett merely lost his balance and fell into a knife sticking out of a kitchen drawer."

"Wait! What? He fell into a knife? Like an accident?"

She placed a hand over her heart. "It was a terrible bit of misfortune for Mr. Brockett. I hope he'll be okay, though."

I wasn't buying it. If Ten Spot PD was calling what happened to Brockett an accident that could only mean one of two things. Either there were dirty cops in the department, or they *had* managed to stumble into Mrs. Whiffletree's patch of hash and were obviously still enjoying it.

Mrs. Whiffletree pulled her ringing phone from a side pocket on her dress. She put an ear to it before excusing herself, leaving the room. I picked up the fresh loaf of bread and put my nose to its cellophane wrapping. It was fresh, still warm to the touch, and had a sweet, yeasty smell. Except for freshly roasted coffee and polished leather, nothing smells as good as baked bread in the morning. I pushed the loaf into my coat pocket.

Brockett fell on a knife, then used his last words to urge me to get out of town? I couldn't see it.

When Mrs. Whiffletree didn't return, I stepped into the main living area. Someone had removed the white rug Brockett had bled on. I walked through the room and back to the bookless library. I opened the doors and walked in. The air was better now, breathable.

I drifted around the room, my eyes lazing across the empty shelves. The grandfather clock stood at attention, watching over the room like a Queen's Guard at Buckingham Palace. In twenty minutes the chimes would ring the half-hour, just like they'd done minutes before Brockett had walked out of the kitchen with a carving knife in his back. Just like they'd done when a 9mm barrel shoved itself into my face at some old, abandoned warehouse. I needed to hear them again, to hear them ring that silly "It's a Small World" song. Just to make sure. I stood in front of the French doors and stared out through their panes, marveling at the impeccable eighteen-hole course only yards away.

"Lose your way?"

I turned to see Mrs. Whiffletree standing behind me. Somewhere between the drawing room and the library she'd abandoned the heels. She had pretty feet, small and slender. Her nails were a light lavender. And a small gold toe ring spiraled its way around the second toe on her left foot. Somehow shoes, even the pricey type, didn't seem appropriate for Story Whiffletree.

"This room smells better than it did last night. Cleaner. Fresher." I watched her face as I spoke.

"You were in here last night?" Whether she was surprised or offended, I couldn't tell. Perhaps both. "Oh, never mind, it doesn't matter." She strode to the French doors and flung them open, flooding the room with sunlight.

In the now opened doorway, she turned to face me. The light behind her filtered through the sheer white dress, revealing a slim, attractive silhouette beneath. I could see the curves of her shoulders, her waist, her legs. The French have a phrase for someone like her. *Haute Bohème*. High bohemian. The moniker fit Story Whiffletree perfectly. Heiress to a family fortune. Eccentric. Free-spirited. She seemed to revel in exposing more of herself than most were prepared to handle.

I motioned to the shelves. "I'm guessing the principal isn't much of a reader."

"We moved here a week before school started," she said. "We had to find a house when Phil got the job at the Academy. The books are in boxes inside the attached greenhouse."

"Read and weed," I said.

She let out a soft, tired laugh. "Will you excuse me for just a moment. I need to check the laundry again."

I walked to the opened doors and looked toward the golf course, as I waited for Mrs. Whiffletree to return. After a few minutes, I became aware of a growing argument in a different part of the house. I went back into the main living room and found Zadie standing at the end of a hall beneath the stairs in a face-off with Mrs. Whiffletree.

"Young lady, what were you doing in my bedroom?" Mrs. Whiffletree shook a long, slender accusatory finger in Zadie's face.

Zadie opened her mouth, but Mrs. Whiffletree turned to me. "I came in here to put some fresh towels in the bathroom, and this young lady was trying on one of my wigs. No doubt she rummaged through my other things as well."

"That's a lie!" Zadie snapped back.

"What *were* you doing in there?" Mrs. Whiffletree asked.

"I was looking for a restroom, came in here, and saw the wig," said Zadie. "That's the only thing I tried on, honest. And I didn't go through your things."

Mrs. Whiffletree clasped her hands in front of her and waited, and Zadie continued.

"It's the color of my hair, and almost as long. I wondered if I would look the same with the wig. That's all, I swear."

I turned to Mrs. Whiffletree. "I'm curious. Why do you have a wig?" The question may not have been fair, perhaps even a bit gauche, but Mrs. Whiffletree hadn't seemed like social graces were all that important when it was just us.

Her eyes narrowed and her lips pursed, and she reached up

with her right hand and removed her long chestnut brown hair. The top of her head was hairless, as smooth as a newborn baby's bottom. Her lips tightened into a thin line, and she flung the brown hairpiece at Zadie.

"Here, little girl, try them both on."

Zadie caught the wig and stared at it with wide eyes. Her gaze trailed slowly up to mine and she dropped the hairpiece to the floor.

"You wear wigs," I said to Mrs. Whiffletree.

She nodded. "I have cancer. I bought two because I wasn't sure which I would wear. I chose brown. The blonde sits on my dresser." She turned to Zadie. "Do you have any idea what it's like to have cancer?"

Zadie was trembling now.

"It's terrible. For me, the worst part isn't the chemo and how sick I feel. For me, the worst was losing my hair. That may sound vain, but it was."

She looked at me.

"This is why I smoke weed. There's been some research—mostly anecdotal, I'll admit—that marijuana has the potential to cure some forms of cancer. If nothing else, it at least eases the nausea I get from the treatments."

She stepped toward Zadie, scooped up the chestnut brown wig that still lay on the floor, and placed it back on her head. Standing in front of a mirror that hung in the hall, she adjusted the piece and combed the strands with her fingers. "I told you, Nacho, I'm an herbalist. Now you know why."

"I'm sorry, Mrs. Whiffletree. It must be…"

She didn't let me finish. "I'd like you and your friend to go. I'm not feeling well."

We followed Mrs. Whiffletree to the front door and stepped outside.

"Nacho," she said, "I'm no longer going to need your services. I can see now this was a mistake. I'll send you a check for what I owe."

She shut the door behind us, and Zadie and I ambled back to the bike.

"I'm sorry, Nacho," said Zadie, tugging at her skirt on the back of the Triumph. "I messed up."

I shook my head and smiled. "You did better than you think."

CHAPTER 19

OPERATION 420

Zadie and I arrived back at school halfway through second period. I parked the bike beneath a pecan tree on the west side of the campus so as not to be seen from the administrative offices.

"What's our next move?" Her face was flushed, her eyes aglow. And that smile was like no other I'd ever seen.

"Actually, we have a small problem," I said. "I've lost access to the Whiffletrees' house. To keep this investigation alive, I need Story Whiffletree to want me back inside her home again."

"Why?"

"I can't say for sure, but something keeps drawing me back to that mansion. The missing photo, a copy of which somebody was ready to kill me over. The fact that Brockett was stabbed in the back there. And the phone call those fake agents got from someone inside their library. Like I said, the clues keep pointing to 123 Castlerock."

"Why don't you give her a reason to rehire you?"

"What do you mean?"

"Simple." She leaned up and deposited a light kiss on my cheek. "Steal something of hers."

I let that thought roll around in my head and then smiled. "You're as brilliant as you are charming."

She let out an affectionate laugh. "You're stealing my lines, Nacho Blanco."

"Yeah, but I actually mean it."

I knew Zadie was talking about getting back in good with Mrs. Whiffletree, and the idea was superb. But Zadie had done something else too. She'd just unlocked a piece of the mystery that'd been bugging me.

"Her pot farm," I said.

Zadie jerked her head toward me. "Wait! What? The principal's wife actually grows the pot she takes?"

"That's why she'll need me." I stood up. "Something's gonna happen to her little herbal garden tonight. And when it does, I'll be right there waiting for her call."

Zadie looked at her phone. "I don't want to go to school today. I want to stay with you and do all this fun mystery stuff."

I sighed. "If I don't get to my next class, Whiffletree's gonna have my ass in a sling in ISS. The real question is do I slip into second period when it's almost over or just wait for third to begin? What are you gonna do?"

She shrugged. "I'm just gonna go straight in. It's Mr. Packard's physics. All I have to say is I had to go to the nurse for some female problems and that will shut him the hell up fast."

"Too bad I can't use that on Calishaw." I shook my head. "Women. You guys know exactly how to work it."

She laughed. "A little sexy, a little sweet, and a little charm, and we can get away with murder." She threw her hands up to her mouth. "Oh my God! Did I just fucking say that?"

I laughed. "Come on. Let's get you inside before you implicate yourself any further."

We slipped through a side door at the school, and she gave me another quick kiss on the lips before running down the hall to Mr. Packard's. I headed upstairs to American History and was still trying to figure out my own excuse when I decided to hit the head first. I ducked into the boys' room to take a leak and for a beat thought about staying there until time for third. I was washing my hands when the door opened. It was Tobias Williams. And he was alone.

He stopped when he saw me, his eyes getting big, and he let the door swing shut behind him. "I been looking for you."

I turned off the water and reached for a paper towel. "Hey, look, man, I told you on the bus I didn't want any trouble. I still don't. You just do your thing in here and I'm gonna leave and we'll all have a great day."

With his left hand, Tobias reached inside his pocket and pulled out a 9mm handgun, black, with a squared off barrel. I hadn't seen Tobias since our fight on the bus. He'd been plenty mad then, even threatened me, and the only thing I could think of was that for Tobias the day of reckoning had arrived.

I didn't wait to find out. I rushed him, knocking him to the ground and the weapon from his hand. It skidded across the restroom floor inside a stall. We both scrambled to get to it first, but Tobias was faster. He snatched the gun from the floor and scrambled up to a standing position. I eased myself up as well, taking a few steps back toward the windows by the sinks. I wondered how far a drop it was to the ground, even if I did manage to get a window up.

"What the hell's wrong with you?" he yelled.

"No more, Tobias." I looked over my shoulder at the window and saw it had screws at the top to keep it from opening.

He took a few steps toward me, placing the 9mm on the edge of the sink's white porcelain.

I looked at the gun just lying there and calculated my odds of grabbing it before he did. I didn't like my chances, and with the window behind me bolted shut, I figured talking my way out was my only way of walking out. "I don't want any trouble from you, Tobias. I'm just trying to figure out who killed Dr. Hardcastle."

"That's why I was coming to see you." He leaned back against one of the stalls.

I gave him a suspicious stare. "You wanted to talk to me about Hardcastle?"

He slid down to the floor, his legs stretched out in front of him. "I wanted to tell you I didn't do it."

I breathed a sigh, then took the pistol from the sink and sat down next to him. The last thing either of us needed was for someone to walk in, see that gun lying on the sink, and throw the entire school into lockdown.

"Tobias," I began, "you can't bring a gun to school. You know that right?"

He scrunched up his face and squinted at me. "It's not loaded, fool. I left the clip at home. Just like Dr. Hardcastle taught me."

I turned the weapon over. Sure enough, the clip was missing from the handle. "Hardcastle taught you how to remove the clip?"

"He's the one who gave it to me. He said I was his favorite patient. He said I wasn't crazy like everyone said. He spent time with me. One of the things we did was shoot guns."

"I'm listening."

"He'd take me outside the city limits to some land for target practice. We would shoot at tin cans and bottles and shit like that. I kept getting better, and he said he wanted to give me a gun." He paused to clear a tear from his eye. "Dr. Hardcastle was my friend."

I turned the sidearm over to get a better look. "This is nice, Tobias."

"I know. He told me it was a Glock. He said the police and the military use it. I told him gangbangers use it too. He said he had a lot of guns. I asked how much it cost, and he said he used to be CIA and got it free."

I handed the Glock back over. "Wait a minute. Hardcastle told you he was CIA?"

Tobias nodded. "That's what he said. At first, I didn't believe him, but he showed me this ID card and it had his name and his photo, and it said CIA on it. It was him."

Hardcastle. A CIA operative? In Ten Spot? Was he undercover or retired?

"Let me ask you something," I said. "Did Zadie or Holiday or Price ever mention something called touch therapy?"

Tobias bent his legs and pulled them up close to his chest. "Man, they never talked to me. My appointment was at the end of his Saturday sessions. I'd get there at one and Aiden would be leaving. I never saw nobody, except Aiden." He rubbed his forehead with a hand. "Everybody's scared of me."

Something wasn't adding up.

"Let's suppose for a minute Hardcastle was CIA. Why would he tell you?" I asked.

He rotated the 9mm in his hands. "I don't know. I guess he trusted me."

I let that roll around in my head for a beat. "Or maybe he wanted you to trust him."

Tobias looked at me from the corner of his eyes. "I already trusted him."

I nodded and tried to get my brain to pull out something that would make sense. "Did Hardcastle ever ask you to do something for him? Favors? Some special assignment?"

Tobias shrugged. "I mean, kinda. Wanted me to ask around at school, see if I could find any girls who might want to learn Krav Maga, some kind of self-defense martial arts shit he learned as an agent. He said it was good for girls to learn how to take care of themselves against strangers. He said if I could find at least six girls that would be enough for a class, and he would teach me too. I was like, hell, yeah, man, I wanna learn some Krav Maga! But these all had to be good-looking girls, too, you know what I mean? He didn't want no ugly ducklings, he said. He said the girls who need to learn how to defend themselves are the beautiful ones. He said if they look like Zadie and Price and Holiday, then those are the ones I could recruit for him."

I was starting to see a pattern with Hardcastle. He recruits five student patients in Ten Spot, three of which, all female, he sexually abuses with some bullshit Touch Therapy. One of the males he recruits to recruit more females who look like the ones he's already abusing. And he bullied the other student, making him wear dresses during his sessions. It was always about power for Hardcastle. He would use, manipulate, leverage, abuse, and humiliate to get what he wanted, which ultimately meant more power.

Tobias let out a long sigh. "I don't know who killed Dr. Hardcastle, but I'm gonna help you find out."

"I'm not sure about that."

"Hey, man, if it's about that shit on the bus, I'm sorry about that." He patted his chest. "My bad."

I shrugged. "It's not that. It's just that I usually work alone."

He pointed a long finger at me. "This time I'm working with you. Tell me what to do."

I let out a deep sigh. "Can I ask you something?"

He waited.

"Why were you seeing Hardcastle?"

Tobias looked down at the weapon in his hands.

"If we're gonna be partners," I said, "I have to be aware of who I'm working with. You feel me?"

He didn't look up and he was quiet for a long time. That was all right with me. Sometimes a person like Tobias needs some space. I stared out the windows and watched the late morning October sun poking its way through. For a moment, it felt good to be still and calm, in spite of the fact that I was sitting on a school restroom floor with someone who was holding a 9mm Glock in his hands.

"I got anger issues," he said at last. "I tried to hurt my mom once. She made me mad, and she did it on purpose. Anyway, the judge said I could either start seeing a counselor or go to juvie. I didn't wanna go to no fucking juvie, so my mom found Dr. Hardcastle."

He looked up, and I smiled.

"This mean I'm in?" he asked.

"Do I have a choice?" I asked.

He raised his eyebrows and wrinkled his forehead. "Hell, no!"

"Fine, but let's get one thing straight, Mr. Williams. You follow my lead. Got it?"

He lifted his left hand like a boy scout swearing allegiance to the Constitution. "No problem, no problem." He flashed a brilliant smile. "Nacho and TDub, partners in crime!"

"Partners in crime-fighting," I corrected.

He shrugged. "Shit. Whatever."

This was gonna be interesting, I thought.

"Okay, TDub, you wanna help solve this mystery? I need you at the principal's house tonight at ten o'clock. Should be plenty dark. Sneak around the back until you find some kind of greenhouse. Destroy everything inside. But you only have thirty seconds. After that, you'll risk getting caught. Get in and get out in thirty. Got it?"

He gave me a suspicious eye. "Why we doing this?"

"Because I need back inside that house and you're gonna help me do it with a little something I'm calling Operation 420."

He flashed a big white toothy smile. "Cool."

"And one more thing," I said as we both stood to leave. "Take this damn gun home right now and don't ever bring it here again."

"You got it, boss." He slipped the Glock back inside his coat and scuttled out.

I stood too. The bell was about to ring for the switch to third period. I needed to get to class. Then I needed a reason to get to the front offices. I had some questions, and I needed some intel, and Ms. Madrid was the only one who had everything I was looking for.

CHAPTER 20

DOPPELGÄNGER

We were well into third period when I asked Mrs. Beck if I could be excused from chemistry to see the nurse.

"Are you sick or just sick of chemistry?" she asked with a look.

"I love chemistry, you know that." I touched my head. "It's my brain. Won't stop hurting."

She let out a hurried sigh, signed a pass, and handed it to me without looking. "I want that signed by the nurse."

A minute later, I was thumping on the door of the principal's secretary.

"Nacho!" She motioned to one of her chairs. "Is this personal or professional?"

I sat down across from her desk. "Ms. Madrid, I must say you look absolutely stunning today."

And she did. She wore a pale pink button-down that fell over a pair of dark blue designer jeans. A silver chain dangled offhandedly from her small wrist. And she'd dropped her hair, allowing it to remain unrestrained, which was uncharacteristic for her.

She blushed and studied me through a small pair of wire rimmed glasses. "I can't imagine what you're up to now, but I like it!" She paused and lowered her voice. "What are you up to?"

"Ms. Madrid, can't a guy pay a gal an old-fashioned compliment without her suspecting anything?"

"Yes, a guy can, but not when that flattery comes from a shady gumshoe like you."

I pulled up my chair, resting elbows on her desk, my chin on my hands. "I need some information. Was a boy named Aiden absent from school on Monday?"

She smiled and shook her head. "I can't give you confidential student information."

I held up both hands, feigning helplessness. "Believe me, I hate even asking. The fact is, I've got a girl who's in trouble. You'd love her. Sweet. Kind. Beautiful. Reminds me a lot of you."

She raised a drawn-on brow. "Another gorgeous damsel in distress?"

I gave a quick look back to the open door and lowered my voice as though making her privy to some hot intel. "Between you and me, this thing has sexual harassment written all over it."

"You will be the death of me, Ignacio Blanco." She opened the attendance tracking program on her computer. "What's his name?"

"Aiden," I said.

She ran a search.

"Two hits," she said. "Ninth grade and eleventh."

"Try the junior."

She did, and I pointed to the screen when his photo populated the field.

She looked at his attendance record. "Looks like he was here on Monday."

"He was?" I asked. "You're sure about that?"

"I'm looking right at it." She pointed to the monitor. "He was here first period and he was here..." She studied the notations.

"The teacher said she marked him present second period, but he left at 9:05, after she took attendance." She read more of the record. "And he was absent the rest of the day. The rest of his teachers marked him as not present."

"Let me get this straight," I said. "He was here for one hour on Monday morning and then he left."

"That's the gist of it." She closed the attendance program, revealing the school's security app still open beneath.

Aiden's story was only partially true, which meant he had a lot more explaining to do, as far as I was concerned.

"One more thing." I leaned over to her monitor. "You mind if I take a peek at your security program for a moment?"

She minimized the window.

"No, you don't!" she said. "You will get me fired, Ignacio Blanco! What if somebody were to come in and see you leaning over my desk. No telling what they would think!" She stood up and pointed to the open door. "That's all for today, you sneaky shamus."

I headed for the door. "You're a doll, Ms. Madrid, and that's why you're my favorite."

She looked over her wire rimmed glasses. "I have a feeling I'm not the only gal who gets that line."

I slipped her a shifty wink and left. But instead of winding back through the office maze, I turned right and into the school's main hallway. The open security camera program on her monitor had given me an idea.

About fifty feet down the main hall was a pull switch for the fire alarm. Taking a quick glance around, I lifted the plastic cover, and gave the hammer a good yank. A high piercing screech cut through the building. I ducked into a nearby teacher's bathroom, locking the door behind me. Within seconds I could hear adults running, yelling, asking if there was a fire, if anyone could smell smoke. Then I heard the hallway fill up as students began evacuating. When the sounds of voices and footsteps had vanished, and with the alarm still screeching bloody murder, I peeked into the deserted hall and made my move, slipping back into Ms. Madrid's office, closing the door behind me. I figured I'd have about two minutes to find what I wanted and get out before the fire department showed up.

As I'd hoped, the security program was still running on her monitor, and from the live shots of the outside campus I could see the teachers and students huddled in the parking lot. A few clicks in the app led me to the archived cafeteria video feed from this past Tuesday. I fast forwarded to 12:52, like the time stamp on Finch's phone. I had to be sure the video Finch had showed me was the real deal. Now, on Ms. Madrid's monitor, I saw a figure walk within complete view of the camera. And just as I had seen on Finch's phone, only this time much clearer, the individual had on a blue skirt, pink leggings, and a pair of red high-top Converse.

And then it hit me.

I'd been wanting to ask Zadie about the video ever since Finch had shown it to me but had hesitated until I'd seen it from the actual source itself. Truthfully, I'd been curious what her reaction would be, what excuse she'd give for being in the cafeteria alone with my grandmother when everyone else was outside. I smiled. Now I wouldn't have to ask her. Zadie Abernathy had a doppelgänger ambling around Ten Spot. This was the proof I needed that Zadie wasn't in the cafeteria during the time my grandmother had been poisoned. I backed up the video and let it play again, this time recording it on my phone.

Sirens from approaching fire engines signaled my time was up. I reset the app back to the home page and was about to leave when I remembered the hall camera. The video had captured me pulling the alarm. I found today's footage from the hallway and deleted it. I was resetting the program when I heard voices on the other side of the door, and one was Ms. Madrid's.

I jumped on Ms. Madrid's desk and popped up one of the hanging ceiling tiles above an adjacent filing cabinet. Sliding the tile to the side, I slipped up to the top of the cabinet and was able to ease myself onto one of the braces that hung down. I slid over and prayed the entire structure wouldn't give under my weight. The door to the office opened and Ms. Madrid entered just as I slid the tile back in place above her.

Then I waited. Waited for Ms. Madrid to notice someone had been tampering with her computer. Waited for her to hear my smothered breathing. And waited for the suspended ceiling to double under the strain of my weight and send me crashing into Ms. Madrid's lap.

My phone buzzed and I wrangled it from my pocket. It was a text from Holiday.

need cu, she wrote.

when, I wrote back.

lunch

Perfect timing.

K

I needed to find a way out.

It was dark where I sat, aside from the little light that leaked up through the tiles around me. I thought about inching along the hanging braces and dropping into a different room, but the chance of Ms. Madrid hearing me, or worse, the whole suspended ceiling collapsing, was too great.

I tapped the phone's light and let the beam search around the darkness. There were fiber optic lines crisscrossing the tiles around me. But there was something else, just a few feet away. It wasn't a great idea, and it would probably send Ms. Madrid into deep therapy. But it was my ticket out, and it was all I had.

It was a dead rat, about a foot long from tip to tail. He'd died only a few feet from where I now sat. I reached for his tail, but it pulled off with one tug. I got a putrid whiff of rotting death, and I held my breath as I clamped my right hand around the rat's fat decomposing torso, positioning him in front of me. With my left hand, I scratched the upside of the tile.

"Is somebody up there?" I heard Ms. Madrid from below.

I scratched the tile again, brasher this time, and longer.

"Hello?" she asked.

Like the world's smartest rat might do, I skidded the ceiling tile open enough to make a four-inch gap and nudged him toward the opening.

"What the…" she began.

The rat tumbled through the opening, striking Ms. Madrid on the right shoulder before landing on her desk and bursting open, his rotting insides spilling over her keyboard.

She let out a murderous scream and fled from the office.

My little friend had come through for me, but I had to move fast now.

I slid the tile to the side, dropped to the desk, and headed for the office door. The hall was empty, but I could hear Ms. Madrid shrieking at Whiffletree around the corner. I headed back into the main hall of the school and again ducked into the bathroom. I wasn't going another step without washing my hands. Half a bottle of soap later, I made for the hall and headed back to chemistry.

I handed Mrs. Beck my hall pass. "Forgot to get the nurse to sign it with the fire drill and all."

Without so much as a glance at me, she crumpled the slip of paper, tossing it in the trashcan. "Just get on with the next part of your assignment, Ignacio."

In fifteen minutes, that's exactly what I'd be doing, meeting with Miss Holiday Le. I just hoped that she had some telling information for me, something that might blow the lid off this case. I also hoped they were serving something good for lunch. A guy can only eat so many chimichanga specials in a row.

CHAPTER 21

MURDER ONE

Bubba's Boba was a tiny fleck of a place, five hundred square feet if that, and nestled smack dab in between the Ace Hardware store and Granny Franny's Antiques on Sumner. I didn't know much about it, except that Holiday's family owned it, and their *piece de resistance* was bubble tea. I'd also heard Holiday worked there part-time after school, most weekends, and any other time school was out. The girl had grit. She also had guts daring to meet me in a crowded cafeteria in the middle of a school day. Something told me Holiday wasn't as timid as she let others think. She was one of those, as the counselor had said, who had a lot more going on under the counter than what's on display, and that impressed me and worried me at the same time.

"How's the bubble tea business?" I asked once we'd both gone through the cafeteria line and found a secluded table in one corner of the room.

"You like bubble tea?" Her voice was soft and high, and she enunciated every syllable carefully. She was relaxed and smiling, not like when I'd last seen her at Price's the night before. She looked cute too, in her jean shorts, light pink tank, and white straw fedora. And this time, she wasn't holding a pillow shield.

"Never had it," I said, squirting one of those little packets of mayo onto my burger.

"You should try it. Come see me. I'll make it special for you," she said. "We have classic Milk Tea. Taro. Thai. Strawberry. Those are the best sellers."

"Okay, I will, but only if you let me pay. Nothing on the house."

"On the house?" She gave me a perplexed look.

I filled my mouth with burger but continued talking. "Yeah, you know, free. You let me pay and I'll come."

"It's no problem. You tell me what you want."

It's quite a feat to move to a new country, leaving everything you've ever known halfway around the world. Holiday was intelligent and diligent, like her family. They were survivors, and I figured it wouldn't hurt to throw some business their way.

She got quiet and I could tell she'd gotten uncomfortable with all the sudden chit-chat over bubble tea.

I wiped my mouth with my napkin. "I'm curious. Is Holiday your real name?"

She covered her mouth with her hand to suppress a timid laugh. "It's my American name. My real name is Thu, which means *fall* or *autumn*. I liked the word Holiday, and autumn is kind of like a holiday, so that's me!"

"Makes sense," I said.

"What about you?" she asked. "Do people call you Nacho because you eat nachos a lot?"

I took a drink from a bottle of Cool Blue Gatorade. "It's a common nickname for Ignacio. You know what? I'm not a big fan of nachos. They're messy. And I can't speak Spanish. Well, not much. My dad could. So could Mom. Maybe I'll learn one day."

She giggled. "I get that. Since coming here three years ago, I'm feeling more American than Vietnamese. It drives my parents crazy."

"The name of your parents' place. Bubba's Bobas. I've met

some Bubbas in my life, but none of them would care the first thing about bubble tea."

She rolled her eyes and groaned. "That was my father's idea. I told him it was stupid, but he said he wanted a name that Americans could relate to."

"At least your parents are here to take care of you." I waited while she finished a bite of her burger, then narrowed the focus of our meeting. "What's on your mind today?"

She glanced around and drew a small red book from her backpack, setting it on the table between us, keeping both hands glued to the cover.

"What's that?" I asked.

"It's a journal, the one Price told you about. The one Dr. Hardcastle took from me."

I sat up straighter in the booth. "This is your journal, the one you wrote about how you wanted to kill him?"

She gave me a vacant stare. "This is Zadie's journal."

I cocked my head, questioning. "I don't understand."

"Dr. Hardcastle didn't take my journal. I don't even have a journal. And if I did, I wouldn't write in English. He took Zadie's." She patted the red book beneath her hands. "Price thought it was mine, and she also saw what was written in it. We were laughing about it just before Dr. Hardcastle stole it. He was crazy mad when he read it."

"How did you get it?"

"The month before he died, Zadie brought the journal with her to the counseling office. She wanted me to hold it while she was in session. I started reading it and so did Price when she got there. Dr. Hardcastle came out of the appointment with Zadie, saw us laughing, and grabbed the journal from me. His face turned so red when he saw what was in it. He called us bitches and whores. Said he was keeping it as evidence against me if I ever tried to do something."

"If you ever tried to harm him?" I asked.

"Yes."

"And you never told him it was Zadie's journal?"

She rested her elbows on the table and placed both hands on either side of her face "I didn't want her to get in trouble. She had to ride home with him and live with him and she already didn't like him. I let him think it was mine. It seemed better that way."

She took a long drink from her bottle of water. "There's more."

"Go on."

She leaned over the table. "She wrote in the journal she wanted to poison Dr. Hardcastle, and while he was out of it, she would cut his wrists."

"Just like they found him," I whispered

"Just like they found him," she whispered back. "She wrote it a month before it happened."

"Why didn't you tell the police?" I asked.

Holiday turned her head toward the window and stared out at the parking lot. "Do you believe in God?"

"I guess so," I said. "I don't think about it."

"My mom is not here legally. Dr. Hardcastle learned this. I was afraid if I told anyone that he was touching me, he would have my mom deported, and I would never see her again. I prayed all the time that something would happen to him. A heart attack. A car accident. Anything. And when he died, I thanked God for answering my prayers. But then I found out how he died, and I thought about Zadie's journal."

All the while she spoke, her hands never left the little red book.

"If Hardcastle took the journal from you, how'd you get it back?" I asked.

"Our last session, the same day he died, while he was with Price, I found it hidden in the storage room in the back and took it."

"Is that everything?" I asked.

"There's one more thing," she said. "It's about the key to the back door of the counseling office. Doctor Hardcastle always kept a key on a tree behind the office for us to get in."

"From what I've heard that key is missing."

"Zadie has it. At least she did."

"You've seen her with it?" I asked.

"A few days ago, we went to her house after school, and she had a hard time finding her house key. She never keeps it on a ring, just loose in her purse. She couldn't find it, so she dumped everything on the ground. And in the middle of all that stuff, there's a silver key with a light pink spot. She tried it and it didn't work so she threw it back in her purse with everything else, and we climbed in through her bedroom window. She leaves the window unlocked all the time. I tell her one day somebody will sneak in and steal something, but she doesn't listen to me."

She rolled her eyes.

"How can you be sure it's the one to the counseling office?" I asked.

"The light pink spot," she said. "I put it there. One day, while I waited for my appointment, I painted my nails. I still had the key and put light pink polish on the key too. I'm sure it's the one."

"How many people knew about that key?" I asked.

"Me, Price, Zadie, Tobias, and Aiden. We were his only patients."

"And you told no one? Not the police? Not your parents? Nobody?"

She shook her head. "I wanted to protect Zadie."

"If you're trying to protect her, why are you telling me about the journal and the key now?"

She let out a long sigh. "I trust you. You're trying to help Zadie. Did she kill Dr. Hardcastle? I don't think so. But even if she did, she's much braver than me, and she saved us."

"What about the others?" I asked. "Aiden, Price, Tobias? What can you tell me about them and Hardcastle?"

"Aiden hated him. The doctor always called Aiden terrible names. Can't say about Tobias. Tobias hates everyone so I guess he hated Hardcastle too. Price did. All the girls hated him."

"Do you think it's odd Price was the one to find Hardcastle dead?" I asked.

"I don't think she realized he would be dead when she came back for her phone."

"Interesting that she left her phone," I said. "She doesn't seem the type to leave her phone anywhere. She's always on it."

Holiday hesitated. "But she didn't leave her phone accidentally that day at the counseling office."

"You mean she left it on purpose? She planned to go back?"

"Her parents put this tracking app on her phone. She left the phone at the counseling office on purpose so they wouldn't know where she was. Later that day, she planned to use the key on the tree to go back and get it. She'd tell her parents she was walking around town and couldn't remember where she'd left it.

Leaving her phone might also be a convenient way of explaining why she goes back to the counseling office after hours, I thought, and why she's the first one to find Hardcastle's body. I took another drink of Gatorade. "I need to talk to Price. Who does she have for fifth?"

"Mr. Packard." She went on. "Please don't tell Price I told you about her phone. And I don't want to get Zadie in trouble for what she wrote in her journal. I mean, so what if she wrote those things. It doesn't prove she killed him. Right?"

Could prove premeditation, but I wasn't going to tell her that.

"Why were you seeing Dr. Hardcastle?" I asked.

She shrugged. "My parents said he could help me learn to be more social in a new country."

"I think you're doing just fine, Thu Holiday Le."

She blushed, then pushed the red journal toward me, lifting her hands from the cover. "Take it, Nacho. Zadie trusts you. She told me."

We stood and she gave me a gentle hug.

"I have to go meet some friends," she said, looking at her phone. "Thank you for talking with me."

"Thank you," I said.

Watching Holiday leave, I sat down again, Zadie's journal in front of me. I folded a piece of Juicy Fruit in my mouth and chewed on what Holiday had said. If it was true, this little red journal would be all the evidence Ten Spot PD would need to file a premeditated murder charge against Zadie. Capital murder. Murder in the first degree. Murder one.

I didn't enjoy thinking about it, and I hoped it wasn't true, but if it was, this journal might also prove to be my golden ticket out of Ten Spot.

I opened the cover and began to read.

CHAPTER 22
PRICE'S EPIPHANY

Zadie's journal began six weeks before Hardcastle's murder. July fourth was the first entry.

Happy Independence Day. MY FAVORITE HOLIDAY!

Counseling session today with Dr. Hard On. He insisted we have our sessions even though it's the 4th of July. He told us a few weeks ago he would start "touch therapy." Today was the day. He made us lie down on this blanket and lift our shirts so he could give us a massage. He even unsnapped my bra. He says he is helping us get in touch with our true selves, our inner child. I think he wants to get in touch with his inner dick.

The following day Zadie wrote the second entry.

Sunday. Lots of homework.

Still thinking about the Hard On and what he did yesterday. Can he do that?

There were more entries, about school, her life, the guys she was interested in. But then there was one dated five days after the second entry.

H. texted me today. OMG! First time. Asked about my day. Told me he can't stop remembering how beautiful I was on Saturday. WTF!

On July 11 she wrote again, after their trip to Ten Spot earlier in the day.

H. is getting worse. During his stupid touch therapy session, he let his hand slip over to the side of my boobs. He asked me if I was ready to turn over. As if! I told him I wasn't ready, and he said we would work up to it. He slipped his hand down inside the back of my panties and told me to imagine my worst fear and exhale it out. Fucking creeper. He's my worst fear! I wish I could exhale him out of my life.

July 13th:

Me and the other girls talked about the best way to kill H. I know how I would do it. Somebody told me antifreeze

I looked up from the journal. My face felt hot. I took a deep breath and looked back down at the page, one fist clenched by my side.

antifreeze is sweet and makes you very groggy, totally out of it. I would put as much as I could in a drink (he would never know it), get him to drink it, and when he was totally wasted, I would cut his wrists and make it look like a suicide. That way he could see everything I'm doing but couldn't do a fucking thing about it, like he does to us!

She'd written a final entry on July 17th, something about meeting a boy named Chris at her school in Austin and liking him. My guess was Hardcastle had taken the journal the very next day.

Maybe I wouldn't need to ask Zadie about the cafeteria video captured the day my grandmother was poisoned, but I would need to question her about this journal. I had Mrs. Cer's English coming up next. Somehow, I needed to convince her that Zadie and I needed to collaborate in the library again.

Adjusting my chair to be as inconspicuous as possible, I pulled out my phone and made a quick call to Chuck.

"How's Brockett?" I asked when he answered.

"Doing better," he said. "The knife just missed his heart and lungs."

"Keep me posted. One more thing. You wouldn't have the toxicology reports on Hardcastle and the Overton student back already?"

"Not yet. I'm expecting them any minute. But there is one thing you might find interesting. Hardcastle was CIA."

TDub had been right. "Undercover?"

"His cover was a teen counselor, but he was working to gain intel on who might've wanted Agent Sullivan dead."

"What was she doing here?" I asked.

"That part I haven't figured out," he said. "Looks like the agency sent in another undercover in the form of Hardcastle. Someone blew his cover too."

"What about Mrs. Hardcastle?" I asked. "You think she was aware of his covert work?"

"Spouses are told very little," he said. "Hard to say without talking to her. I'm certain she's not CIA."

"Anything else?" I asked.

"Hardcastle had an electrical engineering background and was tech savvy. He had some high-tech surveillance weaponry he'd designed and implemented, outside CIA circles. Off the radar. Find that technology and we might find the killer of Agent Sullivan."

"Thanks, Chuck."

I started adding up the clues in my head. For one, Hardcastle was in Ten Spot trying to figure out who killed Agent Sullivan. Most likely, somebody blew his cover, which cost him his life. Second, my client had written the exact means of carrying out his murder a month before his death. The question was, did Hardcastle die because he was CIA or because he was a pedophile? And third, Zadie didn't have her journal with her for a whole month before somebody killed Hardcastle. Was it possible somebody used the journal as a prescription for murder?

The bell rang for me to head to Mrs. Cer's. I grabbed the journal and stood up to leave when I got a call. It was a blocked number.

"Good afternoon, Mr. Blanco." The voice was male and deep.

"I'll let you know if it's a good afternoon when you tell me who you are and what you can do for me," I said.

"My name is unimportant," he said. "What's important is

that there is a brown paper sack behind the large air conditioning units that sit behind the Overton College Library. In that sack is ten thousand in unmarked bills. It's yours. All you have to do is pick it up and head out of Ten Spot by the stroke of midnight tonight. And don't come back."

"That's very generous of you," I said. "And if I refuse?"

There was no response. Mr. Unimportant had ended the call.

Zadie was a no show in English. Odd, since she hadn't mentioned missing some of her classes.

I sent her a text. *U ok? Need to talk.*

The mysterious phone call from Mr. Unimportant had thrown me off and I couldn't concentrate through my last three classes. Ten thousand dollars. That's a lot of beans. Somebody wanted me out bad. I decided to touch base with Finch. I also decided not to mention the ten grand. After sixth period, I jumped on the bike and headed to the Apple Blossom.

It surprised me to see Finch's room open at Ten Spot's infamous motel when I stopped by to report in. Inside I found the place littered with empty beer bottles and abandoned fast food bags.

"Damn electricity is out," he said, wiping his brow with a paper towel. He'd stripped down to a pair of khaki shorts and a sweat soaked ribbed tank top. "What you got, kid?"

"You heard anything about a photograph with a microchip containing government intelligence?" I asked.

"No. What's that got to do with our case?"

"Not sure, but there are some rough people looking for it. It's a photo of Hardcastle with some friends."

"What are you talking about?"

"Two goons posing as feds took me joy riding yesterday. Said they were looking for a picture. Turns out they're working for somebody who wanted to swap my fingers for it."

Finch's eyes searched my hands. "Looks like you made out all right. Did you give it to them?"

"Nope." I helped myself to one of the Dr. Peppers Finch had stocked in the small fridge.

"Who were they?" he asked.

"I don't know." I opened the soda. "But I do know Hardcastle wasn't your run-of-the-mill shrink. He was CIA and working deep here in Ten Spot. Could be that's why somebody killed him."

Finch's eyes had that faraway look in them. The wheels were turning. I could almost smell the smoke.

Standing there I suddenly remembered Price. I pulled out my phone and texted her.

Need to talk.

I wasn't sure she'd answer after my little altercation with her boyfriend. Surprisingly, she did.

Me 2. Texas Theater at 4:30

I looked at my watch. Thirty minutes.

I'll be there.

She sent me back a smiley face blowing a kiss.

I looked up at Finch.

"Doesn't matter," he said at last. "I don't give a goddamn who Hardcastle was, if he was CIA or somebody's fucking babysitter. Somebody killed him and I want to find out who it was so the insurance can indemnify the policy and we all get paid."

I downed the rest of the soda and got up to go.

"That all you got?" he asked.

I jammed my hands into my coat pockets and came across the small loaf of bread Mrs. Whiffletree had given me earlier. After the scuffle with TDub and then breaking into the attic of the school, the loaf didn't quite look as it had only a few hours earlier. It was smashed on one end and starting to crumble apart on the other. I raised it up for him to see. "I got some bread. You want it?"

He gave the loaf a suspicious eye. "Where'd you get it from?"

I tossed it to him. "Mrs. Whiffletree gave it to me. Baked fresh this morning."

He unwrapped it, took a whiff, then took a bite. "Not bad."

———

At four-twenty-seven, I parked the bike in front of the courthouse on the town square and walked the block south to the Texas Theater. Inside the air was cool, cooler than was needed for mid-October, and I felt a chill trickle across my shoulders. The buttery smell of fresh popcorn was enticing, and I bought a small. I got comfortable on a red velvet couch opposite the concession stand and waited for Price to show.

I was starting to get a little worried about Zadie. I still hadn't heard from her. I tried her number again and was sent straight to voice mail. I thought about that for a beat, then shook those ideas out of my head and texted her to call me immediately.

At four-thirty, Price and Holiday danced into the theater's lobby, both in black yoga pants and Nike tees, both singing some song they were into. I watched as Price scanned the room then made a beeline toward me.

"Just the man I wanted to see!"

I stood. "I wasn't sure you'd be so excited after last night."

We sat down on the velvet couch, and she turned to Holiday. "Honey, would you be a dear and get us some popcorn and drinks? I'll join you in the theater in a bit."

Holiday, ever the understanding friend, agreed, and Price turned back toward me, taking both of my hands in hers. "I've had an epiphany."

"Pray tell," I said.

She set up straight, ready to tell her story. "It was right after you left. I looked at Dirk, lying on the ground, his head bleeding from that bottle of Jack Daniel's you smashed him with. And for the first time, you know what I saw?"

"A dumb-ass drunk?" I ventured.

"Oh my God! Yes! And someone way below my standards. And I realized he'd lost to a guy who was smart and strong and not afraid of anything." She squeezed both of my hands. "You!" She said it like I had just won a prize.

She giggled, a silly floating kind of giggle, the kind girls make when they think they're in love, but they're only in love with being in love.

"And I realized he was not the person I want to be with." She squeezed my hands again. "I'm all yours."

I almost choked on the popcorn. "What do you mean?"

"How can I help you with this mystery, silly? I'm ready to answer all your questions now."

I smiled. "Okay. First, tell me where you were on Saturday, August fifteenth, the day Hardcastle died, before you found him."

She rolled her eyes. "What a stupid mistake that was! Dirk wanted to see a friend of his in Austin. My parents have this app on my phone that keeps track of where I am at all times. But Dirk and I came up with this plan that I would leave my phone at the counseling office and drive to Austin. Oh my God, it was so hard being away from my phone for that long! I almost died! Anyway, I left it at Hard-On's because I planned to get in with the key that hung on the tree. Did anybody tell you there was a key on the tree?"

"I'm aware," I said. "You and Dirk drove to Austin that day. What did you do?"

"It was so lame! We drove to his friend's, and he wasn't there. And Dirk got mad because he said he wanted to drink. Plus he wanted to have sex and I'd already told him no. I suggested we go see Zadie because I heard she was sick that day."

"Who told you she was sick?" I asked.

"She didn't come with Dr. Hard-On," she said. "I asked Hard-On about her, and he said she was at home with his wife and she was sick."

"You and Dirk drove to Zadie's house?" I asked.

"Yeah, but here's the weird part. When we got there, at first it didn't seem like anybody was home. I used Dirk's phone and texted her and asked if she was at home and she texted back and said she was. And I was about to text her again and tell her we were at her front door, but the door opened and there is Mrs. Hard-On. She had on her sunglasses and her purse was slung over her arm like she's going somewhere. I asked her about Zadie, and she said she was sick and that she was sleeping and couldn't come to the door. I thought that was odd, but I figured Mrs. Hard-On didn't realize Zadie was awake, so I let it go."

"What time were you at Zadie's house that day?"

Price tapped a finger on her lips, thinking. "About two forty-five? Three?"

"What happened next?"

"Dirk and I left and found another friend of his. This one was home, and we stayed for like half an hour talking and Dirk was drinking. Then he tried to feel me up in front of his friends, so that pissed me off. We had this big argument. I said I had to go because my parents would get worried when I didn't answer my phone for a while, so we left. I had to drive because Dirk was drunk."

"What time did you head back to Ten Spot?" I asked.

"We got back to Hard-On's office around four and that's when I found him."

"And you said last night that you couldn't go through the back door, so you entered through the front door. Is that right?" I asked.

"Yes. The key on the tree was missing but somebody had left the front door unlocked. Which was weird. Anyway, I found my phone where I'd left it under a chair in the corner, and that's when I found Hard-On. I ran across the street to the dry cleaners and told them. I guess they're the ones who called the cops."

"Let me ask you one more thing. What were you seeing Hardcastle for anyway?"

She leaned back and rolled her eyes. "Oh my God. It's my parents. They said I could use a little self-awareness training or some bullshit like that. If they had only known the awareness Dr. Hard-On had for me." She laughed, but it was more like a snort.

"You and Dirk never told your parents what Hardcastle was doing?" I asked.

"Don't you know, Detective Blanco? Bribery is the sweetest revenge."

"You mean blackmail?"

"Whatever." She waved me off. "And seriously, I wouldn't have let him do too much to me, only enough to have something I could use against him. And then I would've bribed or blackmailed the hell out of his ass!"

I looked at the time on my phone. "The previews have started for your movie. You better get in there or you're gonna miss it."

"Yes, sir!" She stood and gave me a salute, then leaned over and gave me a kiss on the lips. "Call me!"

She turned and headed to find Holiday, and I watched her walk all the way to the other end of the theater.

Call it investigative technique. Call it a good old-fashioned hunch. Or maybe it was simply the fact that I hadn't had an 1885 since the party at the Whiffletrees the night before and the popcorn had me crazy thirsty. Whatever it was, I booked it from the Texas Theater to Mr. Dream's and discovered Aiden at the counter ordering a bowl of pink strawberry frozen yogurt. And this time he was alone.

I slapped a five spot on the counter in front of him. "I'm buying. Let's talk."

By the look on his face, I'd either caught him off-guard or red-handed. I guessed it was some of both. He pocketed the five, cased the place, then nodded toward an empty booth. Dream was nowhere in sight.

I took the seat across the table from him. "You wanna go first, or should I?"

He dropped his eyes into the yogurt and began churning it over with his spoon.

"Funny thing about frozen yogurt," I said. "The longer you fool with it, the less it looks like the thing you've been wanting."

While he chewed his bottom lip, the spoon continued to clink the bottom of the ceramic bowl, and the yogurt transformed into the beginnings of a slushy mess.

"I can guess what you're wondering," I said. "The answer is yes, I do. I have enough on you to go to the cops, unless I'm given a reason to do otherwise."

Nothing. Not a word. Not a glance. Not even a fist in my face. I stood up and made for the door.

"He said it would be funny!" Aiden yelled across the diner.

I stopped. Several patrons put down their spoons and looked in his direction. Porter, dutifully behind the counter, stood up, then sat back down. And Aiden stared at me with pitiful eyes.

I paced back over and again slipped into the booth across from him.

"He said it would be funny," he repeated. His voice was low, and the words caught in his throat.

"Who told you to put that blade in Zadie's desk?"

He gave me a blank expression. "I did it."

"You put the blade there?"

"I killed Hardcastle."

"If you're screwing with me, Aiden, I'm out of here."

He dropped the spoon into the melting yogurt and pushed the bowl away. "I told him I had video, of what he was doing to the girls."

"You have a video? How? Who'd you get it from?"

"I made it." He gave me a sheepish grin and snickered softly, and I realized the little pervert was probably just as proud of himself as Hardcastle had been, and now he was smiling at me like I would understand because I was a guy too, and that's just what we guys do. I didn't understand at all, and I wanted to pop him right in the mouth.

"You still have it?" I asked.

"I deleted it when they found his body. I was afraid the cops would search my phone."

"How'd you manage it?"

He shifted his weight in the booth, trying to get comfortable. "Price's session was right before mine. One day, I got there about an hour early. He had to go to the restroom between Holiday's session and Price's. I snuck into his office and hid my phone."

"Did Price see you do this?" I asked.

"Hell no. And I wasn't doing it to trap him. I just wanted to see Price naked. I heard the girls talking about this touch therapy they were doing, and I thought they were taking off their clothes for him."

"Go on. How does that lead to killing Hardcastle?"

"Later, after I got my phone back and watched the video at home, I realized he was only touching them while they lay on the floor with their clothes still on. I almost deleted it. But he started yelling at me more and more. He'd tell me I needed to be more like Tobias."

He stopped and looked away from me, letting his eyes settle somewhere far away outside the windows beside us. His lips were trembling now.

"He made me sit in the middle of his office floor and he'd put women's panties on my head and stick tampons on my face and call me a pussy. He said if I wanted to act like a pussy, I needed to dress like one."

I gave him a pained look. "Keep going."

He turned his face back toward me. "After two sessions of this, I remembered I had the video. The next week I told him if he didn't leave Ten Spot and never come back, I would take it to the police. He told me to go fuck myself, and the next Saturday, when he came back, he said since I was so interested in watching his touch therapy sessions with the girls, he would show me what it was like on me. I told him to go to hell and I got out of there. Later that day, I found out he'd killed himself. He probably figured I'd already taken the video to the cops and offed himself."

"You think Hardcastle killed himself because you had a video of him that would send him to jail?"

"What else could it be?" he asked, his eyes pleading for some other reason.

"If you ask me, I think Hardcastle's death was a murder, not a suicide," I said. "Why were you seeing Hardcastle in the first place?"

He hesitated. "I hear things, Nacho."

I raised my eyebrows. "What things?"

"Voices. Voices telling me things."

"What do the voices tell you to do?"

"I want to tell you something, Nacho," he said. "You're a good guy, and I want to tell you something."

I pulled myself up straighter in the booth. "Go on. Spill it."

"I put the razor blade in Zadie's desk."

"I figured. Why?"

"Because Dream told me. He said he was playing a prank on someone and told me if I'd put the blade and the note in Zadie's desk, I could have free frozen yogurt anytime I wanted."

"Dream wrote the note?" I asked.

"I can't say who wrote it. I didn't. He gave it to me and the box of blades and asked me to put one blade and the note in Zadie's desk." He looked over at the counter where Porter was playing on his phone. "I'm thirsty."

"Never mind that," I said. "Did Dream tell you who he was playing a joke on?"

"No. I figured it was you because you like to solve mysteries."

He looked down and began to rub the temples on either side of his head.

"Did you know that receipt was yours from when you ordered pink frozen yogurt?"

He looked up and gave me a blank stare. "What do you mean?"

"That was your receipt. You dropped it and Zadie picked it up. How'd you manage to get it back and place it in her desk?"

He began to fumble for his words. "Mr. Dream gave it to me. I didn't know Zadie had it. I didn't even know it was mine."

"Let me get this straight," I said. "When Trip found the box in your backpack, you said I must have planted the box to blame you."

He looked up. "Sorry about that. When Trip found those blades, I freaked."

"What about the one my grandmother got at the hospital? Was that you?"

He gave me a puzzled look. "The one you're grandmother got? I don't know nothing about that."

"One more thing…"

He jumped up from his seat. "No. That's it. I stayed. I answered your questions. I have to go."

He bolted for the door.

"I'm gonna need that five!" I yelled after him.

Several patrons turned to look again, but this time Porter didn't bother to stand.

Aiden returned to the table and dropped the Lincoln in front of me.

"Thanks," I said. "After all, you're getting it for free now."

He shot me a glare. "Fuck you." Then he hightailed it out of there.

I eyed Aiden's strawberry yogurt still in front of me. It'd melted, like Aiden's life, like the whole town of Ten Spot had been doing for decades, dripping down the side of the bowl, pooling into a sticky puddle on the table, like Hardcastle's filthy blood on the carpet in his office. I picked up the bowl, tipped it to my lips, and slurped up the murky, sticky mess.

It was past six by the time I parked the bike on the gravel drive at the cabin. Inside, I headed for Brockett's desk. I wanted another look at those surveillance videos. I wanted to compare the person I'd seen on the cafeteria video to the one who'd gone in and out of the drycleaners, the bookstore, and the candy shop on the day of Hardcastle's murder. I had a hunch that Zadie's doppelgänger had been the one skipping in and out of those businesses, and that it was Zadie's doppelgänger who'd sliced open Hardcastle's wrists.

I was standing by his desk when my phone vibrated with a number I didn't recognize.

"Nacho," I answered.

"Mr. Blanco, I see you've made it home. I trust you had a good day at school."

It was the same deep, bass voice.

"What can I do for you, Mr. Unimportant?"

The caller let out a low laugh. "I will miss your sense of humor the most, Mr. Blanco."

"You're moving?" I asked. "Or did you decide to turn yourself in for murder?"

"Mr. Blanco, it's not me that needs to leave. It's you. I am only looking out for your best interest."

"You're the sweetest," I said. "Problem is, I've sorta taken a liking to this place."

His voice was sharper now. "I've given you ten thousand good reasons to leave town. And they are still sitting in a brown paper sack."

"Can't."

"Can't or won't?" he asked.

"Doesn't matter," I said.

"I guess you'll die like your old man."

"What do you know about my father?"

There was a slight pause before he continued. "You and I are not so different, young Blanco. Each of us saddled with both the responsibilities and the limitations of being the sons of, how should I put this, impetuous men. It's trying at times. Cleaning up the messes of others."

"Did you kill my father?"

He laughed. "Me? I barely knew your old man. But I feel a kinship with you, Nacho. We are more alike than you might imagine. People trust us because we excel at solving their problems. The only problem we can't solve is how to get our own asses out of this shit hole town."

"You leaving Ten Spot would solve all my problems," I said.

There was a long pause in our conversation, and I wondered what Mr. Unimportant was thinking. For a second, I thought he might've ended the call.

"You need to go outside, young man," he said at last.

"You didn't answer my question."

"I must insist you pay a visit to the gravel driveway rather hurriedly. The time is ticking, and I wouldn't want you to miss the show."

I opened the front door and stepped out.

"A little further please," he said. "Over by the motorcycle should be sufficient."

I let my eyes scan the entire front lawn as I made my way to the bike. He could see me, but I couldn't see him, and that unnerved me.

"That's perfect," he said.

There was a sudden thunderous roar, and flying wood chips and pieces of log splintered through the air toward me like missiles. I hit the deck and covered my head as debris from the cabin's explosion hurtled past me. When it was over, I poked my head up and saw a gaping hole where the living room of Brockett's cabin had been, a place I had been standing only minutes earlier.

I found my phone on the ground nearby. I didn't even ask if the caller was still there.

"You just made a big mistake!" There was a ringing in my ears, and I had a feeling I was yelling, though it didn't seem like it.

"I own you, Mr. Blanco, like I own everyone in this town. I decide who lives here and who doesn't. You don't belong. We both know it. Take the money. Don't look back, and don't come back."

"I'm coming for you," I said. "And I'm not leaving."

"I respect your tenacity, Mr. Blanco. In fact, I admire it. You remind me of myself. However, I may as well tell you I have something of yours."

I heard a rustling sound on the phone followed by a thin voice. "Nacho?"

"Zadie! Are you okay?" It felt like a vise grip had tightened around my chest. She sounded scared.

"She's okay…for now," Mr. Unimportant said.

"If you touch her in anyway, I'll kill you."

"For God's sake, please, don't be so melodramatic," he said. "Leave tonight with the money and I will let the girl go free. Otherwise you will leave me with no choice but to kill her and dump her corpse onto the side of the road. And I'll kill you too, Mr. Blanco, and throw yours on top of hers. Your bodies will make a hell of a meal for the coyotes. It's your choice, my little problem solver investigator. You have until midnight tonight. I'll be watching. Goodbye, Nacho Blanco."

I looked at the time on my phone. 6:23.

I had just over five and a half hours. Five and a half hours to find Zadie, wherever she was, rescue her from whoever had taken her, and kill anyone who tried to stop me.

Pieces of lumber and logs and cedar shingles dangled from the mesquites like tinsel on a 1950s Christmas tree. Shirts and pants, socks and shoes, all of them ripped or blown apart, along with bits and pieces of lamps and books and other household items, littered the front lawn and gravel drive like popcorn on the floor of the Texas Theater. The explosion had split Brockett's desk, the one I had been standing by when Mr. Unimportant called me. I found it upside-down on the front lawn where I found most of the other furniture. His desktop computer lay on the gravel drive, the bottom of the monitor melted away. Surprisingly enough, his dining room table was still intact, along with his refrigerator, which was still standing, and still plugged in, though I doubted it was still running.

Brockett was gonna need one heck of a handyman to fix this mess.

I called Ms. Baxter and told her about the phone call from Mr. Unimportant, the explosion, and the kidnapping of Zadie.

"Oh my God! Why would someone take her? Any idea where Zadie is or who has her?" she asked.

I could hear the dinging of a car door opening and the start of a car engine. The counselor was already en route to the cabin.

"I have a good idea of both."

"I'm calling the police, Nacho."

A siren wailed in the distance and closed in on the cabin fast.

"Don't bother," I said. "Somebody's already beat you to it."

I slipped the phone into my back pocket and angled my way over piles of smoldering rubble to Philo and fingered the palm's now blackened trunk. The explosion had disintegrated the palm's canopy of leaves, making it look like the long, gray neck of a headless brontosaurus.

"Don't give up," I said, patting its trunk. "Hang in there for Brockett."

My phone vibrated. It was a text from Mr. Unimportant. He'd sent a photo of Zadie. They'd bound and gagged her, and in her lap was a digital clock that read 6:24. One minute ago. Her eyes were wide, pleading, and terrified. And now my heart was pounding.

The heat from the multiple small fires in the wreckage of what had been Brockett's living room stung my face, and the smell from those burning piles was horrendous. I needed my backpack from the bedroom. I also needed to get away from this mess before the first responders arrived. They'd have a lot of questions, and the only question I wanted answered was how to find Zadie.

The blast had upended a small entertainment center, and the larger piece was blocking my path to the bedrooms. I lifted the cabinet enough so it would topple over in a broken heap. On the floor below was a photograph I'd never seen but recognized at once. It was a picture of me and my parents, Dad and I wearing matching swim trunks, Mom in a turquoise one-piece. We were standing on a deck overlooking a lake. Brockett's lake. Brocket's deck. I picked up the picture, and dusted it off, careful to let the broken glass in the frame skitter to the floor. I looked to be about five or six years old. This week hadn't been my first at this cabin. Brockett must've known, but he hadn't mentioned it, and I wondered what else he hadn't bothered to tell me.

I managed my way into the bedroom, found the pack, and

shoved the crinkled photo inside. The sirens had stopped, and I heard voices coming from the front of the house.

"Keep your guns drawn. He's armed."

I slung the backpack over my shoulders and eased up the shattered bedroom window. I lifted myself over the windowsill and dropped to the ground.

"Don't move."

I froze, raised both hands, and turned. It was a cop, large and heavy-set, balding, with a bulbous neck and a thick black mustache. And he had a Smith and Wesson trained on my chest.

"I've got him," he said into his shoulder radio. "He was slipping out a window on the backside."

"Copy that," someone said.

"Okay, kid, nice and easy, drop that pack to the ground."

I did.

"Perfect," he said, motioning with his weapon. "Now put your hands back up nice and high where I can see them."

I did, just before several of Ten Spot's finest rushed me to the ground, kicked my backpack to the side, and pulled both arms behind me. I felt the cold steel of tight hand cuffs pinch my wrists.

"The suspect is cuffed, and I'm bringing him around to the front," said the big cop.

They stood me on my feet and escorted me around the house. Then they mirandized me and plopped me on the ground in front of the charred and smoking cabin.

Two Ten Spot fire trucks and three more police cars pulled onto the gravel drive. I watched as firefighters sprayed a white synthetic foam across the smoldering debris to suppress the remaining flames. The cops stood around watching the firefighters, swapped conquest stories, and took an occasional derisive glare at me. Their good ol' boy assembly came to an abrupt end when a red Hyundai Sonata barreled into the front yard, causing the caucus of cops to come alive and reach for their sidearms.

It was the counselor.

"I'm Darcy Baxter," she said as she got out. "This is my father's cabin. I'm the one who called."

"You recognize this young man?" asked big and balding. "We apprehended him as he was coming out the back."

"Yes," she said. "He's the one I was telling you about. My father and I have been trying to help him, but he threatened to blow up the cabin. We never thought he would do it." She shook her head, pointed toward the house, and brushed away a tear. "What do they say? No good deed goes unpunished."

The moment was surreal, like I wasn't even there, an audience member just watching my own life play out on a big screen and dreading what might happen next.

"Yes, ma'am, something like that." The officer took notes in a little pad. "You want to press charges?"

"Will they take him to jail and lock him up?" she asked.

"If you're pressing charges, one of the officers will take him downtown and book him," he replied.

"Ms. Baxter?" I squinted at the two of them, my ears still ringing.

She didn't look my way. "I'm pressing charges." Her voice was cold, gritty, and cross.

"What's going on?" I struggled to get up, my hands still cuffed behind me. "You don't think I had anything to do with this, do you?"

A cop standing near me jabbed his baton into my gut, and I slumped back to the ground, gasping for air. "Keep your goddamn mouth shut," he said, "or anything you say will be used against you right now."

The big, balding one turned to another, a thin one not much older than me, it seemed, with a shock of bright red hair and a face full of freckles to match. "Take him to the lock up, Billy, and book him for arson and criminal mischief."

Billy grabbed my backpack, dragged me to my feet, and hustled me into one of the waiting squad cars. As we pulled away, I watched the counselor steal a glance over her shoulder at me. Her eyes were emotionless, transfixed on our departing cruiser. With arms crossed over her chest, I saw the smallest, faintest slip of a smile spread over her red, lying Judas lips. She had warned me herself. Not everyone in this town is who they claim to be.

About a mile in, it hit me. Without warning, I fell over in the seat, shaking, gagging, gasping for air.

Billy looked over his shoulder as he judiciously took the curves that led us toward Ten Spot's city limits. "Hey, man, you all right?"

I didn't answer. I started convulsing, like someone had hammered a cucumber down my windpipe. Officer Billy hit the brakes, causing the police cruiser to fishtail on the unpaved road. He jumped out of the front seat and swung open the back door as my eyes rolled back.

"Damn it!"

The convulsions were unrelenting as Billy dragged me out of the car, feet first. He rolled me over to my side to remove the cuffs, tilted my head back, and lowered his mouth to begin CPR.

That's when I stopped him.

"Sorry, Billy, but I don't think I'm your type."

He stared at me, his mouth hanging wide open. "What the fuck?"

Then he heard the click of his own revolver and felt the steely barrel of the weapon burrow into the side of his skinny neck.

I swallowed hard, and I was trying hard to keep my hand from shaking. I couldn't believe I'd actually taken his weapon. Neither could Billy.

"What the hell?" His eyes got big. His body tensed. And for a moment I thought he'd even stopped breathing. And then I thought he might fight.

I stared into Billy's eyes. "If this was re-…" I could feel my throat tightening, "re-reversed, I can promise you I-I…I wouldn't do it. But-But…it's not reversed, and I'm the one with a finger on the trigger of gun pressed to the side of your neck." I tried to sound more confident than I felt at the moment. I suspected Billy was trying to do the same thing.

Another beat or two passed, then Billy let out a sigh. "God-damn you."

I almost laughed. "Yeah, He just might do that, Billy. Now get the hell off me. Real slow-like."

We stood and I motioned with the gun toward some brush in a small ravine.

"I'm not gonna lie," I confessed, wiping the back of my mouth with my free hand. "I'm kinda nervous. It's my first time to pull a weapon on a cop." I motioned toward some brush in a small ravine. "Sorry to do this to you."

He stared at me, unmoving. "What?"

Using the pistol, I pointed to a medium-sized mesquite. "Throw me the key to the cuffs, then cuff yourself to the trunk of that tree."

He squinted his eyes at me and laughed. "You little piece of shit. Fuck you."

I fired off a round above his head, my hand trembling like a wooden barn in Texas thunderstorm.

"Shit! God damn it!" Billy let out a sigh and moved to the mesquite, tossing the key to me, then cuffing himself to the tree.

I lowered the pistol and tossed it and the key into the weeds away from him. I was glad to be rid of Billy's sidearm. My hand was sweaty from holding it, and I wiped my hand dry on the back of my pants. "I'm s-s-sorry, Billy. I—well, I'm just sorry, and —okay, I gotta go."

I climbed behind the wheel of the cruiser and headed toward Ten Spot, the events at the cabin replaying in my mind.

That little stunt of Baxter's was surprising. I wondered what else she was hiding. Then I remembered the puzzle in her office, and something occurred to me. The bulldog wasn't concealing an ace of clubs beneath the table. He was handing it to the other bulldog. The mutts were working together. The real question wasn't what else Baxter was hiding, but who was she in cahoots with? Brockett. Chuck. Finch. Dream. Darwood. Plenty of names and not enough answers. Let them have this town, I thought. Get the money, get Zadie, and get out.

Within minutes, I had pulled up in front of the Overton College Library. With the engine idling, I jumped out and ran to the back of the building. There they were, the two large HVAC systems, and beneath the one on the right was a decent-sized paper sack. I scooped it up and sprinted back to the waiting sedan. Inside the bag were two stacks of fifty Benjamins each. Mr. Unimportant had kept his promise. I had the money. I could leave and never look back.

And I wanted to.

Instead, I fired off a text to Trip and BroFly.

GAZEBO ASAP

I threw the car into gear, peeled out of the library's circle drive, and made for the park. It took only ten minutes to get there. Then I shoved the sack into my backpack and jogged across the field to the gazebo. Trip and BroFly were waiting for me.

I updated them on the explosion, Zadie's kidnapping, and Baxter double-crossing me.

Trip threw both his hands to the top of his head, running his fingers through his hair. "Damn, the counselor's in on it, too?"

BroFly put out his hand, slapping mine. "Shit, bro. You pulled a gun on a cop?" He shook his head. "They coming for you now. Trust me. You one of the brothers, now."

I shrugged. "Probably. Tell me what you guys got."

BroFly went first. "We did like you said. We kept tabs on that detective you told us about and Principal Whiffletree. After school, Trip went to the Apple Blossom and I headed to the school office. I walked in and everybody was like, 'Hey, man, why you here?' And I was like 'Yeah, I'm bored. Do y'all need any help?' So I started sorting through some mail and putting it into the teacher's boxes. I could hear Whiffletree in his office. All of the sudden I hear him on his phone say, 'What do you mean?'

I can't hear who he's talking to or nothing, but he slams the phone on his desk and yells he has an emergency at home. So, I was like, man, I need to see what's going on, right? I pull out my phone, and I'm looking at it like I just got a text, and say, 'Hey, my mom needs me. Sorry, guys, I gotta go too.' Whiffletree gets into his car and drives away, and I run like hell from the school, through the park to his house in Castlerock. And when I get there his car's in the drive and guess who else is there?"

"This guy!" Trip smiled and pointed both his thumbs toward his chest.

"You were at the Whiffletrees' house?" I asked Trip.

Trip took up the narrative. "I stayed behind at the hooker hotel, right? And I'm watching the door to Finch's room and about ten minutes after BroFly leaves, Finch leaves his room, gets into some beat-up old blue piece of shit and takes off. I follow him in my dad's truck. I'm like leaving a lot of space between us so he doesn't catch on and, in a few minutes, he's turning into Castlerock Estates. And whose house do you think he goes to?"

"Let me guess. The Whiffletrees'."

"Bingo!" he said.

They both looked at me.

"What do we do now?" asked BroFly.

I pulled my phone from my pocket and pulled up the picture of Zadie with the clock. "This was taken at my grandmother's house a short while ago."

"Damn!" said Trip.

"How can you tell it's your house?" asked BroFly.

I slid my finger up on the picture, opening the metadata. Beneath the picture was a map showing where the photo had been taken, and the address.

"31 Debra Lane." I looked at them. "That's my grandmother's address. Somebody took this picture inside my house."

"I didn't know phones did that," said BroFly.

"Only if you save the picture," I said. "Many people don't

realize our phones stamp every picture with the GPS data along with the date and time."

"That means all we have to do is go to your house and get her," said BroFly.

I shook my head. "She's not there."

Trip gave me a confused look. "You said they took the photo at your house."

"It was. They planned on me finding the picture's GPS data. In fact, they were counting on it."

"It's a trap," BroFly said, "and Zadie's the bait."

I nodded. "Exactly."

"What do we do now?" asked Trip.

"Listen," I began, "these aren't amateurs we're playing with. This is serious. I'm already in, deep. And if you go into this thing with me, you might not make it out. I'm just saying there's no judgment from me if you guys wanna hang back and let me go it alone. I'd understand."

BroFly pointed an index finger at me. "My granddad was a preacher before he died. He used to tell this story of these five white dudes who traveled to some country in South America where this crazy tribe was running around naked and shit. The white guys were trying to tell them about Jesus, and they all got killed for it."

I put up a hand to stop him. "BroFly, what does this have to do with anything?"

"One of those white dudes wrote in his journal that wherever you are just be all there." He held out his hand toward me. "Well, this is where I am, bro, and I'm all there."

Trip reached out his hand too. "I'm all there, too, man."

I looked out toward Centennial Park, toward the Tower, toward the shadows creepy-crawling over the grassy fields, forewarnings of the night that was coming, the darkness that would cloak everything. There'd be plenty of night to come before the morning would arrive. What I couldn't say was whether or not I'd be around to see the morning. Still, if it wasn't me, others would see it, and I hoped it'd be a better morning for them.

I reached with both of my hands and took hold of theirs. "I'll tell you what we're gonna do," I said. "We're gonna give them what they want. We're gonna visit 31 Debra Lane. You boys ready for a battle?"

"Fuck yeah!" said BroFly

"That's all we ever really wanted," added Trip.

The three of us laughed.

"Perfect," I said. "Let's go find Zadie."

CHAPTER 25
BUMP IN THE GRASS

We heard them before we saw them, Ten Spot squad cars, sirens blaring, winding their way through the streets of Castlerock toward Centennial Park. When they finally came into view, we counted five in total. Three of the cruisers jumped the curb and raced across the field toward the gazebo. Two smartly stayed behind, blocking the exit of the wheels I'd stolen.

"They coming for us?" BroFly asked, his eyes wide.

"They're coming for me," I said. "Split up! Meet me in thirty at Old Gnarly."

We darted from the gazebo and made a hard run to the outskirts of the park, each in a different direction. I made it to the south edge of the field and ducked behind the cover of a grove of live oaks, first to catch my breath, second to check on my pursuers. They were close, but once they'd gotten to the densely treed grove, they'd have to stop their vehicles and follow me on foot.

I pushed on, sprinting toward the opposite end of the grove and through the parking lot of the library. I rounded the corner of the building and tore through the library's front doors. I ran past the stacks to the restrooms, pushing open the emergency door, the same one Darwood had found me at a few days earlier.

For the second time this week, the building's alarm activated. I jumped back into the women's restroom, pulling the door behind me and scrambled into a stall.

Outside the restroom I could hear the melee of desperate runners, commanding voices, and tumbling objects.

"He exited out the back door!"

"Check the cans!"

Somebody opened the door to the women's bathroom.

"Clear! He's doubled back toward the park!"

Within five minutes, the alarm had been silenced. I heard the door open and Mrs. Hazelton's small, raspy voice. "Anybody in here?" When nobody answered, she turned off the light and closed the door.

I waited another fifteen before easing open the bathroom door. The cops had left, and I slipped back through the stacks and out the front and headed for Old Gnarly.

"What's the plan?" asked Trip when he and BroFly found me hiding beneath the tree's low-lying tentacles.

"First, find and rescue Zadie. Second, nab the killer of Agent Stephanie Sullivan. And third, solve the mystery of the murder of Lincoln Hardcastle."

"Easy enough," said BroFly. "How do we do it?"

"We know they took Zadie's picture in my grandmother's house. I'm guessing she's gone now, but somebody's waiting for me to show up. That's where you two come in. I'm gonna slink my way down the back alley and through my window. I never lock it. As casually as you can, you two come to the front door and ring the bell. Ask for me if anyone answers."

They both nodded and we lit out.

I slipped around behind the first house on the street and snaked my way down the alley. It was a quarter past seven and the fall shadows continued their long sag over the rooftops. I hugged the dry, whitewashed wooden privacy fence that lined both sides of the weedy easement until I got to the back of the fourth house. My grandmother's privacy fence was in dire straits. Several of the planks were missing, which made slipping into the backyard an easy task. I skimmed over to my bedroom and peered in through the window. Nobody around. From inside I heard the doorbell. I slipped up the window and scooted in, landing head down on the floor beside my bed. With nobody in sight, I eased over to the door to steal a glance down toward the living room. The coast was clear, and I stepped into the hall.

"Going somewhere?"

I froze. I'd heard that voice before, and when I turned, I faced a 9mm Barretta I'd also seen before. And it was pointed at my chest.

I motioned toward the gun. "You keep waving that thing around and you're liable to get hurt."

He held the piece steady on me and jerked his head in the direction of the living room. I obliged and headed for the front of the house. We were only a few steps into the kitchen when I heard a crash behind me. I whirled in time to see Atkins slump to the floor, blood seeping from a gash across his skull, the sharp pieces of a shattered vase surrounding him.

Trip stood over Atkins' slumped body, proud. "We decided to follow you in through the back window when nobody answered the bell."

I scooped up the firearm Atkins had dropped and stuffed it into my waistband. "Good plan. Thanks."

We relieved our unconscious prisoner of his stun gun as well and secured him to the refrigerator door handle with his own cuffs.

"Time to wake up," I said.

BroFly gave our prisoner a swift kick to the side, and he came to with a start, sputtering, gasping for air. He blinked and took in his surroundings, and discovered his hands bound to the fridge.

"You son of..."

I interrupted Atkins with the stun gun. It hissed and crackled, a jagged blue and white bolt of electricity dancing back and forth between its prongs.

"Listen, kid, this wasn't my idea. I told them…"

I fired up the weapon again to make sure I had his attention.

"This is quite the bug zapper you got here. And let me tell you, it has one hell of a bite. Trust me."

I dropped it between his legs, inches from his groin, and fired it up again. It popped and sizzled and snapped eagerly for his family jewels.

"Oh, shit, please, no!" Atkins shook his head, clamping his legs together, and scooting as far back as he could against the fridge.

"Where's Zadie?" I asked.

He opened his mouth, but his phone rang, and I fished it out of his suit coat.

"Is Nacho Blanco dead?" the caller asked.

"Let me check." I turned to Atkins. "Mr. Unimportant is asking if I'm dead. What should I tell him?"

Atkins said nothing, and he didn't take his eyes off that stun gun either.

I put the phone back to my face. "Atkins is kinda tied up, Mr. Unimportant. But I assure you I am not DOA, although I have been with some girls on dates who I'm pretty sure were."

Mr. Unimportant's voice was calm, deliberate, and even. "Mr. Blanco, what a resourceful little man you are."

I cut to the chase. "Where's Zadie?"

"We had a deal, Nacho Blanco. You leave with the money, and I let you and the girl live. You didn't keep up your end of the bargain. You took the money, but you didn't leave. Now we need a new deal. Bring me my money and we'll talk."

"I bring you the money and you let Zadie and me two-step out of Ten Spot?"

He let out a low chuckle. "I've changed my mind about the girl. She will not be a part of any deal. I've decided to keep her. I'm extremely fond of beautiful young women. Surely a red-blooded all-American boy like yourself can understand. But when she gets uncooperative, as I imagine she will, or when I get bored, as I imagine I will, I'll kill her."

"You're insane."

"You bring out the best in me, young Blanco. I trust I've done the same for you. All that's left is for you to bring me my money and you can leave Ten Spot, never to return."

"If I don't?" I asked.

"I'll put a bullet in your grandmother. And I'll put a bullet in that counselor friend of yours, and her father, too. And I'll put one in you, Mr. PSI."

I was confused. Maybe the counselor wasn't in cahoots with Mr. Unimportant after all.

"Where can I find you?"

"You're the detective. You figure it out," he said and ended the call.

I looked at the phone in my hand. It was half past seven.

I slipped the phone in my pocket and lowered the stun gun to my side.

"I can help you," said Atkins. He tried to sit up a little straighter against the fridge. "I can help you, tell you where she is. Trust me."

"I don't trust you," I said, "but I'm listening."

He pulled against the handcuffs that bound his wrists above his head and grimaced as if to show me how uncomfortable he was. "The first thing you gotta do is take these damn cuffs off me. They're killing my wrists."

I let out a snort. "Start talking, and if I like what I hear, I'll think about it.

"Not one word from me unless you take these things off." He must have sensed my hesitation. "What am I going to do, kid? You got the drop on me, right?"

I didn't have time for negotiations with Atkins. Trip uncuffed him while I held the Barretta steady.

Free now, Atkins stood, rubbing each of his wrists alternately.

I pointed the gun toward a kitchen chair at the red and white checkered dining table, and he sat.

BroFly and Trip manned the front windows of the living room.

I took the chair across from Atkins. "Start talking."

"She's at some big house by the park."

"The Whiffletrees?" I asked.

"I ain't heard of no Whiffletrees. It's this big-ass mansion in Castlerock. That's where they've got her."

"What about the woman? Who's she?"

"The one on the phone? Hell if I know. The man I work for gave me her number, told me to follow what she says. I've talked to her. Never seen her. Hell, I don't even know the man's name. Never seen him either. He calls and I follow orders." Atkins looked around and snickered. "Your grandmother's terrible at keeping a house clean. This place is a wreck."

I wasn't amused. "Was that you that tossed this place this week?"

Atkins clamped his lips shut and looked away. I tapped the pistol on the table and pointed it back at him.

He held up both hands in a show of surrender. "Be cool, kid. Yes, that was me and McKee. The boss told us to look for some picture of Hardcastle and Dream and some other couple. If it's here, you got it well hid."

Trip jumped up from where he'd been sitting on the couch and pointed out the living room window. "We got company, Nacho."

"It's a car," said BroFly. "Black SUV."

I gave Atkins a cold stare. "Why's McKee here?"

He gave me an innocent look, shook his head, and shrugged his shoulders.

I took a quick glance over to Trip and BroFly and regretted it right away. The red and white checkered table flipped toward me, smacking me hard in the face, knocking me to the floor, causing me to drop the weapon.

The next ten seconds reeled off in slow motion. Atkins up and sprinting toward the door. Trip and BroFly turning around, eyes wide. Me yelling something but I wasn't sure what. BroFly and Trip turning back toward the window and shouting something at me.

Then I was off the floor and sprinting toward the door. Atkins was outside and heading across the lawn toward the car. McKee was behind the SUV's wheel, and he must not have seen his partner. Instead, he gunned the SUV toward me. I stopped in my tracks and ran hard toward the other side of the lawn. I could feel the vehicle bearing down on me fast, and I jumped to my right as it plowed into the front left corner of my grandmother's house. Siding splintered and a window shattered as thousands of broken shards hurtled across the lawn. McKee slammed into reverse and the car shot back about twenty feet, jumping when it hit a bump in the grass. It came to another stop and shot out toward the road, drifting to the right as it squealed down the street and out of sight.

BroFly and Trip met me on the front lawn.

"You okay, bro?" Trip asked.

I pointed to a crumpled mass lying on the ground. It was Atkins. He was dead, run over by his own partner, his face pulverized and unrecognizable. There was no right eye, no right nostril, no right ear. The entire right side of his face was a gooey flat mesh, with a discernable tread mark running through it.

"Damn," said Trip.

BroFly shook his head. "You got a dead guy in your front yard, man."

I looked at my grandmother's house. The front left corner had a huge gash, a hole that looked straight into her bedroom.

"I hope you got a maid," said Trip.

I left Atkins' corpse on the lawn and walked over to the hole in the house's front. "We don't."

"Ain't nobody gonna take the job now!" said BroFly.

I turned to them. "I need you to do something. I need you to call the cops and wait here until they arrive. Ask for Detective Larry Books. Tell him what happened. Then wait for me to text you."

"What are you gonna do?" asked Trip.

"I'm gonna find Zadie," I said.

I headed back inside the house, back to my bedroom closet, and lifted three wooden slats from the floor. Underneath, in a small hole, was an olive drab military grade ammo box. Inside were three M84 stun grenades, courtesy of one Steele Buchanan. How he managed to get shit like this I didn't know, and I didn't want to know. I slipped them into my coat pocket. Then I called my grandmother's room at the hospital. To my surprise, she answered.

"Is that you, Nacho?" Her voice was weak.

"What am I thinking, Grandma?"

There was silence on the phone. "What are you going to do, Nacho?"

"*Dime, Abuelita.* Or I will leave your ass in that hospital bed for the rest of the school year. What am I thinking?

"Language, Nacho!" Then her voice got small and afraid. "That you love me?"

"That's right, I love you. And you love me. And nobody will ever take that away from us. Not my mom. Not Dad's plane. Not anybody in Ten Spot or this whole world."

"Nacho?"

"There's something I gotta do, Grandma. I just want you to know…well, thanks for keeping an eye me."

There was another pause. "Thank you, Nacho. You're a good boy, like your daddy was." She paused, and I thought I heard a sniffle. "I'm proud of you like I was of him. He had a great sense of right and wrong. You're like your father in many ways. Go do what he would've done, but I want you to do something he couldn't do."

"What's that?" I asked.

"When it's over, and when you've done what you gotta do, I want you to come back to me."

"I will." It wasn't a promise, but I tried to make it sound like one.

I knew what I had to do, and what it was going to cost me. And whoever was waiting for me at 123 Castlerock knew it too.

I had one more call to make.

"What's up?" I asked when Steele answered. "Well, pause the game. You just found a buyer."

CHAPTER 26

SHE CAN FLY AND SHE CAN SPY

I t was going on half past eight by the time I'd huffed it to Steele's. Sporting a green and yellow Hawaiian shirt and a pair of white Bermuda shorts, he met me on the gravel drive in front of Stanhope.

"You walk?" He looked around for the Triumph. "Where's your wheels?"

"Traded them in for a ride in a Ten Spot paddy wagon. Is it charged up?"

Steele invited me out back to a patio table that sat next to the Olympic-size pool. The whole area was lit up by dozens of lamp posts that dotted the edges of the sidewalks. On a table was a small, silver, metallic object, circular in shape with a hole in the middle, like one of those flat washers in the hardware section of Home Depot, and about the size of a fifty-cent piece.

He picked it up and placed it in my hand. "This is the smallest HD drone available on the black market."

It had one miniature fan blade mounted in the center of the hole. Underneath, on either side of the opening, were two small lenses.

"This is one hundred percent genuine CIA tech," he said. "Like I was saying, she can fly, and she can spy. It has one drawback. No audio."

"I'll read lips. What's the controller look like?"

Steele gave me a wide grin. "That's the best part."

He slipped on a pair of black framed glasses with clear lenses and gave a sudden nod up. The drone came to life. He lifted his head again, this time slower, and the drone ascended about thirty feet. He cocked his head to one side, then the other. The drone mimicked Steele's head movements, left, right, up, down. Then, with precision, he dropped the baby drone back into my open hand.

My eyes widened. "You steer it with the glasses. Is there any visual?"

"Now wouldn't this be a sad little drone if there wasn't?"

He passed the frames to me. At the bottom of the right lens was a small, translucent video. I gave a quick nod up and again the drone came to life. I gave the drone a test run, raising and lowering my head, nodding it back and forth, just as Steele had done. In the glasses I could see a panoramic view of the Olympic-size pool, the blue tennis court, "Santa's Workshop," even the Ten Spot Cemetery, all from thirty feet up. Steele was right. It was a thing of beauty.

"The video is only visible from inside the lenses," he said. "Nobody looking at you would have any idea what you can see."

I slipped the drone in my pocket and hung the glasses on the neck of my shirt. "How much?"

He shook his head. "I'm sorry, man, but this little beauty is hard to get. I mean, I had to give up a year in sales to get my hands on it. Do you realize how many homework assignments I have to complete to…?"

"How much?" I asked again.

He grimaced. "Nine thousand, but that includes the glasses."

I slung my backpack around and pulled out the brown paper bag, setting it on the table in front of us. "Keep the change."

Steele ran through the two stacks of Benjamins. "And this is why I love doing business with you, Ignacio Blanco."

"Do me a favor," I said. "Don't mention this to anyone. I don't need anyone knowing I have this little gadget. And trust me, you don't need anyone knowing where you got those Benjis."

"Gucci."

He walked me back around the house to the front drive.

"Be careful, Iggy. I'm gonna be pissed if you get hurt."

"Not as much as I will."

"And take care of my little buddy," he added. "I'm gonna be more pissed if you let something happen to that drone!"

I laughed. "Can I ask a favor?"

"I'm down."

"I need a ride to Castlerock Estates."

***

It was past nine when Steele dropped me off three blocks from the Whiffletrees. I had less than three hours to rescue Zadie. After that, I'd just be daring Mr. Unimportant to do the inevitable sooner than later. There were three cars parked on their circle drive. One was the black SUV that had driven over Atkins. One was Darwood's blue beater. The other was the principal's green Volvo.

Two doors away from the Whiffletrees, I hopped the wrought iron fence of a much more modest home and scooted around the back. The moon was full, giving me just enough visibility to make my way through the wary darkness without having to use the light on my phone. After managing several more adjacent fences between houses, I found myself in the backyard of the Whiffletree mansion.

To my left was the golf course, quiet now as it slept and recovered from the day's traffic. To my right, the back of the Whiffletree house, and the two French doors where Mrs. Whiffletree had stood in that translucent white dress. Through the doors' opaque windows, I could make out the steady pacing of a shadowy figure.

Further to my right, jutting from the house like some emerald cathedral, was the attached greenhouse, tall and thick, buttressed with multiple lines of green arching steel, and wrapped from top to bottom in crystal-clear green glass. I assumed this was where Mrs. Whiffletree cultivated her cannabis. I tried the door and found it unlocked. No wonder there were trespassers helping themselves to her weed, I thought. I slipped in and crouched down behind a long row of wooden tables filled with hundreds of brown pots.

The pungent, sulfuric air hit me hard and I fought the need to retch. It was skunk, Mrs. Whiffletree's stash for her so-called herbalist hobby. The more stinky the weed, the more potent the high, and from the way this place smelled, Mrs. Whiffletree could've floated to the moon and back. I wound my way through the long tables in the oversized grow house and discovered another door that led inside the main home. I opened it an inch and, satisfied I was alone, slipped into the darkened room, grateful for fresher air.

I turned on my phone's flashlight to case the place. I was in some kind of storage room. Metal shelving with an assortment of pantry items and office supplies lined the wall, and boxes marked "PHIL'S BOOKS" lay jumbled in the center. I felt my way past ghostly obstacles to another door where light seeped in around the edges from the other side.

I slipped on the glasses Steele had given me and pushed the little drone through the luminated crack at the bottom of the door.

"Time to go to work, little fellow. Go find Zadie."

With a quick upward nod, the video feed awoke, and in vivid HD I could see a long white hallway, thirty feet or more. I lifted my head and the drone followed, stopping about six inches from the ceiling.

Steele had been right. The little bug was CIA all the way.

Using the drone, I discovered the hall tipped into the large airy living room where Brockett had fallen with a knife in his back not twenty-four hours earlier. The room was unoccupied, and I continued toward the open library, bringing the drone to a quiet hover, allowing it to settle into the room, and hoping against hope nobody would realize my little spy.

I landed the drone on the mantle of the library's stone fireplace and kept the video feed running. I couldn't hear anything, but I could see Zadie sitting in a metal folding chair, her hands and feet bound with zip ties, wide green doe eyes blinking back tears as they tracked McKee who stood guard over her while he paced the room like some caged animal. There was another metal chair to her right, two more on her left. Every few seconds McKee would check his watch. I checked my own. Almost nine forty-five.

A few minutes later, Mr. and Mrs. Whiffletree entered, followed by Rachel, Finch, and Darwood. The latter two forced the Whiffletrees and the housekeeper to sit, and then they took up posts on opposite ends of the room. McKee continued to hold court in the center. I watched Zadie turn to Mrs. Whiffletree on her left, to the housekeeper on her right, then back to Mrs. Whiffletree. A puzzled expression spread across her face. She turned back toward the fireplace.

"Oh my God," she mouthed. At least I thought she said that. She was shaking just slightly, her eyes fixed straight ahead. And she was biting her lower lip.

What are you thinking, Zadie Abernathy? What did you just notice?

I pulled out my phone and dialed Finch's number. He fished his own from his pocket, looked at the screen, and answered.

"My boy! It's about time you reported in. Where are you and what have you been doing?" He left his post by the door of the library to stand by McKee.

"Oh, you know, just getting ready for the party."

"Nacho!" Zadie screamed. "Don't come! It's a..."

I watched as Finch's backhand came down hard across Zadie's left cheek, snapping her head toward the housekeeper who watched in horror.

I willed myself to stay hidden.

Finch cupped Zadie's chin with his hand, using his thumb to stroke the red imprint on the side of her face. "Where are you, Blanco?"

"I know who you are, Finch, or at least whose you are," I said. "You're working for a man and a woman who tried to kill a federal agent, not to mention my grandmother, and has now kidnapped a girl you all want to frame for murder."

There was a long silence. At last, Finch said, "I tell you what, kid, just bring the money and get out of town. That's your best play if you want to walk away from this thing alive."

"I have a better idea," I said. "How about you and McKee and that psycho Darwood turn yourselves in."

"Listen, kid," he said, "be reasonable. When it comes right down to it, all the boss wants is the money. Drop it off at the principal's house and get the hell out of here."

"No can do. Already spent it. Ten grand doesn't go as far as it used to."

Through the drone, I watched Finch walk to Darwood, and through the phone, I heard him ask, "You have your knife?"

Darwood pulled a silver switch blade from his pocket and popped it open for everyone to see. "Never leave home without it."

"Excellent," Finch walked back to the center of the room. "Would you be so kind as to cut off her hair?"

Darwood snickered, and a smile curled across his lips. "With pleasure."

He swaggered over to Zadie, grinning, the knife's blade open, the glare of the lights flicking off its deadly steel. He grabbed a large handful of Zadie's hair on the right side of her face and held it steady.

Zadie shook her head with dreadful anticipation, her eyes filling with large tears that spilled over her cheeks.

"Please don't do this!" the housekeeper begged.

The blade came up with a violent thrust, slicing through the hair, the long platinum strands falling from Darwood's fist to the floor.

Zadie's shoulders shook as she continued to sob uncontrollably.

"Oh my God, help us!" the housekeeper prayed aloud.

Mr. Whiffletree lunged toward Darwood, but Darwood side-stepped him and he landed in a heap on the ground. McKee took his 9mm and slammed it against the back of the principal's head, knocking him out cold. Mrs. Whiffletree screamed as the body of her unconscious husband fell to the floor.

"Mr. Darwood just cut off some of the hair on your beloved princess, Blanco. I'm giving you five minutes," said Finch. "After that he cuts up the rest of her."

Zadie's head dropped to her chest as she continued to sob. Tears rolled down her face, her hair a lopsided mess.

"Finch," I said, "I wanna make a deal."

"I had a feeling you would."

"My life for hers," I said. "You get me and the money."

Finch laughed. "Well, let me…"

But Finch didn't get to finish. Every head turned toward the open door as another person now entered the room.

It was Brockett.

He was moving slow, limping, no doubt still besieged with pain from the knife he'd taken to the back. But he was standing, and there was a 9mm semi-automatic in both hands.

He fired a shot at McKee, just over his head, causing McKee to drop his gun.

"I've got a bullet waiting for all three of you," he said. "Drop that knife, kick it toward me, and back away from the girl."

Darwood complied and he and Finch took several steps away from Zadie.

Finch dropped the phone down by his side, but I was just barely able to continue making out the conversations.

"I'm taking the girl with me." Brockett turned to the housekeeper. "Pick up that knife and cut her free!"

Her hands trembling, the housekeeper cut the zip ties that bound Zadie, then flung the knife to the floor, hurrying to sit down.

Zadie rushed toward Brockett, pressing herself between his outstretched arms.

Brockett struggled to maintain his balance as he tried pushing her away.

Zadie fought to maintain her position next to him. "Don't let them take me again!"

"Back up!" he yelled, and he tried again pushing her to one side.

Zadie spun and pushed herself further into Brockett's outstretched arms, knocking one weapon to the floor, nearly making him lose the other. But that was the only opening Finch needed. He lunged at the pair, and during the tussle, knocked the remaining 9mm from Brockett's hand, sending both Brockett and Zadie sprawling to the ground.

Finch scooped up both firearms, stuffed one in his waistband and held the other on the pair as they lay tangled.

"Get up," he told Zadie.

She did and he motioned for her to retake her seat in the metal folding chair.

Finch raised the phone back up to his face again. "Mr. Blanco. You still there?"

"Yep."

"We've had a most unexpected surprise in the last few moments. It would seem your friend Mr. Brockett attempted to play the role of hero." There was a poignant pause. "It didn't work."

Through the drone, I saw Brockett struggling to get up, his arms bracing his body as his chest and head sagged over the wood floor. McKee walked to Brockett's crumpled body and gave him a solid kick to the ribs, sending Brockett reeling to the floor, and gasping for air.

"Mr. Blanco," Finch continued, "I need you on the front steps of this house in five minutes with the money."

"And if I don't?" I asked.

"I'll put a bullet in everyone in this room."

"Do us all a favor," I said. "Start by eating one yourself."

He walked over to Brockett's struggling body and pointed one of Brockett's own guns at him. "Why don't I start with your friend."

"Wait!"

It was Darwood. Everyone's head turned to him in surprise, and he ambled over to where Brockett lay.

"Let me do it for you, boss," said Darwood.

Finch gave Darwood an appreciative smile and placed one of the 9mms in the understudy's hands.

Darwood pointed the gun at Brockett and shot point blank into his back. Brockett's body flopped from the impact of the slug, and a pool of red formed beneath him, trailing across the mahogany floor toward the fireplace.

Mrs. Whiffletree clamped both hands over her mouth, her eyes wide with horror.

The housekeeper screamed.

Zadie closed her eyes.

And Mr. Whiffletree began stirring back to consciousness but did not try to get up.

"Thank you, Mr. Darwood," said Finch.

"You just murdered a federal agent." I was struggling to maintain my composure, but I was hoping Finch couldn't tell.

"Former federal agent," he corrected.

I saw Darwood smile as he pushed Brockett's 9mm into the front of his waistband and took up his post across the room again.

"You now have four minutes," Finch advised. "After that, Mr.

Darwood puts a bullet in your fearless principal." He turned to McKee. "You stay here. Darwood, follow me. It's time we took everyone up to higher ground."

Darwood helped the principal to his feet and shoved him toward the door.

Finch jerked Zadie up by the arm and led her out. She let out a scream and struggled against his grip.

Darwood motioned for Mrs. Whiffletree and the housekeeper to get up and they followed behind Finch.

I wasn't sure why Finch had moved the group upstairs. My guess was he expected me to show up within a few minutes and he wanted his prisoners safely tucked away where I couldn't find them.

I watched McKee shut the door of the library after everyone had left the room. Now the fake FBI agent was alone with the lifeless body of a man who had been a real federal investigator, and probably the closest thing I would've ever had as a mentor.

I opened the door of the storage room and sprinted down the long white hall, skidding to a stop in the living room. The place was empty, but I could hear voices upstairs. I slipped over to the library and tried the handle. The door was locked. I took a step back and kicked it open.

McKee, standing by the French doors, phone in hand, looked like a man who'd been caught with his pants down. "What the...?"

I'd tossed one of the flash bangs into the library, and high-tailed it across the living room, the explosion behind me rocking the house. I threw another of the stun grenades into the kitchen for good measure as I sprinted for the stairs.

I didn't get far.

Finch was storming down and when he saw me, he squeezed off several rounds from a silver revolver.

The bullets whizzed by my head, and I ducked back into the white hallway that led to the storage room. I pulled my final flash bang and tossed it around the corner into the living room, the explosion rattling the walls.

Poking my head around the corner I saw Finch and McKee lying face down on the floor. The blast had flattened them. I ran toward the stairs and took them two at a time to the second level.

The hall upstairs was long as the house was from front to back, with four or five rooms peeling off on either side. They were holding Zadie in one of the rooms, and I began with the first on my right. It was dark and unoccupied, and I fumbled my way across it. From the hall, I could hear Finch. He'd recovered, and he was fuming, yelling my name, and mixing in a nice set of obscenities to boot. I ducked into a bathroom and slipped into the bottom of an oversized linen closet. It was time to make good use of the 10k I'd paid Steele.

I gave a quick nod up and the drone, still perched on the ledge of the library fireplace, came to life. With the glasses, I scanned the room. The door was open. McKee had left, and so had Brockett's body.

I flew the drone out of the library and across the living room to the bottom of the stairs. Finch was at the top, his phone to his ear. I couldn't hear him, but I watched him say something, then head downstairs.

I tucked the drone under the stairs and watched Finch go to the front door and open it. It was Dream, and he had Trip, BroFly, Aiden, Price, and Holiday with him. Finch welcomed them in with a smile and shook their hands. But when Dream closed the door, Finch whipped out his revolver and motioned for them to walk. They dropped their smiles and trooped across the living room, disappearing into the library. My phone buzzed. It was Finch.

"Show yourself, Blanco," he said. "I have your friends. You have one minute until one of them takes a bullet."

"That's no way to treat one of your operatives," I said.

I flew the drone to the open library door, keeping it high, just below the ceiling. The new arrivals sat on the floor, huddling together, it looked like BroFly and Trip might spring at their captors at any moment. I prayed they wouldn't.

"Forty-five seconds," Finch said.

He stood by the fireplace, Dream by the French doors. The ice cream man didn't look good. He was wringing his hands, and his face had gone ashen white.

"By the way, Finch," I said, "I've changed my mind about working for you. Something tells me you wouldn't be a good career move for me."

I brought the drone into the room and settled it again on the mantle above the fireplace. Five more people now entered the library. McKee made Zadie, the housekeeper, and the Whiffle-trees join the others on the floor. Darwood, behind them, posted himself by the open door.

"Mr. Blanco, in a different time, a different place, I think you and I could've been something special. You've got great raw talent, kid, the best I've ever seen. No offense to Mr. Darwood." He looked at his watch. "Thirty seconds."

I eased out of the linen closet and slipped across the darkened bedroom to the hallway at the top of the stairs.

"The thing is," I continued with Finch, "I'm a problem solver and you're a problem maker. I don't do drama, Finch, and you're about as screwed up as they get."

In the translucent monitor in the bottom right corner of the glasses, I watched Finch point to Trip.

"Get up," I heard him say.

Trip stood, settling his gaze on Dream. "You told us Nacho had solved the mystery and needed us here. You're a fucking liar, Dream."

The ice cream man looked away.

"Ten seconds, Blanco," said Finch into his phone.

McKee raised his weapon and held it inches from Trip's head.

"No! Please, for God's sake!" yelled the housekeeper. "Don't do this!"

Finch cut his eyes toward Trip. "Five seconds, Mr. Blanco. Four. Three. Two…"

"Keep your panties on, Finch. I'm here."

I walked into the library, pushing past a startled Darwood, and stood in the center before Finch and McKee.

McKee turned the gun on me and told Trip to sit.

Finch pointed to one of the folding chairs. "I had a feeling you'd show."

I decided the best thing I could do was keep my mouth shut for once. So I did.

Finch had me right where I wanted him.

"I'm disappointed," he said. "You had one job to do and that was to find the evidence against this young lady right here to prove she killed Lincoln Hardcastle. You failed."

"I didn't kill Hardcastle!" Zadie looked around, pleading for someone to believe her.

Finch waved her off. "Water under the bridge."

He started to say something more but stopped. There was a noise coming from another part of the house, a crashing and thrashing sound, like someone taking a battering ram to the walls. The clamor was coming from the east side of the house, the side with the storage room, and the greenhouse.

I looked at my watch. Ten twenty-five. Operation 420. I hadn't remembered. TDub was late, but he hadn't forgotten. And I wished now I had just said no when he'd wanted in on solving this mystery.

"I'll check it out." McKee left the room, his weapon drawn.

Within minutes, he'd reappeared holding his firearm on TDub. He motioned for him to sit with the others and turned to Finch. "The gang's all here."

"Perfect." Finch looked around the room. "Any more surprises we need to take care of before we move on?"

"Where's the old man?" asked McKee

Finch looked around the room. "I thought you moved him."

McKee cocked his head and squinted. "Why the hell would I do that?"

I was just as confused as Finch and McKee. Where *was* Brockett's body?

"Find him!" yelled Finch.

McKee sneered. "I don't take orders from you."

Finch turned to Darwood. "Would you be so kind as to find our missing friend and take care of him? He couldn't have gotten far."

If nobody had moved Brockett's body, it could only mean one thing. He was still alive. But how? And could he have made it out of the house in time to stay alive? I wanted so badly to believe he was okay, but I was afraid it would hurt even more if I did and he wasn't.

Darwood spun and left the room.

McKee lowered his face to mine, his teeth gritted. "Are there any other copies of the photo?"

"There are," I said. "And I figured out why it's so important to you. It's the smoking gun. It's the evidence that leads right back to the murder of the CIA operative."

Outside the library, two shots were fired in rapid succession. Everyone jumped, then turned to the door as Darwood entered.

"Found him," he said.

"Good work, Mr. Darwood," Finch said.

I looked up at Dream. "Do you see what's happening here? Is this what they promised you? Kidnappings. A murdered CIA agent. A murdered FBI agent. You want more blood on your hands?"

Dream stammered for an answer. "I don't...I..."

"What'd they promise? They would forgive the debt if you did the job?"

Finch grabbed my collar and pulled me forward. "Who do you think you're fucking dealing with! You're just a pawn."

I gave my head a sudden nod up and watched the video inside the spectacles on my face come to life. I tilted my head to the side bringing the drone fifteen feet above Finch's head.

"Last chance to give up, Finch."

"Give up?" He snorted. "Fuck you, Nacho Blanco."

I brought my head down with a sudden jerk, and the drone hovering above Finch dropped into a free fall. It bounced off Finch's head, surprising him, giving me just the slightest bit of opening I needed to make a jump for his gun. I put both my hands on it and twisted the barrel toward Finch. He let go and I pushed him in front of me with the gun shoved into his ribs.

"You fool!" McKee yelled.

I wasn't sure if he was talking to me or Finch.

"Drop it," I said to McKee, "or your partner eats one right now."

McKee didn't even blink. He raised his pistol and fired at Finch. The private eye doubled over when the slug hit him in the gut, and I let his body drop to the floor.

A collective gasp filled the room, as well as a couple of screams.

I pointed my gun at McKee.

"I wouldn't do that." McKee looked to my left.

Zadie was standing now. Behind her was Dream, and he had a gun pointed at the back of Zadie's head.

She stared at me, eyes wide, a silent tear rolling down her cheek.

I looked at Dream and shook my head. "No."

"I'm sorry," said Dream. The gun in his hand was shaking.

I nodded and dropped Finch's weapon to the ground. Darwood picked it up, putting it inside his waistband next to Brockett's.

"Tell me this, Mr. Dream. How did you get the receipt Aiden

put in Zadie's desk if she's the one who grabbed it from the floor?"

Dreams eyes were blinking, like someone does when a light is suddenly thrown on in a dark room. "She dropped it on a table. I figured it had her prints on it, so I grabbed it."

"Shut the fuck up!" McKee yelled. "This ain't no question-and-answer forum!"

"What do you do now, McKee?" I asked. "Kill us?"

McKee motioned for Dream to step away from Zadie. "Thank you, Mr. Dream. That will be all. Little lady, you may sit down."

Dream took a step back and Zadie fell to the ground with the others, tugging at her skirt. I breathed a sigh of momentary relief.

The gun in McKee's hand barked, and Dream now doubled over just as Finch had, hitting the floor hard.

There was another round of gasps, but no screams this time.

"For the record," McKee said, "I didn't kill the CIA operatives."

"Sullivan. And Hardcastle, too. He was CIA, wasn't he?" I asked.

"Yes, albeit not a very good one," said McKee. "He had some disturbing proclivities toward young ladies, not unlike our dearly departed friend Finch."

Everyone's eyes fell on the body of Finch lying in a bloody heap.

"What about Finch?" I asked. "What was his role in this?"

"His job was to get you to find the evidence against the girl that would send her away for the murder of Hardcastle."

I understood now. "If it looked like someone murdered Hardcastle because he was a pedophile, his death wouldn't be tied to the photo you were missing."

McKee smiled. "Now you're catching on."

"And the imbedded data chip? That was just a cover?"

"You're not as dumb as you look, Blanco."

"Who hired Finch?" I asked. "And what about Dream?"

McKee shook his head. "Fuck this! Did you make a copy of the photo?" He stood in front of the group. "Has he given any of you a photo in recent days and asked you to keep it for him?"

They shook their heads, turning to each other with questioning faces.

"I believe you. I believe all of you." He turned to me. "The picture?"

"Take me to your boss," I said. "Take me to Mr. Unimportant and let the others go. I'll tell him where the copy is. You have my word."

McKee shook his head. "You tell me where the copy is or I kill everyone in this room, starting with your little girlfriend."

"Please no!" Tears drizzled from Zadie's eyes. "Tell him, Nacho. Tell him!"

McKee pressed the muzzle to the crown of her head. "Last chance, Blanco."

Zadie's body trembled as her sobs grew louder. She lowered her chin and waited for the end to come.

I stood. "There's no copy."

McKee pulled the weapon away from Zadie and searched my face. I watched him search for even the slightest hint of deception. He wouldn't find it. I'd played my last card, and McKee had called my bluff.

"There's no hard copy." I pulled my phone from my pocket and tossed it to the floor. "It's on the phone. Let Zadie go. Let them all go."

He lowered the weapon and Zadie crumpled to the floor. He picked up my phone, found the picture I had taken of the photo in Mr. Dream's office, and deleted it. Then he tossed the phone back to the floor.

"There isn't another copy, is there?"

I shook my head. Then I turned to Zadie. She'd stopped crying and I felt her eyes pouring deep into me. I nodded at her before turning back to McKee. I couldn't look at her another second.

He let out a brash laugh. "You little devil. You were stalling, buying time, until you could figure out your next move."

I bit my lip and looked him in the eye.

"But you don't have a next move, do you?"

I didn't say anything. McKee held all the cards now.

He leered at me and raised the pistol. "That's too bad."

The blast caused me to suck in and tighten my body as I braced for the slug. I closed my eyes and clenched both my hands. I waited for the fire in my gut, a burning that would consume me, kill me, as it had Finch and Dream who now lay dead on the floor.

But the fire didn't come.

There was no exploding pain inside me.

My legs didn't give way.

And I opened my eyes to see the collapsed body of McKee crumpled on the floor next to Zadie.

"I knew you couldn't do fuck without me."

I turned around and saw Darwood, his arm outstretched, and Brockett's gun in his hand, still pointing toward where McKee had been standing.

I looked down at my body. There was no gaping hole, no blood. Nobody had shot me. Darwood, at the last second, had taken out McKee.

He pulled his phone from his pocket and jabbed at a number. "It's Darwood. All targets down."

CHAPTER 28

DARWOOD LAYS IT OUT

"Mind telling me what's going on?" I asked.

Darwood massaged his forehead with his left hand and sank down in one of the oversized leather chairs, his right hand still clutching Brockett's 9mm.

"I'll tell you," said a familiar voice behind me.

I spun to see half a dozen Ten Spot police officers, firearms drawn, enter the room. Behind them limped Brockett, his shirt soaked in blood.

I struggled to find my voice. "You're alive."

"Back and better than ever." He put an arm across my shoulder then winced in pain. "Well, almost." He pointed toward Darwood. "Nacho, meet Special Agent Jamison Darwood."

Darwood didn't look up, but he extended his right hand, and we shook.

"I'd like to see some ID," Mr. Whiffletree demanded.

Darwood rolled his eyes, fished a small black wallet from his pocket, and tossed it to the principal.

Whiffletree studied the badge. "He *is* FBI."

Everyone in the room wanted to see the ID and passed it around.

"But you were dead!" Zadie said to Brockett. "I saw him shoot you! I saw the blood. It's still on you!"

Brockett smiled and unbuttoned his shirt to reveal a bullet resistant vest.

"Kevlar," I said.

"Which is why Darwood volunteered to shoot me," he said.

"But the blood?" asked Zadie, feebly running a hand through her mangled, chopped hair on the right side of her face.

"Specially designed optics packet in the bulletproof vest. When a bullet strikes the vest, the packet releases a certain amount of blood to give the impression the victim is dead." He turned to Darwood. "Still hurts to take a slug even with the Kevlar."

I turned to the housekeeper and pointed to Zadie. There were red blood splatters across the front of her black sweater. "Rachel, do you have a top she could borrow? I promise to get it back to you."

Rachel nodded curtly and left the room.

I turned back to Brockett. "How did you get out of the library?"

"When McKee left the room, I slipped out, but I couldn't make it to the front door. I didn't realize how weak I was from the knife wound. The impact from the shot to the vest only intensified the pain. I ducked into the kitchen and that's when you guys all moved into the library. I waited until I heard Jamison tell everyone he would finish me off. When he came out, he helped me to the front door, and I rounded up the police."

"I heard two pops," said TDub.

"Straight into that white sofa out there," said Darwood.

I looked at Brockett. "All this time he was undercover?"

Brockett gave me a sly smile. "All this time."

"I was already here investigating Hardcastle's murder when you stumbled onto the scene," Darwood explained. "Once we realized you weren't backing off, and that you might have an advantage over an outsider like me, my role changed. They gave me the assignment of keeping tabs on you. When things started getting hot, I got worried. I kept trying to convince Finch to fire your ass to extrapolate you from the danger."

"That's why you were spying on me when I was with Zadie in the back alley," I said to Darwood.

"Where's that business card Darcy gave you?" Brockett asked.

I dug it out of my wallet.

"That isn't your normal Office Depot special," he said. "It has a GPS tracker inside, and with our phones Agent Darwood and I could track you wherever this card went. That's why Darcy insisted you take it."

I looked at Darwood. "You tracked where I was all the time."

"We both did," said Brockett. "Which is how we were able to follow you to that warehouse. We had eyes on you the whole time."

"What about the knife in your back last night?" I asked. "Despite the police report, I'm guessing that wasn't an accident."

Brockett shook his head. "I don't know who got me. Whoever it was waited for me in the kitchen. Could've been one of them." He pointed to the bodies of Finch, Dream, and McKee.

"There's something else I don't understand," I said. "What happened at the cabin between Ms. Baxter and me?"

Brocket chuckled sheepishly. "We were trying to get you away from the danger we saw coming. Darcy was with me in the hospital when you called to say the cabin had blown up and they had taken Zadie. I told her we needed to get you to a safe location. We both assumed you wouldn't volunteer to go, so it was my idea to have you arrested and locked up until I could get you out."

He paused, I waited, and he continued.

"Anyway, we heard you'd escaped. Big surprise there! I told Darcy, 'That boy will be the death of me!'"

"I almost was." I let out a shaky laugh.

The housekeeper returned and handed me a gray hoodie. I

handed it to Zadie, and she slipped into the restroom and changed. When she came out, she looked fresh and alive, the hoodie snugging her perfectly. She'd also cut the other side of her hair to even up both sides. She sidled up to me and I wrapped my arm around her waist.

"You saved me, Nacho." There was a sparkle in her beautiful green eyes, and I savored her now familiar but no less amazing scent of rose petals and sweet almond milk.

"You look great with short hair, too," I said.

She laughed. "I almost asked to wear Mrs. Whiffletree's blonde wig but decided I wasn't gonna go there again!" Her voice took on a more serious tone. "There's something I need to tell you. It's about…"

"Sorry to break up this little reunion," said a paramedic across the room, "but we will need everyone to get into an ambulance or a police car and head to the hospital. The doctors will need to check everyone before being cleared."

"Not yet," I said.

An officer I didn't recognize approached me. "I'm Detective Larry Books. We spoke on the phone." He extended his hand to me as a peace offering, and I accepted it. "We need to get everyone to the hospital."

Darwood stood and leaned toward me. "What's going on?"

"I know who did it," I said.

He cut his eyes at me. "Who killed Hardcastle?"

I nodded. "Agent Sullivan, too. I can prove it, but not here."

"Where do you want us to go?" asked Brockett.

"Back to Mr. Dream's Ice Cream. That's where I'm gonna explain the entire mystery of the murder of Dr. Lincoln Hardcastle."

CHAPTER 29

M.O.M.

What should have been a three-minute trip from the Whiffletree's house to Mr. Dream's took much longer. Darwood and I had to put everyone into groups, and we assigned each group to someone in law enforcement who transported them in a Ten Spot police cruiser. Mr. and Mrs. Whiffletree and Rachel rode together with Darwood. Trip, BroFly, and TDub were a group, with their own officer, as were Aiden, Price and Holiday. And Zadie and Brockett and I rode with Detective Books. During the drive, I called Chuck and asked him to meet us. Forty minutes later everyone assembled in the dining area of Mr. Dream's now long-lost dream.

"This place gives me the creeps," said Zadie. "It feels dead now."

She was right. Dream's murder, not to mention his duplicity, hung like a pall over the place, making the restaurant feel more like a lifeless mortuary than a tasty gallery of frozen art.

I walked to the center of the room. "Let's get started. I want to explain to you who murdered Dr. Lincoln Hardcastle, how it was done, and why. The M.O.M."

"The mom?" TDub scrunched his face.

"Means. Opportunity. Motive."

Price jumped up. "Oh my God! Is the murderer in here right now?"

Darwood moved over to Price and pointed to her chair. She sat down to pout.

"Let's begin," I said, "on the day Hardcastle died, Saturday, August fifteenth. The coroner estimated his death to be around two or three o'clock that day. Somebody had cut both his wrists as he sat in his favorite chair. And as he sat there, he bled out. He was discovered later that day about four o'clock."

"That was me!" Price's arm shot up. "I was the first to see Dr. Hard-On dead."

I continued. "Price was the first to find the body of Dr. Hardcastle. She had left her phone in the counseling office that day after her appointment and had gone back to the office at four to retrieve it.

Price beamed, as though thrilled to be a part of the dramatic narrative.

"Every Saturday morning Hardcastle made a trip from Austin to Ten Spot for individualized counseling appointments. He had five patients, all of them in this room right now. Zadie's appointment was always at nine, followed by Holiday at ten, and Price at eleven. Aiden came in at noon followed by TDub at one. My guess is when TDub's appointment was over, Hardcastle hung around the office for an hour or two doing paperwork and whatnot since he wouldn't be back again for a week." I paused and looked at Hardcastle's five clients. "Do I have the schedule correct?"

"Except," said Zadie, "that Saturday I wasn't there. I was sick and stayed in Austin."

I snapped my fingers and pointed at her. "That's right. That morning Price asked Hardcastle about Zadie, and the doctor said she stayed at home because she was sick."

The front door of the restaurant opened, ringing the bells above it. Everyone turned to see the newcomer. It was Chuck.

He flashed a manila folder for me to see, then quietly settled into an empty chair at the back with Brockett.

"Keep in mind," I continued, "at first blush, one might assume his death to be your run-of-the mill suicide. He's by himself. He cuts his wrists. He sits quietly until he bleeds out and dies."

"But why would he want to kill himself?" asked BroFly.

"I'm glad you asked," I said. "It would seem that the good doctor wasn't so good." I turned to each of Hardcastle's five patients and added, "Was he?"

Zadie, Holiday, Price, and Aiden shook their heads.

"We'll get to that in a moment," I said. "For now, let's just say somebody had some compromising information on Hardcastle, information that most likely would send him to jail for a very long time. That's something that could lead a person like Hardcastle to commit suicide. Or at least that's what somebody might want us to think."

"Are you saying somebody killed Hardcastle but tried to make it look like a suicide?" asked Aiden.

"That's what I'm saying. And that person came close to getting away with it."

"How can you be certain it wasn't a suicide?" Holiday asked. "I mean, if somebody had something on him and if everything looked like a suicide, what makes you think it wasn't?"

"Because of the cuts on his wrists." I looked around the room. "Does someone have a wristwatch I can use, the kind with a traditional face and hands?"

Brockett did and passed it up to me. I put it on, fastening it so the face was on the inside of my wrist.

"If I wanted to slice my own wrists," I said, "I would take the blade in my right hand and I might make a cut from left to right, from nine o'clock to three o'clock. If I was in a hurry and I wasn't paying attention, the cuts might be at an angle, from the top left to the bottom right. Or you might say from ten o'clock to four o'clock."

I held up my right hand and pantomimed the motion as though holding a blade. Everybody did the same. Brockett and Darwood looked at each other and nodded in agreement.

I turned to Holiday. "What would you do if you wanted to cut your right wrist?"

"Put the blade in my left hand," she said.

"Exactly. And again, you might cut in a straight line, from right to left, or from three o'clock to nine. But if you were in a hurry, you might cut from top right to the bottom left, from two o'clock to eight. Like this." I pantomimed this motion also.

Again, everybody copied the motion on his own wrists, and agreed.

"He's right!" said BroFly. "At an angle, the marks on the wrists would be opposite each other. Like mirror reflections."

"Only Hardcastle's cuts weren't like that," I said. "Somebody had sliced both wrists from the bottom right to the top left. From four o'clock to ten o'clock. That would be very impractical for Hardcastle to do, if he was making the cuts himself. Both cuts start from the bottom of his wrists and go up and angle the same way."

"What does that mean?" asked Mr. Whiffletree.

"It means somebody stood in front of him and sliced his wrists," I said. "This wasn't a suicide. It was homicide. It was murder. And that person was in a hurry, so much so, they didn't think about which way the cuts should go."

"But why would he just sit there and let someone cut his wrists?" asked Trip.

"Maybe somebody tied his ass down." said TDub.

"I thought about that," I said, "but there were no ligature marks on his wrists from a rope or zip ties or whatever."

"He just let someone cut him?" Trip looked around the room at everyone, his mouth open. "Damn!"

"I'll get to that," I said. "There's one more thing I want to say before we move on to my next point. The killer had to be right-handed."

"Why?" Holiday asked.

"A left-handed person would have made both cuts from eight to two, from bottom left to top right. But the forensic photographs show us Hardcastle's cuts go from four to ten on both wrists, and that tells me that the murderer was right-handed."

"That leaves me out." TDub raised his left arm. "I'm left-handed!"

"That's right," I said. "TDub punches with his left and he holds a gun with his left. Trust me on that one!"

I sat on top of a table, propping my feet in a chair.

"This past Monday afternoon, Zadie told me somebody had put a note in her desk along with a razor blade." I pulled the note out of my pocket and read it aloud.

Cutters get what they deserve

"That's all it said. Plus it came with razor blade. There was what appeared to be blood on the blade, and my friend Chuck had that blade and one other analyzed." I turned to Chuck. "What did you find?"

"No blood," he said. "The best we can tell it was some kind of red syrup."

"Like strawberry syrup, the kind you might find in an ice cream shop like this one?" I asked.

"Yep," Chuck confirmed.

"At first," I said, "I thought this was a simple case of high school bullying. But then I found out Hardcastle had died from cuts on his wrists, and my client, Zadie, had been one of his patients. I had to ask myself the question: Was somebody trying to point a finger at Zadie?

"Aiden got one too," said BroFly. "In fact, somebody put a whole box in his backpack."

Everybody looked at Aiden.

"Go on, Aiden," I said. "Now's the time."

Aiden looked around the room, and after a deep sigh he said, "I put the razor blade in Zadie's desk."

"You lied to us?" Trip asked in surprise.

Aiden dropped his eyes to the floor.

"Who gave you the box of razor blades?" I asked.

"Mr. Dream."

"But why would you do that?" Zadie asked Aiden.

Aiden fought back the tears. "Dream said he would give me free frozen yogurt for the rest of my life if I pulled a prank for him. He gave me the note and the blade and said he wanted me to put them in the Zadie's desk." Aiden paused, choking back his emotions. "I swear I didn't give anyone else a razor blade."

"I believe that," I said. "Most likely Dream put the other blade in my grandmother's flowers. Or maybe it was Finch or Atkins or McKee. Doesn't matter. But it was just one more link in a case they were trying to build against Zadie."

"But why would Mr. Dream ask Aiden to do that?" Holiday asked.

"Because Mr. Dream owed $30,000 to someone for an ice cream business that was failing. When he couldn't pay it back somebody made him an offer he couldn't refuse. They told him the debt would be forgiven if he did this one little job."

"I still don't understand," said Price.

"At first I didn't understand," I said, "until Zadie mentioned something to me earlier today. She said if I wanted someone to hire me for a case, I needed to give that person a reason to do so. That made me think about this business with the razor blade. When Dream asked Aiden to plant that blade in Zadie's desk, he gave Zadie a reason to hire me, or at least get me in her life."

"Why would Dream want you and Zadie together?" Price asked.

"For me to find the evidence someone planted that would implicate Zadie in the murder of Lincoln Hardcastle."

The room got silent and I could see it in their faces. The dime had dropped.

"Let me get this straight," said BroFly. "Somebody wanted you to find planted evidence that would convict Zadie of the murder of Hardcastle. So they tell Dream to make it happen and they would wipe out the $30,000 he owed. He agrees and hires Aiden who puts a razor blade in Zadie's desk. She comes to you, you take the bait, mission accomplished."

"Exactly!" I said.

"But why would someone want to point the finger at Zadie?" asked TDub.

"Somebody wanted Hardcastle dead but needed a scapegoat to take the blame," I answered.

TDub stood. "Who's the motherfucker that wanted Dr. Hardcastle dead?"

"We all did," said Holiday.

"What?" TDub scrunched up his face again. "Why'd y'all want him dead?"

I didn't wait for one of the four to speak. "Now we're talking about motive. Remember I said we would talk about means, motive, and opportunity. Who had a reason, a motive, for killing Hardcastle? Aiden did. He suffered from the constant belittling and bullying from Hardcastle. The three girls did too, because of something Hardcastle called touch therapy."

Now Darwood spoke up. "What the hell is touch therapy?"

"He told the girls touch therapy was a way to get in touch with their inner selves. In reality, it was Hardcastle's way of manipulating his female patients into letting him sexually abuse them. Hardcastle might have been a licensed counselor, but he was also a narcissist, a misogynist, and a pedophile. He probably felt entitled to take or do whatever he wanted. It's been stated he recorded the sessions as well, although nobody has recovered any video evidence."

Price lifted her head and wiped the tears from her eyes. "I hated him. I was glad he was dead. But I didn't kill him."

Zadie put an arm around Price. Holiday put a hand on Zadie's arm.

I went on. "Hardcastle was emotionally abusive and a sexual predator, but there's another reason somebody wanted him dead. There is somebody else in this room who had a motive, and it had nothing to do with bullying or touch therapy."

I looked at Brockett. He was smiling. And for just a moment, I had a feeling Dad would've been too.

"TDub, did Hardcastle ever tell you anything about himself you found interesting?"

"He said he was a spy or a secret agent or some cool shit like that."

I looked back at the group. "TDub's right. Hardcastle was CIA. He was deep undercover, working as a counselor, but searching for a killer."

"Somebody else got killed?" Zadie asked.

I leaned back and crossed my arms. "About five years ago, another agent came to Ten Spot. Her name was Stephanie Sullivan. Somebody poisoned her with ethylene glycol, or antifreeze, as we know it."

"Like your grandmother!" said Zadie.

I turned to Chuck. "And unless I missed my mark, like somebody else too."

"You've missed nothing," Chuck said. He opened the manila folder and pulled out some papers. "The toxicology report on Hardcastle says he also had ethylene glycol in his blood stream when he died."

I turned to Trip. "There's your answer. Hardcastle was most likely given some kind of drink that had a large dose of antifreeze in it. He would've never noticed the taste if the drink was sweet. Shortly after drinking it, he would've become loopy and disoriented. That's how the killer could cut his wrists without a struggle and without his arms tied."

"But who else would want Hardcastle dead?" asked BroFly.

"The person who wanted him dead," I said, "was the same person who'd killed CIA operative Stephanie Sullivan. Hardcastle, despite his depraved appetite for underage women, had found the evidence he needed to arrest Sullivan's killer. But instead of handing over the suspect and the evidence to the authorities, he waited."

"Why?" asked Trip.

"I can't explain it," I said. "I mean, we're talking about someone who was CIA and a licensed counselor. But I think he used those positions and his power for his own thrills. He wasn't a good person. He wanted money, sex, and power, and he was willing to do whatever it took to get as much as he could of all three."

"Wait a minute," said BroFly. "Are you saying in this room right now is the person who killed two people?"

"In a manner of speaking, yes." I stood up from where I'd been sitting on the table. "Follow me. I'll prove it."

CHAPTER 30

ROSE NOIR

I led the group down the narrow hall on the back of the restaurant to what had been Dream's small office. The lock on the door still hung limply in several tangled pieces. I squeezed into the room, positioned myself by his desk, and waited until everyone had crowded in.

I pointed to the photograph of Mr. Dream, Mr. and Mrs. Whiffletree, and Dr. Hardcastle standing together with big smiles and arms around each other. "That's your evidence."

"What's that prove?" asked Mr. Whiffletree.

"You all went into a business partnership with Mr. Dream when he began this ice cream shop," I said.

"That's correct. We've known Mr. Dream for several years now," he said. "We only met the Hardcastles that one time."

"And you and Mrs. Whiffletree, along with the Hardcastles, loaned him the money to build this place. Is that correct also?" I asked.

He nodded. "Damn skippy."

"Had he paid you back any of the money?" I asked.

Mr. Whiffletree shook his head. "I figured it would be quite a while before I would see that money again."

"What has this got to do with us?" asked Mrs. Whiffletree.

"Agent Sullivan also had ethylene glycol in her system, but

that was not the cause of death. Somebody strangled her with a thirty-two-inch sterling silver chain necklace from Tiffany and Company. But her killer made a mistake by leaving that necklace, the murder weapon, around her neck. That was unfortunate for the killer because she'd been wearing that same necklace in a photograph like this one." I pointed again to the picture hanging on the wall.

"Nobody in this picture is wearing a necklace," said Price.

"Not in this picture," I said. "Somebody swapped out the photos. I saw the original and snagged a shot of it before someone traded it out for this one. That's the photo McKee kept asking me about, the one he deleted from my phone. In that original photo, there are not four people present, but five. And one of them is wearing the same Tiffany and Company necklace used to kill CIA agent Stephanie Sullivan. I know because the heart pendant on the necklace was flipped over. And anyone who saw the photo would've easily read the engraving on the back. *Act as if.* That's what it said. The same words on the back of the heart pendant attached to the necklace used to kill Agent Sullivan." I paused and looked at Rachel. "Isn't that right, Mrs. Hardcastle?"

Everyone turned to look at the housekeeper.

Her face reddened. "I don't understand."

I moved my way through the group crowded into the small office until I was standing in front of her. "I believe you do. That was your necklace used to kill Agent Sullivan. You were wearing it in the first photo I saw in this frame. I don't know who gave that necklace to you, or maybe you bought it yourself, but the inscription on the back of the little heart, would make sense. *Act as if.* That fits you, doesn't it?"

The housekeeper didn't say anything. She tried to take a step back from me, but the room was so full there was no place for her to move, and I pressed into her with more accusations.

"To the Whiffletrees, you are Rachel Bates," I said. "But beneath that wig you're Gloria Burton Hardcastle."

"That is absurd!"

"I don't think so." I took an exaggerated whiff of the air. A mixture of rose petals and sweet almond milk filled my nostrils. "Zadie, do you recognize the cologne she's wearing?"

Zadie, who was standing only one person away, breathed in and nodded. "That's what I was going to tell you back at the house. I knew it was Mrs. Hardcastle the moment I saw her. The perfume? It's the same one she gave me. It's called Rose Noir." She leaned in closer to the housekeeper. "I recognized it when those guys made us all sit in the library at the principal's house. I also recognized her when she came into the room."

"Rose Noir," I repeated. "Black Rose. You both wear it."

Zadie nodded.

I looked at the housekeeper. "And when I had you find a top for Zadie, you didn't go to your boss, Mrs. Whiffletree. You gave me one of yours because you knew it would fit Zadie perfectly. It's yours, isn't it, Mrs. Hardcastle? You and Zadie wore the same size. That's why I asked you to help her tonight. It even smells like Rose Noir."

The housekeeper performer was shaking. Her bottom lip quivered. Her eyes darted around the room to the faces watching her final act.

"I think you'll also find she's not as old as she pretends. It's amazing what a little stage make-up can do for a person these days. But you know all about that sort of thing, being a theater major at Overton. Right, Mrs. Hardcastle? *Act as if.* Makes sense that'd be your necklace."

She was on the verge of tears now, her voice quiet and small. "I didn't kill my husband. I swear."

I went on. "Either you or Finch told Dream that if he helped cover up the murder, you'd forgive his debt."

She closed her eyes tight and shook her head violently.

I continued. "When I asked Dream about Hardcastle's death earlier this week, he told me you called him at three o'clock that day to tell him your husband was dead. But Price didn't find the body until four, and the police got there after that."

She was crying softly now. Her eyes were shut, and silent tears flowed down her cheeks. "No. No. No. No. You can't prove any of this."

"Detective Books, did you bring in your fingerprint kit?" I asked.

"Like you said." He pressed his way through the group until he was standing beside me.

"Would someone hand me that photograph on the wall?" I asked.

BroFly handed it to me. I gave it to the detective who removed it from its frame and glass and began dusting it.

"What are you doing?" Mrs. Hardcastle complained more than asked. "You won't find my prints on there."

"I'm not looking for your prints." I said. "I'm looking for mine."

"Wait…what…I…"

"The other day, I saw a photo in the Whiffletree's house, a photo of Mr. Dream, the Whiffletrees, and your husband. I'm guessing you were the one holding the camera the day it was taken. I picked up the picture and I said that I'd seen another almost like it. Only two people heard me say that. You, Mrs. Hardcastle, and Mrs. Whiffletree. One of you came over here in the middle of the night to swap out the photos."

"But how can you be sure it's the same one?" Mrs. Whiffletree asked.

"I got a print," said the detective. He held up a white card to show the print he had lifted from the photo.

"Now take my thumb print," I said.

The detective inked my thumb and I placed it on a separate white card. He held the two prints side by side. "Perfect match," he said.

"That proves it," I said. "This is the photo that was in the Whiffletree's house, the one I touched, which means that either Mrs. Hardcastle or Mrs. Whiffletree swapped out the pictures."

"You can't prove I was here," Mrs. Hardcastle said defiantly.

Gone now was the self-effacing, meek servant of a lady she'd pretended to be as the Whiffletrees' housekeeper. "How do you know it wasn't her?"

I pointed my index finger in the air and wagged it. "It's not her because she's not the one who hired Finch. You did."

Mrs. Hardcastle shook her head. "I'd never even heard of him before today."

I pointed at her. "That's a lie. Last night at the party, you asked all of us what we wanted to drink. Finch was there being his usual obnoxious self. He said nothing, and yet you brought him his favorite, the old bartender's special. You knew his drink because you knew him."

She dropped her head to her chest. "Please stop."

"Mrs. Whiffletree gave me one of the small loaves of bread you'd baked for the school. I gave it to Finch. He was deathly allergic to nuts, and he asked me where I got it in case it had nuts in it. I told him it came from the Whiffletrees. He smiled and took it, knowing that you were the one who'd baked it. He told me just a few days ago you vowed never to put nuts in bread again."

"She could've baked it!" Mrs. Hardcastle pointed to Mrs. Whiffletree.

"But I can't bake or cook," Mrs. Whiffletree said.

"That's right," I said. "She can't. She's a restaurateur who can't bake or cook. Mrs. Hardcastle, you were the only one in the house who could cook. Finch took the loaf because he knew it was from you."

A heavy pall hung over the quiet room now.

"You were Stephanie Sullivan's roommate," I went on. "Somebody found out she was an undercover agent working a case here in Ten Spot and that person put you up to killing her. But you made a mistake. You left your Tiffany and Company chain necklace, the one with the heart pendant, the murder weapon, at the scene of the crime. Later, you remembered there was a photo of you wearing it, a photo taken only a few months earlier when Dream opened this place. And with that pendant and its inscription on the back, there would be no mistaking who it belonged to. As long as nobody discovered that photo you were fine."

I paused to take a deep breath.

"But somewhere along the way a man named Lincoln Hardcastle comes to Ten Spot. He's CIA and he's also undercover. He's trying to figure out who killed Sullivan. My guess is you were the Agency's number one suspect. You were the roommate. He begins a relationship with you, ends up falling in love with you, and you two get married and settle in Austin. And then somewhere along the way he finds the photograph and realizes he has the proof he's been looking for. But he doesn't turn you in. And he also doesn't destroy the evidence, either. He's playing both ends against the middle. He gives the photo to the one person nobody would suspect for safekeeping – Mr. Dream. But somebody, I'm guessing it was a man known to me as Mr. Unimportant, was unhappy with your mistake. So you had Dr. Hardcastle, your own husband, killed. And you hired Finch to help pin the murder on Zadie." I paused for a moment to collect my breath and my thoughts. "If you just hadn't left that beautiful, expensive, necklace."

With both hands, Mrs. Hardcastle smeared the tears on her cheeks. "You can't prove any of this."

"Look at this video." Using my phone, I played the security video of someone who looked like Zadie going into the cafeteria. "That's you. You and Zadie are the same size. She told me she would borrow clothes from you. And Mrs. Whiffletree has a wig that is remarkably similar to Zadie's hair. Somehow you slipped into Zadie's room, through a window she never locks is my guess. You got Zadie's clothes, you put on the wig, and you came into the school to murder my grandmother. Do you know what outfit Zadie wore Tuesday?"

I didn't give her a chance to respond but kept going.

"I do. I notice things like that. She had on a grey sweatshirt and blue jeans rolled at the bottom. That's the day my grand-mother was found on the floor of the kitchen. But we just saw this video. This person is wearing the outfit Zadie wore on Monday. I'm guessing you figured nobody would notice the change in the outfits. You just thought if you could kill my grandmother and pin that on Zadie too, we would have an airtight case against her, and you could send her to jail for the murder of Hardcastle. Isn't that right?"

"I think I need an attorney," Mrs. Hardcastle said softly.

I nodded. "I think that would be a very wise idea."

"Come with me," Books ordered. He led her through the group that crowded the room. "Darwood, I'm taking her to lock up. You can find her there if you need her." As they passed through the door, I heard him begin to Mirandize her.

When they'd gone, the rest of us headed back down the hall toward the dining room. I drew in a deep breath and sighed, happy to be back in less cramped quarters, ready to begin the last and hardest part of the narrative.

I turned to the Whiffletrees. "You're gonna need a new housekeeper."

"Mrs. Hardcastle killed Mr. Hardcastle?" Trip asked.

"In a manner of speaking," I said. "Actually, she was a part of an elaborate…"

Darwood interrupted me. "We're missing two."

Everyone began looking around.

"Who's missing?" TDub asked.

"Zadie," I said, "and Holiday."

"They must've slipped out the back door in the hall," said Darwood.

"I think I know where they went," I said. "Come on!"

CHAPTER 31

THE SCOOP

I broke out in a full sprint from the parking lot of Dream's to Hardcastle's office. Two blocks south on East Travis and a block over on Sumner. Darwood paced me the whole way. Inside the office suite we found them, Zadie in Hardcastle's brown leather high back chair, Holiday standing by the terrycloth blue one.

That's when I noticed Zadie had a single, flat edge razor blade in her right hand.

"What's going on, Zadie?" I asked, panting, still trying to catch my breath from the run.

She didn't look up. The deadly sharp thin piece of metal flashed just above her left wrist, like a copperhead waiting to strike.

"Zadie," Holiday said, "put the blade down and let me hug you."

She looked up, confused, as though only just aware that she wasn't alone. "She told me it was the only way."

"Will you give me the blade?" I asked.

"We teach people how to treat us. I told you that. Remember?"

"I remember," I said.

"It's my fault." She lowered her head but kept her eyes up. "That's what Dr. Hardcastle said. He said I was teaching him to take me."

I shook my head. "No, Zadie, it wasn't your fault. He was rotten. You didn't teach him that."

She lowered the blade to her wrist and allowed the thin edge to touch the transparent layer of skin above the bulging purple vein below it.

I took a step closer. "Please don't!"

Holiday inched closer to her, a few feet from Zadie. "It's not your fault, Zadie. He did it to me too. Please don't hurt yourself. He's not worth it."

Darwood tapped me on the shoulder. "Holiday's too close, Nacho. She needs to move back."

I reached out for Holiday's arm, but Zadie was already out of the chair. She lunged for Holiday, spinning around behind her, thrusting the deadly steel to Holiday's neck, just above her jugular.

"Stop!" Darwood yelled.

I took a step forward, but that only made Zadie tense, and she gripped Holiday tighter with her free arm, scraping the blade across Holiday's neck.

"She has to pay!" Zadie screamed. "She did this to me!"

Holiday was trembling, and her eyes pooled with tears. She was trying not to move, but she couldn't stop shaking.

I lowered into the leather high back and crossed a leg over the other. "I don't understand."

"You don't understand?" Zadie knit her brows and glared. "She gave my journal to that fucker! He read it. He read the whole fucking plan!"

"Hardcastle's wife told you to do it, didn't she?" I asked.

Zadie let out a deep guttural laugh and lowered her eyes at me. "I never heard anything about the picture or the agent she killed. Her husband was a monster, and he wanted to adopt me so he could rape me whenever he wanted. She didn't protect me. She said the only way I could ever be free was to kill him. She's the one who told me how to do it."

While she talked, she kept the blade pressed tight against the side of Holiday's neck.

I folded my hands in my lap and casually swung the crossed leg back and forth over the other. "I'm listening."

"She made this drink. She told me to give it to him. She said it would make him sleepy. After that, I could cut his wrists and it would look like a suicide. She said if I did it, she and I would be free for the rest of our lives."

I stood up.

Zadie smiled at the blade threatening Holiday's neck. "It's your fault, Holiday. If you hadn't been so careless with the journal, he wouldn't have seen it. It would've been so easy. But you let him find out. Do you know what I had to do because of you?"

She pressed the blade in further and a thin trickle of blood seeped down Holiday's neck.

Zadie looked affectionately at the silver blade. "I'm good at knowing how much pressure I can get away with before the blade cuts, and the blood drips. I have so much experience, so much practice." She laughed again.

I took a step toward the pair. "Zadie, listen. You're hurting Holiday. You've cut her. It was Mrs. Hardcastle's fault. When the coroner didn't rule his death a suicide, she pinned the whole thing on you. She wanted the insurance money and she used you. She's the one that needs to pay."

I slipped Hardcastle's ring from my pinky finger and held it out.

"Take this," I said. "This is him. This is the one who hurt you. Cut this ring. Stomp it. Bite it. Break it. Do to it what you want to do to him."

With the blade still firm against Holiday's neck, Zadie took the ring, rotating it around and around.

"You think this is what I need to feel better? Are you that fucking stupid, Mr. Problem Solver Investigator?"

She hurled the ring across the room. It smacked the wall hard and broke apart, the two pieces landing a few feet from each other. I walked across the room and picked up the two halves and noticed what looked to be a small black data chip inside the ring's crown. The end of the chip had the same connector as an iPhone cable.

Zadie loosened her grip on Holiday. "What's that?"

I held up the chip so she could see it. Her breathing had gotten more even, and she dropped both arms to her side, letting go of Holiday who ran to Darwood.

"Looks like a storage device," said Darwood. "Will it plug into your phone?"

I pulled my phone from my pants and flipped the chip around. It plugged into the charging port perfectly. I thumbed through several pages of apps until I came across an unknown file titled "Sessions." I opened it and a menu of recorded videos populated my screen. I tapped the last one. It was time stamped as two fourteen, Saturday, August fifteenth.

All four of us watched the video unfold on my screen.

It was the last few minutes of Dr. Hardcastle's life, and he and Zadie were in the same office where we now stood. The recording showed Hardcastle sitting in his brown leather chair in the center of the room. He had on a pair of blue jeans and a black short sleeve button down. He was talking and I turned up the volume as high as it would go.

"You want me, don't you?" Zadie said off-camera, elsewhere in the room.

"I always want you," said Hardcastle, stroking the salt-and-pepper beard. "You can be my mistress."

She laughed as she came into view on the screen. She was naked from the waist up, standing in front of him wearing a pair of tight red shorts. She leaned over him, her breasts in front of his face, and whispered something in his ear. He grabbed at her, but she was too quick, and jumped back before he could cop a feel.

"You're a naughty doctor." She wagged an index finger at him. "Or should I call you daddy?"

He licked his lips. "Your shorts look uncomfortable."

She put a finger to her lips, bit, and sucked. "Oh, doctor, you're right," she said with a sultry, pouty kind of voice. "I am so uncomfortable."

We watched Zadie peel off the red shorts and kick them to one side. She had on a white thong, and she adjusted it for his benefit.

"Is this better?" She twirled around in front of him, her breasts bouncing.

He reached for her, but she backed away from him again before his hands could take her.

She giggled. "Do you want to play doctor with me, daddy?"

He grinned, watching her with devilish eyes, and adjusted his tightening pants.

She reached behind her and picked up two drinks, handing one to him. They clinked their glasses and drank. Hardcastle downed his in one large gulp, then wiped his mouth with the back of his hand.

"What a thirsty boy you are," she said, still using her pouty voice. "Would my favorite doctor like more?"

She refilled his glass, and he downed this one too, his eyes fixed to her playful breasts.

She refilled the glass yet again, and he drank it all. Having had enough, and eager for her, he tried to stand but couldn't find his legs. Still Zadie filled his glass a fourth time, lifting it to his lips.

"Drink up, lover," she said.

He did, but by now, it was obvious he was unaware and didn't care.

We watched on the screen as Zadie set the glass down behind her and walked over to Hardcastle who sat motionless in his chair. Standing in front of him, she stretched out both of his arms, his palms up. She pulled a thin, silver, single-edged razor blade from the pocket of her discarded shorts and made a quick slash on his left wrist, from bottom right to top left. From four to ten. Then she did the same on his right.

Hardcastle said nothing. He didn't move. He didn't cry out in pain. He didn't look at his wrists. He sat in his chair and stared ahead like some comatose zombie, unaware that his life was now going to leak from his veins onto the carpet below.

Zadie leaned over him, her naked breasts in front of lifeless eyes. "Are you in there? Do you still want to touch them? They're beautiful, aren't they? Do it. You know you want me." She moaned into his ear and giggled. Then she stood and faced him. "I guess not. Have it your way. Good-fucking-bye, Dr. Hard-On."

From an oversized purse, she pulled a long red wig, a Texas Rangers baseball cap, a pair of blue jeans, and a red hoodie. She dressed, slipping the wig over her own hair before putting on the cap. She put the t-shirt and red shorts she'd been wearing in the handbag. She poured the remaining contents of both glasses into a wine bottle, stuck on the cork, and put the glasses and the bottle into the bag. She wiped both sides of the razor blade with the bottom of the red hoodie, placed the blade against Hardcastle's left thumb, before letting it drop into the gathering pool of blood below him.

She took a step back to admire her work. Then, almost as an afterthought, she removed a pinky ring from his left hand and slipped it on her right forefinger, holding it up to the light to see it better. It was a signet ring, silver with a flat onyx adorning the top.

"A little reminder of our dearly departed doctor," she said.

She gave the room one last look before leaving.

The last image on the video was Hardcastle sitting alone in

the brown leather high back, silent and unmoving, unaware and dying. At last his eyes closed and his head slumped to his chest.

I turned off the video. Zadie collapsed to the floor. She was sitting on the same blood-stained area of the carpet she'd created only two months earlier.

"It was his only weakness," she whispered. "Sex was the only thing I had over him. He wanted to teach me to be his slut. I became one to teach him how not to treat me. I had to do it. It was the only way I could be free."

Hidden leverage. Just like Steele had said. And Hardcastle had never seen it coming.

The razor blade that Zadie had held against Holiday only minutes earlier now lay on the floor. I kicked it across the room and dropped down beside her on the carpet. She put her head on my shoulder. I put an arm around her and pulled her close.

"I'm sorry, Zadie. I'm so sorry."

The street outside Hardcastle's counseling office looked like a set straight out of Hollywood. A dozen cop cars blocked the road on either side with some pulled up in the middle. The alternating red and blue lights cast an ominous glow on the exteriors of the surrounding businesses. Ten Spot PD had once again hung yellow crime scene tape around the exterior of the counseling office, as it had a mere two months earlier. There were half a dozen cops outside patrolling the area, keeping the curious onlookers at bay. It surprised me to see so many people up as it was already well past midnight. News travels fast in Ten Spot, especially if it's grisly. Nobody wants to miss the worst in others.

Leaning against one of the patrol cars parked near the yellow tape, Darwood and I found ourselves as outsiders looking in. The cops were inside the office now, questioning Zadie, processing the scene. They'd interviewed Holiday, and she stood tucked in a blanket next to a female officer at an adjacent car, a bandage wrapped around her neck. We stood there, Darwood and I, quietly, and I was glad for the chance to think.

At last the door to the counseling center opened and Zadie came out, her hands cuffed behind her, an officer on either side, each with a tight grip around her arms. I saw several flashes from the small crowd that had assembled to the left of us. Macabre photo hunters.

One officer opened the back door of the police cruiser and covered Zadie's head as she slipped into the back seat. I waited to see if she would look at me. The door closed, and the car made a slow U-turn as it headed toward central booking. Zadie's window was on my side, but she never looked, and the car pulled away and disappeared into the night.

Darwood must've sensed my disappointment. "You did good, Nacho. You got them both."

"Doesn't feel good. Feels rotten. And there's still another. Mr. Unimportant. Whatever his name is. You think Mrs. Hardcastle will roll on him?"

"Don't hold your breath. She's probably faithfully waiting for him to legally extract her from this mess. I suspect you won't hear from him for a while," said Darwood. "He'll go dark, lick his wounds. But he'll be back. And you'll need to be ready for him." He placed a hand on my shoulder. "Unless you move."

Ten Spot, I thought. What to do about Ten Spot.

"Did you ever figure out how she got back to Austin?" Darwood asked.

"My guess is Mrs. Hardcastle picked her up at the end of the street. Price said she saw Mrs. Hardcastle with her purse in her hand and sunglasses on at the Hardcastle home in Austin. She thought she was going somewhere. More likely she'd just come back from Ten Spot with Zadie. That would've been around two forty-five or three." I shook my head. "Zadie almost got away with it and would have if Mrs. Hardcastle hadn't double-crossed her."

"By the way, where's Hardcastle's ring?" he asked.

"Ten Spot's investigators have it. You got anything on the technology behind that ring?"

Darwood rubbed the back of his neck. "Bureau doesn't have anything like it. Maybe CIA has that kind of hardware. Hardcastle was a technological whiz. There's a good chance he designed and built it himself. Most likely the camera in his office sent the video wirelessly to the ring's memory card. Little did Zadie realize Hardcastle was recording her that day. Little did Hardcastle realize he was recording his own murder."

I heard my name called and turned to see Steele waving madly at me from the other side of the yellow tape. With him were Trip, BroFly, Price, and TDub. I motioned to the officer in the area to let Steele come through and he ducked under the tape and trotted over, Nikon in hand.

"How'd you hear?" I asked.

"Police scanner. Doesn't everyone have one?"

Darwood stood to go, but I grabbed his arm. "Don't leave. I don't think I can do this one without you either."

"Listen, boys," Steele said, "I need an exclusive with you for tomorrow's Academy News, and a photo," said Steele. "You guys are going above the fold."

"He wants the scoop," I said to Darwood. "Okay, Steele, but only because I owe you one. Make it snappy."

Steele asked me about a dozen questions, most of which Darwood wouldn't let me answer for legal reasons.

I yelled for the officer to let the other four inside the restricted area and they pounded over. When the officers were finished with Holiday, they let her join us as well.

"Are you saying this is your investigative team?" Steele asked.

"Yes, we are!" Price confirmed. "We are all a part of the Nacho Blanco Detective Agency."

I shook my head. "Don't put that in there. There's no such thing. I work alone!"

"Let me get a picture of everyone together," Steele said. "Squeeze in."

We posed for the photo op. Everyone said "cheese." I hated it.

"I got the photo for tomorrow's headlines," said Steele. "I may even try to sell it to the *Ten Spot Tribune*."

"I'm sure you will." I looked around. "Where's Aiden?"

"The police still have him," said Trip. "They're questioning his role with Dream. What an ugly mess."

I watched as Ms. Baxter slipped beneath the yellow tape and made her way over to me. She had a cup in her hand. "You're coming home with me tonight, kid. I've got a nice clean spare bedroom with your name on it."

"Thanks. I'll sleep good tonight," I said, but I wasn't so sure.

"I also brought you this." She handed me the cup.

I took a drink and smiled. "An 1885. That's all I ever really wanted."

"By the way," she said, "I'm sorry about what happened at the cabin. I was just trying to keep you from getting hurt."

"No worries," I said. "Your dad explained the whole thing." I took another drink and smacked my lips. "This makes up for it."

"I don't know how you drink that!" We walked to her car, and she got more serious. "Listen, Nacho, I want you to know your father would be proud of you. You're everything he'd hoped you'd become." She paused, then added, "That's not true. I think you're more than even he imagined."

I stopped her. "You knew my father?"

"He was a great man, like you."

I had more questions for her, but they would have to wait. Somebody was calling my name. I turned around and saw Holiday coming toward us.

"Do you mind if I catch a ride with you, Ms. Baxter?" she asked.

The counselor looked at me and winked. "Our pleasure, honey."

At the car, I held the door for Holiday. She smiled, stood on her toes, and kissed me on the cheek. "Thank you, Nacho, for saving my life. I will never forget it."

"I'm glad it all worked out."

We slipped into the back seat. I buckled and felt Holiday's hand slide over into mine. We held hands as Ms. Baxter drove, and I thought about Zadie.

FRIDAY

CHAPTER 32
PIPER STRANGE

"**D**amn, dude, I can't believe Dream's a floater."

Trip slurped up the last of a strawberry shake from The Dirty Diva where we'd had our fill of burgers and fries, compliments of Miss Fitts. Word had gotten around about the arrests for the murder of Lincoln Hardcastle and Stephanie Sullivan.

BroFly bobbed his head. "I can't believe he was hustling for that murdering bitch."

"What are you talking about?" asked Trip. "He *was* her bitch. The bitch's bitch!"

They both laughed and Trip tossed his empty cup into a trash can on the sidewalk as we continued down Main.

"People'll do anything for thirty K, bro," said BroFly

They'll also do anything to stop the abuse, I thought.

I pushed the button on the crosswalk. "You guys go on. I've got an appointment at the police department for a little Q and A with the District Attorney. Might take a while."

"You sure you can't make it to the movie, bro?" Trip gave me a fist bump.

"Highly doubt it. Pretty sure this little meeting is gonna take longer than thirty."

While Trip and BroFly headed toward the Texas Theater, I crossed Main and headed back down the other side toward the police station. The air was crisp, the sun was out, and for the first time in a long time Ten Spot seemed to be glowing. Either that or this place was finally growing on me.

My phone buzzed and I slipped it out of my back pocket.

"Ms. Baxter." I slowed my pace.

"Have you seen the paper?" she asked.

"Nope."

"You're the *Ten Spot Tribune's* three-inch headline. Listen to this, and I quote: LOCAL SLEUTH SOLVES HARDCASTLE MURDER. There's a long article and a picture of you and your friends from last night."

Steele. Always looking to turn a buck.

"You made a difference in Ten Spot," she said, "the kind this town hasn't seen in decades."

"I guess so." Using just my right thumb, I twisted the ring on my right hand, Dad's ring, so that the silver diamond logo was on the topside of my finger.

"Thanks for sticking around."

"Somebody had to water the grass, right?" I'd reached the station and stopped at the bottom step. "What are the authorities saying about the cabin?"

"They're saying it was a gas line explosion."

I laughed. "You didn't mention that little call I got before the blast, did you?"

"Dad said to leave that one alone for now. He said he'd explain when he gets out of the hospital."

About thirty yards away sat the bench where I'd seen Zadie stop to befriend an old woman just a few days ago. An unsolicited, sympathetic act of kindness toward a fragile, forgotten human being. Not everyone does something like that. And now she was in jail for first degree murder. Not everyone does something like that either.

"Your dad's a brave man," I said. "How's he doing?"

"Not too shabby," she said. "I'm here with him now. He's strong, much more so than most men his age. The doctor said he'll let him go sometime early this next week. I saw your grandmother this morning also. She looks good. She's going home today."

"The sight of the home she's going to might put her back in the hospital," I said. "I haven't had the time to fill her in on all of the details."

"Don't worry. I told her everything and she's coming to stay with me. Both of you can crash at my house until yours gets repaired. Rusti too. I've already filled her in. She'll be here tomorrow." There was a slight pause. "There's one more thing I need to tell you."

"Yes?"

"Gloria Hardcastle is dead."

"Are you kidding?" I asked. "What happened?"

"She hung herself in jail this morning," she said. "God knows how she got a rope in the middle of the night."

Gloria Hardcastle had weaponized Zadie, using her to take out her husband. Now somebody else had taken out Gloria Hardcastle. That somebody had just saved the taxpayers a lot of money. They'd also just saved Mr. Unimportant as well. Whatever secrets Gloria Hardcastle held had been taken with her to the grave.

We ended the call, and I made my way up the steps of the police department and into the front lobby. The DA was waiting for me.

"Great work, Nacho. Thanks for coming by." He pumped my hand and guided me along a hallway on the first floor. "I need to get your version of the events that took place over the last few days."

"No problem." He buzzed us through a secure door that opened to the back of the building. "Out of curiosity, how are you going to try her?"

He snapped his head toward me. "If I have my way, I'll try her as an adult. And I guaran-damn-tee I'll do my best to send her to death row."

I swallowed hard and fought the urge to lay one across his chin. It wasn't easy.

We walked down a long corridor that opened to a rather small day room filled with black plastic chairs, a soda machine, and two interview rooms. Inside the first was Zadie. She was sitting across the table from Detective Books. There was a yellow legal pad between them, and a pen in Zadie's hand. She'd drawn some kind of diagram on the paper. Her face was splotchy, the area around her eyes swollen, and she was drowning in an over-sized orange jumpsuit.

"My office is this way," the DA said, urging me on.

I stood my ground, watching her. "I want to talk to her." She still hadn't notice me.

The DA let out a low sigh. "I don't think that's a good idea, Nacho."

Zadie had put the pen down now and was using her hands to demonstrate on Books wrists how she'd used the razor blade on Hardcastle.

"Just one quick minute," I said, still facing the window that separated me and Zadie. "Just a minute. I promise."

The DA let out another sigh then used his keyless entry to swipe the door open, and we entered.

Zadie looked up. Her eyes got big, she drew in a long deep breath and jumped up, throwing her arms around my neck, burying her face in my shoulder.

"Help me, Nacho!" She was shaking, and large tears spilled over her cheeks, sinking into my shirt. "I'm so scared!" All the emotions from the last twenty-four hours poured out in a disheveled heap.

The DA had joined the detective and together they tried to pry her loose.

"Let her go!" I yelled.

They stopped pulling but they didn't let go. Each kept a firm grasp on an arm.

She loosened her grip enough so we could see each other face to face.

"Nacho?"

I knew I had to be strong. For her.

"He wants to send me to death row."

I nodded but said nothing.

"I'm so scared."

I bit my lip, blinked back a tear, then another.

"You can't help me now, can you?"

I shook my head. "I can't, but don't think I don't want to."

She popped one of the pink rubber bands on her right wrist. "I'm going to miss you. You're the best friend I've ever had."

I reached a hand to her face and wiped a tear from beneath each eye. "Yeah, well, like you said, we teach people how to treat us. You're a good teacher, Zadie Abernathy, even if I am a rotten student."

She raised both eyebrows. "Do you think you could love me again?"

"Oh, for God's sake!" the DA burst out. "The only love you'll be getting is from your new girlfriends at Mountain View."

I shot the DA a "go to hell" glare, then I looked at Zadie. "I never stopped."

She leaned forward and placed her lips on mine. We breathed the other in one last time. I took in as much of her as I could, letting the scent of rose petals and sweet almond milk fill me.

When our last goodbye was over, the DA and Detective Books retreated with her back into the room and snapped a pair of steel handcuffs around her wrists.

As I stood at the door and watched, she flashed me one last smile.

"I was wrong about you," she said.

"How so?"

"You really are as brilliant as you are charming. But mostly, Nacho Blanco, you're kind."

Then they closed the door of Interview Room 1.

The DA shook his head. "I gotta hand it to you, Blanco. You're the last of the real ones."

I waited for her to look at me through the window. She didn't, and I continued walking with the DA.

My mind was a blur of memories from the last few days. The first time we'd met. The ride we'd taken together on the Triumph. The moment when I looked at her just before I thought McKee would kill me. And now her in a prison jumpsuit. I just wanted to rewind back to the beginning, put Zadie on the back of that bike, and take her away with me forever.

We settled into a room with black plastic chairs pulled up to a table that wobbled on it's one center-pole leg. The DA pulled out a yellow pad and took notes. He asked the questions and I gave the answers, and we covered every detail that had led to the discovery of who killed Dr. Lincoln Hardcastle.

When it was over, I stood up to leave. "Who's her attorney?"

The D.A. waved it off. "The court will appoint her one. She doesn't have money, so she'll get whoever they give her. It's her right as a citizen, even if she doesn't deserve it."

I left his office and began my long walk back to the front where I'd come in. Interview Room 1 was empty now. I wondered where they had taken her. I wondered if she was still shaking.

My heart felt like it was crushing in on itself. I wanted to hold her. I wanted to make it right for her. I wanted to do anything at all for her.

A court-appointed attorney. You get what you pay for. When it came to her criminal defense, Zadie didn't just need a lawyer, or even a good one. She needed the best, someone who could get an acquittal in their sleep. But Zadie couldn't afford the best and that left her with only one other option. An acquittal based on the grounds of ineffective counsel. The best thing for her now was to find the worst damn lawyer this side of the Red River and convince him to come to Ten Spot and put on the worst damn defense this town had ever seen.

Stepping back outside, I grimaced at the sudden glare from the sun and slipped my Maui Jim's over my eyes. A timid voice called to me and I looked down and noticed a girl standing at the bottom of the steps. She was thin and small-chested, athletic-looking, blonde, and cute. She had on a heather-grey t-shirt and running shorts that snugged the longest, most toned and tanned legs I'd ever seen. Her blonde hair was in a pony and she had on little to no make-up which gave her a fresh, natural, girl-next-door look.

I stepped down toward her.

"Nacho?" she said again. "You are Nacho Blanco, right?"

"Last time I checked."

"I thought it was you. I saw your picture in the paper today." She stood up and looked around. "I need your help. I think I may have stumbled onto something bad."

"Like what kind of something bad?" I asked.

"I think somebody killed somebody," she said. "A long time ago."

I jerked my head back over my shoulder toward the police station. "Why not go there?"

She took a step toward me, whispering. "I can't. It happened sixty years ago, and I think the police may have covered it up."

"How'd you find this out?"

"Somebody called me," she said. "I've been checking into it, but I need help." She paused. "Will you take my case?"

"I don't..."

"Please. I think somebody else will die, and if you don't help, it might be me."

She must have seen the hesitancy, the reluctance, the skepticism in my face. "Please?" She bit her bottom lip. "You're all I've got."

I sighed and shifted from one foot to the other. "There's a place down the street called The Dirty Diva."

"I'm familiar," she said. She stuck out her hand and we shook. "I'm Piper. Piper Strange."

ACKNOWLEDGMENTS

It takes a village to raise a child and to write a book. I've done both now, and in both instances I've had to rely on some very knowledgeable people to bring both into maturity. I always say collaboration breeds quality, and the following people really helped make this book what it is. Without them there would be no *We Planned a Murder*.

First and foremost there's Jimmy Calloway. I met Jimmy in February of 2021. Jimmy works as the submissions manager at a well known literary agency in San Diego. Over the course of that year Jimmy did three developmental passes through the novel. He told me to cut some chapters, bring some characters more to the foreground, had me tone down some lines that were too strong, and so much more. His work was both developmental and copy editing. But as valuable as I found his critique and corrections, equally prized was his constant encouragement. Jimmy's belief in the story was a source of strength to me and I continued to believe in the novel because Jimmy believed in it. Unequivocally, *We Planned a Murder* would not be the same without Jimmy Calloway. I'm already working on the second Nacho Blanco novel and you can bet your sweet bippy I'll be sending that one to him too. If you're a writer and in need of an amazing developmental/copy editor contact him at jimmycallaway@yahoo.com.

I would still be floundering with novel in hand if it weren't for best selling author William Bernhardt. Bill is the authority on self-publishing. I emailed him so often and each time he answered with the most gracious of responses. His wisdom and knowledge are priceless and he is the most generous man with time I've ever met. I already felt I knew Bill when he and I started corresponding due to his wonderful and very informative podcasts which I listen to regularly when I walk. Besides his writing and his podcasts Bill also hosts his annual WriterCon in Oklahoma City (www.writercon.com). Without Bill *We Planned a Murder* wouldn't be a book. As thousands of others would also say, whether he knows it or not, Bill has become my writing mentor. I aspire to be like him.

There are a lot of people in a village but finding just the right ones to help you raise a book is not always easy. I went through three other developmental editors before I found Jimmy. Thanks to Bill, finding Maria Novillo Saravilla at BeauteBook (www.beautebook.com) was a breeze. Whether we want to admit it or not, we actually do judge a book by its cover. Maria did the cover artwork for *We Planned a Murder*. She asked me some questions about the story, I gave her the synopsis, and voilà, just like that she had the perfect cover art. I loved it the moment I saw it. The cover is exactly what I pictured when I was writing the story. It was almost as if she was reading my mind! She and I have already talked about the sequel to the story and what that might look like. I can't wait to see what she comes up with next! The day I met Maria the book became even better because of the cover work she did. Another example of collaboration leading to better quality.

Of course I would've never even written one word of *We Planned a Murder* and I certainly would've never met Jimmy, Bill, or Maria if it hadn't been for my wife Tiffany. On Monday, March 7, 2016, she and I were sitting on a beach in Hawaii and I was reading *Writing with Quiet Hands: How to Shape Your Writing to Resonate with Readers* by Paula Munier. At some point I turned to Tiffany and said, "This is what I want to do. I want to write." Without the least bit of hesitation she said, "Then do it." So I did. I left educational administration two months later and began the journey into writing. She has been my biggest supporter from day one.

I am indebted to all those who read the work and gave me feedback, encouraged me to keep writing, or sometimes just listened to my progress (or lack thereof!). My daughter Brooke and her girlfriend Bethany. My son Bret and his wife Lauren. Her parents. My parents. My two little ones, Landry and Presley. My in-laws Paul and Charla. Uncle Joe. There are so many more. Their encouragement has meant the world to me.

A village. And not just a village, but the right people in that village. I am eternally grateful to all of them. Together we raised a book.

As Nacho would say, all of you are all I ever really wanted.

ABOUT THE AUTHOR

Derek lives in Frisco, Texas, with his wife Tiffany and their two girls Landry and Presley. He graduated from Baylor University and has been a public classroom teacher and school administrator. His journey into mysteries began on his 10th birthday when his parents gave him his first Hardy Boys book, *The Mystery of the Aztec Warrior.* That was January 12, 1976, the same day the Queen of Crime, Agatha Christie passed away at 85 years of age. That was the day he fell in love with reading mysteries. That was also the day he knew he wanted to write one. He still has that book in his office. It sits on his shelf in plain sight. He sees it everyday when he sits down to write. Derek has also written the short story "Think of the Children" in the Sisters in Crime North Dallas chapter's recent anthology *Malice in Dallas*. *We Planned a Murder* is his first novel. Find out more about him and what he's working on at www.DerekDWheeless.com or on social media.

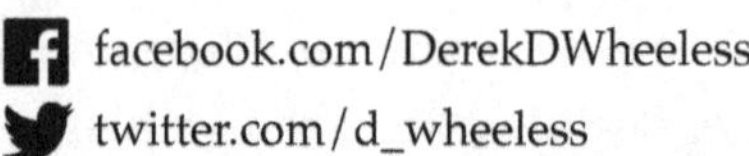

facebook.com/DerekDWheeless
twitter.com/d_wheeless
instagram.com/d_wheeless